that I know what happened at Massingham that night; what Sugden's part was, and poor Amy's; or whether the old woman was lying in her last words to me?

Mr Jobling could make nothing of it. He was a newcomer to the district and had never even heard of Massingham. And though the twenty closely typed pages opened his eyes to many things and helped to make him in future years perhaps the most cautious of a notably cautious breed of men, it gave him no insight into the secret heart of Mr Derry. He understood the lawyer's problem and missed the man's. But then perhaps there would have been no problem for Mr Jobling. He would never have given house-room to the Massingham Affair.

"OLD father antic the law," says one of the characters in *King Henry IV*.

One day in the late nineteen-forties, a young solicitor in Smedwick, near the Scottish border, happened to be going through some papers left in the lumber room by his predecessor from whom he had bought the practice, a Mr Justin Derry, recently deceased, when his attention was caught by a folder marked in Mr Derry's rather crabbed handwriting *Summary of Facts in In Re Milligan* and containing carbon copies of some twenty typescript pages, the originals of which the old man had probably taken away with his other possessions at the time of the sale.

Young Mr Jobling had a quick eye. It had led him to the cobwebby but immensely lucrative practice in the 'historic ducal town' (as the municipal guide book had it), and where most men would have passed on with a cursory nod to *In Re Milligan*, he looked closer and saw that what he had stumbled on was a personal confession of the most beguiling kind. Nor had he read far before he suspected that the carbons, which must have been left behind by accident, had been typed by Mr Derry himself, not entrusted to the somewhat formidable lady who had passed with the firm and was now designated, in Mr Jobling's idiom, his P.S.

12th July 1936

Something that has happened recently [he read] had decided me to write down all the facts of what came to be called the 'Massingham Affair'. It is still not quite forgotten in Smedwick, though it ended in 1899, nearly forty years ago, and poor Milligan and so many of the others are dead. I would have said only last week that it *ought* to be forgotten. Now I am not so sure. I shall write it all down first and then decide what to do. It will not be an easy decision. There are still people alive who could be hurt most deeply by what it is in my power to say. And can I even be sure it is true? Can I say with absolute certainty

THE LETTER
1936

CONTENTS

	Page	
The Letter: 1936		7
The Crime: 1891		11
The Quest: 1899		49
The Trial: 1899		169
The Verdict of You All: 1936		211

Connoisseurs of crime will notice certain resemblances—though the differences are greater—between this story and the celebrated Edlingham Burglary that convulsed Northumberland towards the end of the last century and in time achieved a national fame. I dedicate the tale to the late CHARLES PERCY, solicitor of Alnwick, the hero of the real-life struggle that ended so triumphantly and helped towards the creation of the Court of Criminal Appeal.

Copyright © 1962 by E. D. Grierson Ltd.
All Rights Reserved
Printed in the United States of America

The Massingham Affair

EDWARD GRIERSON

DOUBLEDAY & COMPANY, INC.
GARDEN CITY, NEW YORK

THE MASSINGHAM AFFAIR

THE CRIME
1891

I

THE young woman came to the head of the stairs and peered down into the darkness. From there the sounds from the drawing-room were much more audible. Rats, most probably. The Rectory was plagued with them: 'like Hamlin town', her father would complain as they set off on their nightly pilgrimage, candles in hand, up the stairs and along the narrow, shadowy corridors of the house. Only last year young Merrick from the bothy by the bridge had found a nest of them behind the cistern in the attics, and on his advice there had been imported, despite the Rector's marked repugnance to the tribe, a large and somnolent tom-cat that dozed all day by the fire and did his duty, one supposed, by night. Not in the drawing-room, apparently, where the sounds persisted even more loudly than before.

Miss Verney stamped her foot imperiously to stop them. She was an imperious girl: it came of being an adjutant in the care of souls. The Rector was a widower, and in the remote parish lost in the wilds of the Northumbrian hills he had no other helpmate. He would not have desired one. He would certainly not have been permitted one.

Below the stairs the passage stretched out to the front door with the two main living-rooms on its right. All was dark down there. The moon was full, but the hall had no windows and all the doors into it were closed. Suddenly Miss Verney was aware of a shaft of light shining diagonally across her view like a sunbeam through cloud, marking the wall of the passage on the left, and she saw that it was coming from the drawing-room door which had begun to open.

She drew back from the stairhead, but not hastily, for she was not a timorous or hasty person. The Rector's room was next to her own, and she entered it, knocking gently at the door.

"Father."

He too had been awakened. She heard the scraping of a match

and by its glow she saw him sitting up in bed, a Biblical figure with his ragged white beard, wearing a flannel nightgown of the same stuff as her own and a cap with a tassel that dangled down over one ear.

"Father," she said, "there are burglars in the house."

Mr Verney was nearing seventy, but a man of spirit, and he received this alarming news with something approaching relish. "Where's my sword?" was his first remark as he jumped up. Some time elapsed before he got his candle lit and found it, but he was armed at last and was just starting for the door when he was firmly ordered back to bed.

"Didn't you call me, my dear?" he protested, taking the logical point as he usually did in their arguments, without much noticeable success.

"Perhaps I did," she answered. "It was foolish of me. Please don't go out."

"But I will," he said, taking a good grip of the sword.

He had got the door open by this time and their raised voices, still arguing earnestly with one another, had already roused the cook in the servants' wing. But from below the sounds continued uninterruptedly, and as they went down the stairs, the Rector leading with his drawn sword in one hand and a candle held high in the other, they saw the drawing-room door wide open and, nearer at hand, a shaft of light shining from the dining-room and moving along the wall. From the landing half-way down the stairs they could look directly into the room, and there, between them and the table, they glimpsed the figures of two men, one with a candle and something like a gun or an iron bar. Next instant the intruders had seen the light on the stairs, and their candle was snuffed and thrown under the table.

"Who are you?" Mr Verney called out, and repeated it as the dining-room door was seen to close towards them. He went on unhesitatingly and had almost reached the door when there was a loud explosion and the candle fell from his hand, leaving them all in almost total darkness.

"Are you hurt, Papa?" Miss Verney cried.

"Merely grazed," he answered. "And you?"

Before she could reply, a man came out at them, crouching low and making for the drawing-room some yards away, only to be seized by the militant Miss Verney, who shouted out, "You scoundrell!" while the Rector slashed with his sword in all directions. The fugitive darted from her grasp into the drawing-room, and by the light of the moon she saw him disappear through the window into the grounds. Returning into the passage, she took her father round the waist from behind and tried to drag him back from the dining-room, into which he sought to hurl himself against the armed and desperate man whom they could hear beyond the door blundering up and down and vainly trying to open the shutters and get out. But the Rector's blood was up. He thrust her from him roughly, shouting to her to leave him, and she obeyed out of half-forgotten habit. From the landing, in painful agitation, wounded by far the more severely, she heard him go, and listened to the macabre game of blind man's buff proceeding in that room, in which one powerful fellow with a gun went dodging from corner to corner, pursued by an old gentleman who lunged out at shadows in Byronic style—

> Arras they prick'd and curtains with their swords
> And wounded several shutters and some boards

—a table cloth in this instance, as she found when she came to the reckoning.

She could see nothing but a faint glow where the moonlight shone into the passage through the drawing-room door. She heard the sound of heavy breathing, the crash as a table went over, a sudden cry of triumph, or so it seemed, and then the door was wrenched open, and in the uncertain light she saw the figure of a man come bursting out in one tempestuous rush to hurl himself into the drawing-room, from which came the tinkle of broken glass and the thud of a body landing in the flower-bed below the windows of the house.

Above her a light was shining on the stairs as the cook came wavering into view, uttering cries of alarm and clutching her dressing-gown around her. "Be quiet, Jane," Miss Verney commanded her. She could feel in her thigh the slow welling of blood, but there was no trace of it to be seen on her gown and she had no intention that it should be seen. Seizing the candle, she ran into the dining-room, fighting back the rising tide of panic. Her father was slumped against the table, head thrown back, eyes open and staring. For a moment she thought that he was dead, and a fierce, uncontrollable anguish filled her heart. Then she saw him move and his gaze came down to hers, and she rushed into his arms as she had not done since she had been a little girl frightened by some sound in the night.

"There, there," he said, trying to comfort her, not knowing that it was for him that she feared. They were interrupted by a cry, as the cook, following cautiously into the light, caught sight of the blood flowing from the wound on his shoulder where a few scattered pellets from the charge had struck.

"Only a graze. Surely you've seen blood before. Be a good sensible woman," the Rector admonished her in a firm voice. "I'll take no hurt. Are you sure you're all right, my dear?"

"Quite sure, Father."

"The scoundrels!" the Rector said as she began to lead him into the drawing-room, where the bandages were kept. "They fired on us. There were two of them, you saw that?"

"Yes."

"Have they taken anything?"

She glanced around her, not really caring, for the blood seemed to be coming faster now and she feared that at any moment he might discover it. The room was in turmoil: the desk rifled, drawers open, papers strewn everywhere. Something was missing; she sensed it even before her eye detected what it was; and she said: "They've taken my watch. The one with the seal. From the mantelpiece."

"The one poor Davey gave you?"

"Yes."

"My dear!"

"It's all right, Father. It's no matter. Now stay still while I cut away the cloth from your shoulder."

Working deftly, she soon had him bandaged and dosed and tucked up in bed with a hot-water bottle. From the pillows, with his long beard straggling down over the sheets, he watched her anxiously as she bent down to kiss his forehead under the white woollen cap. "Are you sure you're all right, dearest? You look so pale. You're sure they missed you?"

"Of course. Now lie down and try to go to sleep like a good papa."

"Don't you go out," he said suddenly with anxious awareness of what she would do.

"I'll behave sensibly, you can be sure."

"But you'll go running out. I know you."

"Only to Tom's dear. We must have the doctor fetched from Smedwick. And the Police must be told."

Avoiding his gaze, so filled with dismal forebodings for her safety, she kissed him again before going to her room, where she stood in front of the mirror in the candle-light and let down her gown. The shift beneath it was soaked in blood. Calmly, with the detachment of a nurse, she examined the wound and dressed it with linament. It was not as bad as she had feared. Then she threw on some clothes and ran down the stairs to the front door.

Outside, the moonlight shone down on the Rectory in its garden among the bare trees, with the one straggling street of the hamlet on rising ground behind it under the rim of the moor. Below her, as she hurried down the hill, she could see young Merrick's cottage, set in the narrow valley beside the church and ruined castle, and beyond it a bracken-covered fell topped with a line of crags, along whose face lay pockets of snow glittering with a silvery brightness.

She felt no fear. It never occurred to her to think that the men who had broken in on them might still be lurking in the hedgerows. She came to the cottage in a mounting clamour from the dogs, and knocked loudly at the door. When young Merrick came she gave him her message and walked back up the hill, refusing all help. Only when she had reached her own room and got herself tidily to bed did she faint clean away.

II

SUPERINTENDENT BLAIR, stationed in Smedwick, six miles off across the moor, was awakened at half-past three on the February morning. He came downstairs muttering to himself, fastening his belt and tunic buttons, a burly, square-jawed man with an iron-grey moustache that drooped round the corners of the mouth, giving to his face a petulant and disapproving expression.

At young Merrick's news, however, his eyes kindled and he nodded his head several times portentously.

"Two men, eh, Tom?"

"So Miss Charlotte says, sir."

"And armed, you say. A shot-gun?"

"Seems it was, sir."

"Poachers," announced the Superintendent with profound conviction. He knew his district and its besetting sin, which was an inordinate love of pheasants and coneys. As in so many other towns surrounded by large estates, poaching in Smedwick had achieved the dignity of a profession, diligently pursued, night after night, by groups of men and dogs roaming as silent as shadows in the woods and straying sometimes, when game was scarce, to the scattered farmsteads on the fells. Only a few months earlier a police constable by the name of Luke had been shot and killed by gentlemen of this kidney who had never been brought to justice, and the memory of that crime was still fresh in Blair's mind.

"Let's see now," he mused, stroking his moustache with the back of his hand. "It was done about two, you say. And you'd heard by half-past and rode straight over here."

"I went to Doctor first, sir."

"You went to the doctor first," the Superintendent repeated, though it could be seen that this was not a commendation. "And now it's three-forty. Those beggars could be home across the moor and safe and snug by now. And they could still be out of their bolt holes and in the haughs. We'll get the nets down."

No sooner said than done with so efficient a machine. The Headquarters staff was alerted, constables were sent running to every outlying officer, and within half an hour the roads into the town were guarded and patrols had begun the rounds in the Bewley and Pelegate sectors where all the more notorious poachers were known to live. Having thus galvanised his force to deal with what he saw as a heaven-sent chance of smiting the Amalekites, the Superintendent got into his gig and drove by the Deeping Road to Massingham which he reached about half-past five, while darkness still lay over the countryside.

He found the villagers swarming in the Rectory and its grounds in a pleasurable state of ghoulishness. No doubt it was felt that after thirty years the Rector and his family had at last edified the neighbourhood. "Can't have this, now can we?" the Superintendent reasoned with them as he began to shoo them out. "Destroy the clues you will, if any, and then where'll we be?" With tact and good humour he got the place cleared of all but the Verneys, who were under sedatives in their bedrooms, and the household staff, which consisted of a cook, two daily maids and a general handyman by the name of Bell who did not sleep on the premises.

"Now see here, Jane," the Superintendent said, waylaying his quarry in her kitchen, "you're the one to help me, you are. Did you see or hear anything?"

"Just a noise like, and the gun going off—and then the master hollering."

"I want you to show me where they got in."

Preceded by a constable carrying a candlestick, they went into the drawing-room. One of the sash windows had been forced with some instrument and panes of glass had been broken. The window stood open. The Superintendent leaned through it over the flower-beds, but it was still too dark to see anything out there, so he turned back into the room, following the trail of damage that led towards the central table lying on its side and the bureau against the far wall, all its drawers open and littered with paper.

"Seems they couldn't have found much," he said. "Anyways, they went next door."

"That's right, sir. Into the dining-room."

The confusion was even greater there. The dining-table had resisted stoutly, but almost every other stick of furniture had been overturned in the course of that frantic mêlée in the darkness, and the plate from the sideboard was strewn around the room. Under the table, where it had been thrown, lay the burglars' candle, and the Superintendent bent to pick it up. "There's this, sir, I was looking round before you came, sir, and I found this," the cook announced, handing him a chisel with paintmarks on it that might have come from the forced window in the drawing-room. "Found it here, sir, near the door."

"Find anything else?" said the Superintendent, grimacing slightly at this amateur detection.

"There's this sheet o' paper, sir. Jim Bell found it in the hall."

The Superintendent, muttering a little louder to himself, accepted it. He seemed to be accumulating clues at second hand. But on his way out of the dining-room he stopped and pointed triumphantly to a mark about shoulder level on the door jamb where part of the woodwork had been blown away. Beyond him on the passage wall and considerably higher was another mark where the rest of the charge had struck. The shot must have been deflected from the door jamb, to pass close to Mr Verney's head before embedding itself, a few pellets ricocheting on the way. A sporting gun had caused it—a poacher's gun, most probably, as he had cleverly divined.

Furthermore, when dawn came and he went outside, he found in the soil of the flower-bed a set of marks made by the second burglar who had hurled himself through the window on all fours. These the Superintendent covered over carefully with boards. His case was taking shape, and he returned in excellent humour to his headquarters in the Lawnmarket and to the discovery that in his absence a first-class pair of suspects had been unearthed for him.

III

THAT morning, soon after five o'clock, while the Superintendent was driving down to Massingham from the moor, the poaching fraternity in the Bewley Road and Pelegate received unwelcome visitors, the 'Poliss' in the shape of pairs of burly constables. In the fraternity, certain personages stood out by virtue of their skill and the number of their convictions. George Sugden was certainly one of them: a wiry man in his late thirties, about the average height, a famous runner, with a reputation for artfulness. He received his visitation about five-fifteen in the room in a tenement house which he shared with his wife and infant child. It was a brief visit. Sugden was asked to show his boots. He did so and they were seen to be dry. The trousers were inspected and they were dry also. "You'll know in the morning" was the only answer he got when he asked what the visit was about, and the constables then left.

Another likely candidate, Joseph Henderson, was seen about the same time in his house in Pelegate. It was of this stalwart fellow with the shoulders of a pugilist that the Vicar of St Bede's, the Reverend Walter P. Beaumont Lumley, whose agreeable name was a byword in the district for his eloquence and charity, wrote with unmistakable feeling: "He is a parishioner of mine. I have sometimes wished it otherwise." The constables that morning, however, found his trousers, boots and clogs were dry. They retreated empty-handed.

Yet, as it happened, not all these visits were in vain; not all the Smedwick poachers were at home that morning. Patrick Milligan, labourer, was not with his wife and two small children in their room in Bewley Street. Michael Kelly, his young workmate, was not in the house next door where he lodged *en famille* with his fiancée Amy Dodds, his sister Eliza Jean, and her protector, an old half-blind reprobate by the name of Piggott. Soon after seven o'clock both these men, accompanied by their terrier Matt, were seen coming into town near the Methodist chapel by P.C. Lang and P.C. Buchan, who stopped and searched them, but finding nothing incriminating on them, allowed them to continue home. The hunt was up, however, and no sooner had the two suspects begun to change their clothes than they were told to get dressed at once and were marched off in custody to the police office in the Lawnmarket, where Blair awaited them.

The Superintendent's sense of triumph had been growing steadily all morning. For months he had been plagued by this feckless community living by its wits, and here at last he held a couple of the most notorious—held them on a charge which, if proved, would put them away where they would never trouble him again. Surprise at the identity of his suspects was the last thought in his mind. He knew too much about them. Only a matter of weeks earlier he had lost a case on prosecution thanks to the evidence of Kelly, and the experience had not sweetened his regard for him.

Once at the Lawnmarket, the prisoners were immediately stripped and searched, Blair personally performing this office for Kelly, much the younger man, who had some bruising on his body, though nothing in the way of the sword thrusts that Mr Verney's testimony had led everyone to expect. There were no marks of any kind on the bearded, middle-aged Milligan. "Never mind, I've plenty of grounds to lock them up," the Superintendent confidently remarked. Certain articles of the prisoners' clothing were removed, and when they were dressed again, Blair for the first time revealed his hand—"Come here, you damned rascals, while I tell you what you are charged with. You are charged with breaking into the Reverend Mr Verney's house at Massingham last night and shooting at him with a gun with intent to murder him." To which Milligan, the spokesman, said that they had never been near Massingham at all but rabbiting on Bridewell Moor, six miles or more to the north-east, returning by the Coomber Road and the wall of the Duke's park to Pear Tree Lane, where they had been seen at dawn by witnesses. "Perhaps you'll be naming them," the Superintendent replied, suffering this with difficulty, for the whole breed was anathema to him after the murder of P.C. Luke at Hannington.

"It was young McGuire and Andy Reede. They was comin' in to work, sir."

"Coming from the same sort of work, you mean. I know your kind. Scoundrels the lot of you."

That evening the prisoners were dressed in the clothes they were thought to have been wearing when seen near the chapel, and were driven over to Massingham and placed in the dining-room between the table and the door.

The grand moment of confrontation had arrived and old Mr Verney was seen, candle in hand, peering at them from the landing at the turn of the stairs. "It's like them, very like them," he was heard to murmur.

"You identify them, sir?" Blair called out encouragingly from the passage.

"There were two of them and they were standing just where these are now, like drilled men, like soldiers in a line. One had something in his hand—a gun it must have been. It was the bigger man."

"This one, sir? The prisoner Kelly?"

"I think so, yes, I think it was. He is very like him—the same build. Of course it was candlelight."

"Of course, sir. Do you identify the accused?"

"Well then . . . yes . . . yes, there are resemblances. I think these are the same men, I feel that increasingly. I go partly by the faces but more by the shape of them and the way they stand, like drilled men. One had a gun and he fired at me. I saw the explosion plainly—a most extraordinary effect, like a meteor, yes, like a meteor of transcendent size. . . ."

"I'd better see Miss Verney, if you'll allow it," the Superintendent said to Dr Higson, who stood beside him.

He had no great hopes of the encounter. He thought of women as unpredictable, wayward creatures with little understanding and less respect for the majestic processes of the law. Also he was apt to be intimidated by them. It had been one thing to examine the garrulous old Rector, but it was quite another to beard his daughter in the mysterious surroundings of a lady's room, with the brocade and taffeta dresses behind the door, the buttoned boots in a row, the silk curtains, the engravings and devotional pictures. It was a relief to him when he had got his suspects marched up and paraded at the foot of the bed where she could see them as she lay with only one pillow behind her head, the dark eyes seeming enormous in the parchment coloured face under a cap of Brussels lace.

She looked at them for a long time without speaking, and everyone in the room kept silent. "I had hold of the man who had the dark coat on who passed me in the passage," she said at last. "I had hold of his hair."

Now Patrick Milligan was wearing a dark coat. His head was close cropped, a style he had acquired while serving along with Kelly in the militia. He stooped down by the bed and asked her to take hold of his hair and compare it with that of the man she had touched that morning, and she did so, remarking that the burglar's hair had seemed a little longer.

"Seemed?" enquired the Superintendent, looming in the background.

She turned her gaze on him with an expression of surprise, as though grieved at finding so uncouth a person in her room. The doctor started towards her, but she stopped him with a gesture. "No, it doesn't tire me. Let me go on. It seemed to me that the man who darted past me in the passage was slighter than the man here, and the hair longer, as I have said, because no doubt he was stooping as he passed me and I never had a proper hold on him. Yet I believe they are one and the same. I feel sure these are the men we saw; it's coming back."

"Should make a fair witness for a woman," the Superintendent remarked to his attendant constable, P.C. Pugh, as they went downstairs. "If we can trace the chisel to these damned ruffians, and maybe that bit of paper too, and if the footmarks fit the bill, they'll not poach another rabbit this side of Paradise."

IV

YOUNG Mr Justin Derry sat in his corner of the railway carriage reading the depositions taken by the Smedwick magistrates. It was the first time that he had encountered *'In Re Verney'*, as the case was known in the highly respectable offices of Rees and Featherstone where he was articled, and he was only attending the Assize trial at Belcastle Moot Hall because another of the clerks had been taken ill and Mr Rees liked company. It seemed an unrewarding case. Not many firms would have bothered with it, seeing that the combined resources of the accused men would not pay counsel's fee, never mind the railway fares, yet the old solicitor had come in person, leaving the practice to chance and his partner Featherstone. Such cases were his one concession to philanthropy.

Reaching the end of the file, Justin glanced out of the window at the sea and the romantic silhouette of Rayworth Castle which had just come into view. He hoped he had mastered the rudiments of the brief. He would certainly be asked about it and he had better be ready with his answers to satisfy the exacting old gentleman in the corner opposite.

"Care to review the evidence, my boy?"

He began rather desperately to marshal his facts. There were the Verneys to begin with: identification: not certain by the best standards, but damning enough.

There was evidence of opportunity, for both the accused had undeniably been away from their homes at the material times.

There was the evidence of the chisel found in the Rectory dining-room by the cook. An old man by the name of Piggott, who lived with Kelly's sister in the house where Kelly lodged, had identified it as a tool he owned. Which was bad enough. But a torn sheet of paper, found on the morning of the crime in the Rectory hall by the handyman James Bell, had been proved to fit exactly into a smaller piece discovered by the Police Surgeon in the lining of Kelly's coat, and a button and a shred of cloth, fitting just as neatly into a tear in Milligan's trousers, had been unearthed a month later from the flower-beds under the drawing-room window.

Most damning of all: footprints, which casts of the men's boots showed conclusively to be theirs, had been traced on the crown of the lane leading from the Rectory to the main Deeping Road and along a mile of that road in the direction of Smedwick across the moor. No prosecution could really hope for better. It was almost too much to expect of luck and the criminal classes, Justin thought, and paused in his review.

"Well?" prompted the senior partner, apparently much edified by this proof of what his firm's training had accomplished in a once slipshod lad.

"I was just thinking, sir."

"A very desirable exercise, my boy. About what, precisely?"

"About coincidences, sir. Take the piece of paper. The Police have that coat of Kelly's in their keeping for two weeks and find nothing. They give it to the doctor, an independent witness, and immediately the paper's found. Same with Milligan's button. They find a tear in his trousers, and a month later the missing bit obligingly turns up."

"What about the chisel? Can you get over that?" Rees said. "And the footprints. They're conclusive, surely?"

Justin was about to admit that the footprints certainly were conclusive, when he had an idea and changed his mind.

"Thought of something?" asked Mr Rees.

"Just this, sir. The footmarks were mostly in the lane. What about the ones under the window, the ones Blair discovered first and covered with boards? We don't hear of *them*. Why not? Seems rather selective evidence. Then take the nature of the crime itself. How comes it that two men commit a burglary at two in the morning, are interrupted, and instead of running home to bed before the hue and cry, go poaching and walk into town in broad daylight with their terrier at their heels?"

"I thought we'd come to little Matt in time," said Mr Rees in a soothing voice. "He's certainly our most engaging witness."

"Who'd take his dog out burgling, sir?"

"Oh, come! They were poachers first, remember."

"Then where's their gun? No gun's been found. Miss Verney's watch and seal were stolen. Nothing's known of them."

"They could easily have cached them."

"Like the rabbits they told the Police they'd poached on Bridewell Moor and buried there at dawn? Those rabbits were there all right, just as they said; they've been dug up; that's proved."

Mr Rees conceded the rabbits with a generous flourish of the hand. "Not that they're worth much," he remarked, "when you remember that those fellows could have got across the moor from Massingham and buried them with time to spare. Or they could have hidden them beforehand to stage an alibi. Nothing else supports it. The men who are supposed to have seen them at first light near the Duke's Wall have not come forward. But have your rabbits by all means," Mr Rees said, settling back in his seat.

For the remainder of the journey Justin sat and wondered what brought an elderly, overworked man forty miles to help defend two penniless clients in whose innocence he seemed profoundly to disbelieve. Nothing would have been easier than to have sent the managing clerk or some other minion; yet here he was in person on the Belcastle train with his gout and his scepticism rampant. He must have an admirably abstract love of justice. Or perhaps he just liked travelling and a day free of Mr Featherstone, a worthy person but one whose nature it was to fuss in a teapot.

It was not a long walk from the station to the Assize court, a porticoed building, several shades grimier than the waters of the river flowing beneath its walls. By some archaic fancy it was known as the Moot Hall, though it had in fact been erected at the beginning of the century in the profoundly un-Saxon days of the Prince Regent. The place was swarming with people. Witnesses huddled together in the hall on either side of the staircase up which marched important dignitaries and Grand Jurors on their way to their panelled room and box on the first floor. Policemen, carrying their helmets under their arms, stood guard outside the two courts opening off the hall, while immediately to the right of the main doors a bleakly appointed room had been set aside for solicitors and clients, who could be perceived sitting about in resigned attitudes waiting for Justice to begin.

Mr Rees, with a sigh, was about to enter it when he caught sight of a tall figure in a wig forcing his way through the crowd near the bottom of the stairs.

"Mr Gilmore."

"Mr Rees. How fortunate."

They shook hands: two professional men on parade and aware of it.

"You've not met young Derry. He's articled with me. In his last year now."

Justin found himself presented to a frock-coat of exquisite distinction adorned with a watch-chain and beautifully laundered bands and cuffs. The trousers were of bold grey check, narrowing above a pair of very slim elastic-sided boots. Such elegance was not to be found in Smedwick, even on the back of its resident duke, but belonged quite clearly to the world of *Spy* cartoons of statesmen and rising legal luminaries, with a dash of the *Tailor and Cutter* thrown in. Gilmore himself seemed plain by comparison, though he was an alert young man, already gifted with the sagacious expression that barristers must either have by nature or practise daily in front of a mirror if they are to survive. "First on the calendar, I see," this paragon remarked briskly. "Are the witnesses here?"

"Young Kelly's sister."

"Good."

"And his fiancée, Amy Dodds. Their evidence is something. It's about the only evidence you've got. Apart from some rabbits. Mr Derry sets great store by the rabbits."

At this moment they were interrupted by the arrival of the judges, and Justin found himself staring at a range of a few yards at the robed figures under the full-bottomed wigs advancing like images being borne in procession. He wondered to which of them Milligan and Kelly had been consigned. A couple of Molochs. That was apparently how Justice saw herself, to judge from the ceremonial and the craggy, impassive faces that might have been carved from stone. There was little to choose between them, though one idol was larger than the other and older, its eyes more deeply sunk between the massive nose and cheekbones, and the honour done to it seemed to be the more absolute, as though this were some particularly trusty and devouring idol that worked great works.

"Looks sleepy today," Gilmore remarked as the procession departed from them into the robing-rooms. "Not a good weather sign with Garrowby. He won't take to things too readily."

"He's a sound man," said Rees.

"Oh quite, quite. Very fair according to his lights. We could have done with someone a little less Messianic though. It's a case that wants understanding."

"A very clear case, surely? All too clear."

Gilmore considered this. "In a way," he admitted at last. "The crown's evidence is very strong: identification, motive, opportunity, Piggott's chisel, the footprints, the piece of paper and the button. It all adds up. Yet somehow the total seems wrong. If only I dared take a flyer at that evidence."

"It would be dangerous."

"Oh yes. There's not the shadow of a proof anywhere that anyone is lying. Why should they lie? The Verneys are transparently honest. Piggott was a friend of the accused. To attack the purity of the Police evidence is the simplest thing, and we all know it's usually the silliest. No one would believe me. Besides, Garrowby wouldn't like it. It could mean a stiffer sentence."

There was a flurry of movement near the doors and Justin perceived that the crowd had begun to press into court. He followed, and from just behind Mr Rees he heard the Queen's commission read and saw Mr Justice Garrowby take his seat in the chair under the royal arms between his marshal and the High Sheriff. "He was born in the Rectory," Mr Rees whispered over his shoulder.

"Garrowby? You can't mean in Massingham?"

"Certainly: in that very house. A strange coincidence, wouldn't you say? I wonder what he'll think as he sits up there and hears the story told . . . how much he'll remember?"

Justin wondered too. But all at once a number of things were happening. Mr Rees was elbowing his way forward towards the benches behind Gilmore; the Clerk of Assize was reaching for the court calendar; and soon there appeared in the dock a middle-sized, wiry fellow with a domed forehead and a fringe of whisker under the chin, and on his left a much younger man, not yet twenty, from whose lumpy, unformed face the ears stood out like jug handles.

"Patrick Milligan, Michael Kelly, you are jointly charged . . ."

They might be innocent. Yet it would have been a comfort, Justin thought, if they could have looked the part a little better. Where virtue had so lamentably failed to announce itself by outward and visible signs there was obviously a great need for cynicism in a young man, and he was easily able to maintain the mood through prosecuting counsel's opening for the Crown and the arrival of Mr Verney.

The Reverend Thomas James McMichael Verney. Aged sixty-eight. Rector of Massingham since 1859. Yes, he remembered the early hours of February 7th. His daughter woke him with certain news. He found a candle and an old sword, came down the stairs, saw through the open door of the dining-room the two men standing 'like soldiers in a line'.

As he told the story, his earnest eyes fixed on the judge, his white beard wagging above the witness-box as it must have done above his pulpit in the Norman church on score upon score of unremembered Sundays, the simplicity and courage of his actions came home to everyone. There had been no hesitation. He had come down with his candle and his blunt sword, and when the shot was fired and he felt his wound he still lunged out against his enemies, but gently, he insisted again and again, as though he fancied that those in court might make an aggressor of him. And then, when the first burglar had decamped through the window and he heard the second—the one with the gun—quite distinctly ramming home another charge of shot, he had struggled with his daughter to get free and had gone in alone to him, to what seemed likely to be his death.

The court stayed absolutely silent through all this. Mr Verney had risen above farce. It was impossible not to respect him. Justin could feel Mr Rees moving uneasily on the seat beside him. "You'll have to be careful with him, Mr Gilmore," he heard him whisper.

"I know."

"A highly respected man. A good witness too."

And a dangerous one, from the Defence point of view. For the Rector had moved on to a description of the visitors in the night, and whereas at the famous confrontation scene he had seemed doubtful, now, under the questioning of Edward Paget for the Crown, he was far more certain:

"As I came down the stairs I saw the lower parts of the men distinctly, but not the upper parts. One was dressed in a light coat, more of a grey colour. The other man had a dark coat. The men were just the same size and dress as the prisoners. I identified them by their height and bearing and the military positions they took up, as if they were trained men."

This was not altogether new: some of it was on the depositions. Nor did Justin find anything surprising in this hardening of opinion, since he knew it was what so often happened to the thing men call memory, which is less a snapshot of an event than a mosaic made up of all sorts of bits and pieces of hopes, prejudices, facts, imaginings. It was Gilmore's turn to sift them, for Paget had sat down and the judge, high up on his bench, was looking at him with his lowering expression.

"Mr Verney," Gilmore said.

Justin saw him shift a little in the box to face this new antagonist and one could see what a benevolent old man he was.

"Mr Verney, I am sure that everyone in court feels for you and your daughter in the grievous circumstances that befell you both, just as everyone rejoices in your recovery."

"It should be a matter for general satisfaction," remarked the judge, with a sharp look at the prisoners in the dock. "This might have been a capital charge."

"As your lordship so truly says, and no one would minimise the gravity of what happened." He turned to the witness. "Mr Verney, you have told us that you lunged out several times with your sword at the man in the dark coat? And you felt the blade penetrate some inches, as you thought, into the flesh?"

"Of his breastbone, it felt like."

"Then you had wounded him?"

"So I believed."

"Later you lunged at the other man, the one in the light coat who had remained in the dining-room. Did you wound him too?"

"I believed it at the time."

"Are you surprised today to learn that no wounds were found on either of the prisoners?"

"The sword was blunt. Some kind of mark was found on Kelly, I believe."

Gilmore was glancing at the jury. They were listening intently. "But not the wounds you had imagined?"

"That is so."

"Let me go back a little. You saw the intruders for the first time from the landing half-way down the stairs. You saw them through the open door of the dining-room?"

"I did."

"And you saw the lower parts of their bodies?"

"Distinctly. I had a candle and so had they."

"Mr Verney, do you remember writing a letter on February 17th to the *Smedwick Mercury*?"

He replied at once: "I do. I wanted to put a stop to all the idle and misinformed talk."

"So you wrote this letter to clear things up, to put the truth of the matter on record?"

"That exactly describes it."

"Thank you. Now in this letter did you use the following words: '. . . the lower parts of their bodies being all that I could see, *and that not distinctly*'?"

There was a stir of excitement in court of the kind usual when a question explodes under a witness, and in the public gallery it may have been believed that counsel had quite blown the old man up. Gilmore knew better. It was a score, but a small one.

"You did write that, Mr Verney?"

"I did. The light wasn't very good."

"So now we arrive at this—correct me if I am wrong. You saw only the lower halves of their bodies 'and that not distinctly'? And the top parts of their bodies not at all?"

"That is so."

"How did you identify the accused?"

"Partly by the clothes they wore. Partly by their bearing, the way they held themselves, like trained men."

"And by their height also, I think you said just now?"

"Certainly."

"Pray tell me, Mr Verney, how you manage to judge the height of a man when you can't see the top half of him?"

Justin saw a dawning smile on the faces of some of the jurymen, until they caught the judge's eye on them.

"I had an impression of size," the Rector managed to get out lamely.

"When did you get it?"

"At the time, naturally."

"Isn't it a fact that on the evening after the crime you hesitated to identify the two accused?"

"I was doubtful, slightly doubtful."

"But you're not doubtful now? Your memory gets better and better as time goes on?"

Again that laugh—and this time Garrowby took note of it and looked very deliberately round the court like an old lion that has been stirred up. Before he had got as far as Gilmore, that wary gladiator had sat down, well pleased with himself, as he had every right to be; but when Justin glanced round behind him he saw only the impassive faces of the prisoners in the dock and poor Rees looking quite flustered at this success. 'God knows what he'll think if Miss Verney gets the treatment too,' he said to himself. 'Another highly respected one, I shouldn't wonder.'

Just then he heard her name called and saw her coming past the press into the witness-box, which was on the judge's right and on the same level as the bench. She was about twenty, with dark hair and fine brown eyes which hardly seemed to belong to the tight angles of the mouth and jaw below them. A strange personality, he thought, studying her as she took the Book in her right hand: impulse and determination at war with one another. There could be no doubt which side of her character was winning.

"Miss Charlotte Matilda Verney?" Paget was booming out with the greatest gallantry.

"Yes."

"Miss Verney, will you tell my lord and the jury in your own words of the events of the morning of February 7th?"

She did so very factually without a flourish of any kind, doing her distasteful duty in a low incisive voice, very well bred. At the dramatic moments Paget would utter small exclamations of astonishment and admiration, as though drawing the jury's attention to her many excellencies, but she ignored him every time and spoke to the court as she might have spoken to some rather backsliding parishioners who had missed Matins three Sundays running. The substance of what she said was not as damaging to the prisoners as that given by her father in his evidence in chief, for she had only had the briefest glimpse of them before their candle was blown out, and after that had seen only one man by the light of the moon through a window still partly shuttered. Yet she too had the Verney memory which seemed to thrive on the passing of time. Her assailant, she said, resembled the prisoner Milligan whom she now saw. The resemblance was something that had struck her forcibly when he was paraded for her in her bedroom. Paget was nodding his head at this and commending her quick eye to the jury along with her pluck and good breeding. And still nodding, he sat down and left it to the Defence.

"You have spoken of resemblances," Gilmore began. "Was the resemblance you observed between your assailant and the accused man Milligan one of size?"

"It was a general impression," she corrected him severely.

"But size was part of it, surely?"

"Yes."

"Were there any other elements in your 'general impression'?"

She thought for a while and produced the word 'bulk', then corrected it to 'build'.

"Size again, surely?" Gilmore remarked. "You are saying that your assailant and Milligan were much of a size?"

"I suppose I am."

"Very good. Will you please look at the man, Miss Verney?"

She did so very calmly with her 'parish visiting' eye, and Milligan, finding it fixed on him, glanced nervously away.

"You'd hardly call him a particularly small man, would you?" Gilmore said, watching the two of them.

"No, I wouldn't."

"Yet I think you told us that when you reached straight out ahead of you in the darkness you grasped him by the hair?"

She saw the point at once and answered: "Of course he was stooping—doubled up—and that accounted for it."

"Why 'of course', Miss Verney? Did you *see* him stooping as he came towards you?"

"That was my impression."

"Pray what is an impression?" Gilmore said.

"An impression is simply an impression."

"But surely it can't exist in a vacuum? To receive an impression of an event one must presumably hear it, or see it, or smell it, or touch it. Would you agree?"

"I suppose so: yes."

"But your assailant never spoke, and what you saw of him was seen in a room lit only by moonlight shining through one window? In near pitch darkness?"

"It was nearly dark."

"Smell we may ignore. But you touched your assailant. You held him by the hair?"

"I did."

"Which assumes, does it not—forgive the levity—a certain length of hair to hold?"

There was a titter in court as everyone took in the point and Milligan's bristly crop.

"Perhaps he's had it cut," she said.

"Is that another 'impression', Miss Verney? You must forgive me. More is at stake here than a discourtesy or two. Let me ask you this. You remember that on the evening after the crime the accused man Milligan was brought to your room and he asked you to take hold of his hair and compare it with your assailant's?"

"Yes."

"What were your comments on that occasion?"

She didn't hedge, as so many would have done, but replied straight out: "I said that I thought the man in the passage had the longer hair."

"And didn't you say that you thought him broader in the shoulder too?"

"I did."

"More like Kelly, more Kelly's build?"

"Yes."

"But of course you don't claim to have touched or been near Kelly at any time?"

"No."

"Thank you, Miss Verney."

There followed her into the box the witnesses who formed the link between the Verneys and the Police evidence to come—the 'odd job men and discoverers', as Justin dubbed them. On a technicality the judge refused to have the evidence of Bulwer, the tailor who had examined the rent in Milligan's trousers and had compared it with the piece of cloth found in the flower-beds. But James Bell deposed to finding the torn sheet of paper in the Rectory hall. Dr Higson, the Police Surgeon, had unearthed the missing scrap of that same paper from the lining of Kelly's coat. The cook, Jane Clegg, produced the chisel: the same chisel which old Piggott (in whose house Kelly lodged) had identified in the depositions as his own. But where was Piggott himself? Not at the Moot Hall, apparently: they were tendering a medical certificate, along with the old man's sworn evidence before the magistrates. "You mean my friend is not calling this vital witness before the court?" Gilmore exclaimed in outraged tones.

"The man is destitute."

"Can't the Crown afford his fare?"

Mr Paget managed a sickly smile. "If my friend will but exercise his patience," he lamented. "The old man is too infirm to make the journey here. I have the doctor to testify to that."

"You're saying he's physically and mentally infirm?"

"Physically at least."

"And you want to read his deposition—on which I can't in the nature of things cross-examine. When did he make it?"

"Nine weeks ago."

"Was he less crazy then?"

Justin, in high glee, was just applauding this, when the judge had the doctor called and admitted Piggott's deposition on the spot. "The damned old Moloch!" muttered Justin fiercely under his breath. There had been nothing in Piggott's deposition to suggest that he could be cross-examined to any useful effect, but the way the thing had been done rankled and left the feeling that the law had been unfairly stretched in favour of the Crown. The Crown needed no such patronage. It had the evidence on its side; it had Superintendent Blair, who now advanced into the box, a huge man but walking delicately, like Agag.

Now Justin had set out that morning because the managing clerk had detailed him. Like most pupils, he was a disenchanted soul who guarded himself against enthusiasms. Yet already he was changing. Reading the depositions in the train, he had felt a quickening of interest that had surprised him, and now, at sight of Blair standing in the box with the Testament raised high, he had the strangest feeling of personal involvement in what was about to happen, as though he were at the beginning of something that would claim him one day, perhaps after a long time.

The Superintendent's evidence when it came was in amusing contrast to such thoughts. It was banal to a degree: more like an official circular than anything else:

"As a result of certain information I went to Massingham Rectory at about five a.m. on the morning of the 7th February. I found the drawing-room window had been forced open. From the witness Clegg I received a chisel and a piece of newspaper which I now identify. Under a window I saw certain indentations in the soil. I covered these with boards. Going out of the grounds into the lane leading past Merrick's bothy I saw sets of footmarks. I traced these marks from the lane to the main road and along that road towards Smedwick for the best part of a mile. On the 7th February and again on the following day I took plaster casts of these footmarks and I produce these casts with the boots of the accused. They correspond exactly. I found it impossible to take plaster casts of the marks under the window. On 13th February I gave the chisel in question to Inspector Mathieson and P.C. Pugh with instructions to show it to the witness Piggott. On 20th February I was present when Dr Higson was examining Kelly's old coat (which I now identify), and a piece of paper (which I now identify) was found in the lining of the coat. It fits exactly into the larger piece given me by the witness Clegg. The accused when charged denied all knowledge of the offences."

"Time for luncheon," murmured Mr Rees as the judge closed his notebook and laid down his pen. Justin allowed his thoughts to wander agreeably in the same direction. Lunch. A large one. Steak, kidney and mushroom pie for choice. With a pint of beer and apple tart and cream to follow. He had some hopes that the 'old buffer' would rise to that, and it was with a most grievous sense of deprivation that he saw they were not going out of court at all, but through the gate into the dock and downstairs into the bleak echoing world of cells, filled now with an aroma which he recognised authoritatively as Irish Stew. 'At least those two poor devils will be fed,' he thought, as the warder unlocked the grille, and with Rees leading they went in. A sad looking pair, though. Seen at close quarters they had an unprepossessing look. 'Capable of anything,' he noted to himself, 'though I expect it's only the knowledge that they're prisoners that makes me think so. A great leveller the dock: makes everyone look guilty. What villains we'd seem if we were there. And Garrowby. I know what a jury would think of *him*.'

"Now Milligan, you're much the older," Gilmore was saying, "so I'll address myself to you. You've heard the evidence. Have you anything to say about it?"

"It were lies, sir," the man said.

"Was Piggott lying about the chisel? Wasn't he your friend?"

No answer.

"Was Dr Higson lying about the paper in the coat? Or the Verneys? Why should they identify you if it wasn't you?"

"Because the Poliss had been talkin', sir. Poliss was sure we done it from the start. 'Come 'ere, you damned scoundrels,' the Superintendent says. That's the way 'e talked, sir. Then 'e comes back after a bit and knocks me down, sir. Says I been smokin' in me cell."

"And had you?" Gilmore asked, his face expressionless.

"May 'ave 'ad a bit o' baccy like."

"Why should he have a 'down' on you?"

"We done a bit o' poachin' like."

"Why should the Police risk their careers and conspire against you?"

They stared at him, unable to answer. It was fortunate, thought Justin, that the law as it stood would not allow them to be called as witnesses in their own defence. He felt sorry for them and for their story. By all the processes of law it was untrue. And it *sounded* untrue—he could not avoid that feeling, however much sympathy he might have for the two forlorn and ignorant men. It was an instinctive feeling and he tried to analyse it, puzzling over in his mind the paradoxical fact that the Crown's case should have suggested to him the accused's innocence and the Defence case even more certainly their guilt. He wondered if he was alone in these feelings. He could see on the faces of his colleagues none of his doubts but only an enviable calm and attention to business.

"Now see here, Milligan . . ." They were at bay now, just as they had been in the dock. "I want you to listen carefully. If you tell me that the Police abused you, and beat you, and had a grudge against you, then that's your case and I can put it to the Police witnesses in the box."

"It's for you to say, sir."

"No, it's for you. I'm your counsel. You instruct me. I must tell you, though, that in my opinion such accusations won't be believed, nor will an attack on this Police evidence as such. That cock won't fight. Ask Mr Rees."

"No one will believe it," the old man replied.

No one asked Justin his opinion: he was obliged for that. As he went up the stairs lunchless, with nothing in prospect but a sandwich before the judge descended from the grandiose meal the county had provided, he wondered what he would do in Gilmore's shoes. Fight, as Milligan and perhaps Kelly wished, and risk the heavier sentence? But with what? One had to have *some* weapons. A dead case. And yet the inner prompting of mind that had said to him at the beginning, 'Something is wrong', returned, and not all the magisterial appearance of Blair in the witness-box could quell it for an instant.

Gilmore started quietly with the witness. "Correct me if I am wrong," he said, "but as I understand the matter a large sheet of newspaper was found in the Rectory on the morning of the crime, and later there was found a scrap of paper which fitted exactly into the jig-saw, if I may call it that?"

"Exactly," Blair intoned.

"Found in the presence of the Police at Police headquarters by the Police Surgeon in the lining of the prisoner Kelly's coat?"

"In Kelly's coat."

"Now you and your subordinates had searched that coat?"

"Yes."

"Several times?"

"Several times."

"And found nothing?"

"Nothing at all."

It was like a duet—one really needed and expected a chorus, Justin thought, though perhaps it was asking too much of the jury to fill the bill.

"How long, Superintendent, had that coat been in the possession of the Police?"

Blair began to think this out and Gilmore said: "Consult your notebook if you like."

"I don't need to, sir. We had that coat between the 7th and the 20th February."

"And in all that time you found nothing?"

"We didn't search every day," Blair said.

"Of course not. But you searched it. Did you search it thoroughly?"

That was a clever 'Morton's Fork' kind of question, reflecting on Police skills, and Blair, forgetting other things and remembering honour, retorted hotly: "We try to be thorough, sir."

"Of course you do. I've no doubt you were thorough. No one doubts it. You and your men searched thoroughly and searched several times and found nothing. Then you hand the coat to Dr Higson, an independent witness, and immediately something is found."

"Don't know what you mean by that, sir?" Blair said aggrievedly. He would have done better to have kept silent. "Don't you?" Gilmore said. "Weren't you glad to have an independent witness to bolster up your case?"

Paget lumbered to his feet as though he would object. Gilmore ignored him entirely and remained facing the Superintendent. "Because your case *did* need some bolstering, didn't it? You had two suspects and a scrap of paper—and what else?"

"We had the chisel."

"Oh yes: Piggott's chisel. And some marks in the soil under the drawing-room window. Aren't we to hear of those?"

"I could make no casts from them," Blair retorted.

"Why not? Is soil not a receptive medium for footprints? Is a lane better?"

"As it happened, sir."

"How did it happen? I am puzzled. Please enlighten me."

Justin began to grin delightedly as he felt the old solicitor beside him moving restlessly in his seat.

"You see I am puzzled, Superintendent," the gentle, insistent voice went on, "by certain factors in this case. I am puzzled about the delayed discovery of that paper in Kelly's coat; the even more delayed finding of the cloth and button; the casts that were never made of the marks under the window. I must ask you formally if a mistake may not have been made about the guilt of the accused?"

"Impossible, in my opinion," the Superintendent said.

Gilmore smiled at him almost benignly. "You have a very decided opinion, have you not?" he remarked. "Didn't you have a decided opinion about this case from the start?"

"On the evidence as it came in, sir."

"Even before it came in, surely? Didn't you charge these men with this crime in the forenoon of the 7th February, *before* the Verneys had identified them?"

"Yes."

"*Before* you'd taken any plaster casts and compared them with the prisoners' footwear?"

"That is so."

"Before Dr Higson found the paper in Kelly's coat?"

"Yes."

"Before Piggott had identified the chisel or you had found the rabbits, buried, as the accused had said, on Bridewell Moor?"

Blair nodded.

"Isn't it a fact, Superintendent, that you charged these men with these crimes *solely* on the fact that your officers had discovered they were abroad on the night of the crime and might conceivably have done it?"

"There's the other evidence, sir."

"Try to be fair. That came afterwards, didn't it—after you'd arrested and charged them and made up your mind that they were guilty?"

"I'd not made up my mind, sir."

"Hadn't you?" Gilmore said, and Justin saw him turn directly to the jury. "You knew they were poachers, didn't you?"

"I knew them for poachers, sir."

"As a police officer you have a natural animus against the breed?"

"One would scarcely expect a fraternal devotion," remarked the judge to sycophantic laughter, in which, Justin observed, only a few jurymen joined.

"I would expect a proper attitude, neither more nor less, my lord," Gilmore replied, very grim, not smiling at all. "I would expect fair play: not prejudice."

"I wasn't prejudiced," the witness said.

"Try to remember. Didn't Kelly give evidence for the defence in another Police prosecution some weeks ago?"

"I believe he did."

"Didn't you lose that case? The man was acquitted?"

"Yes."

"What were your words to Kelly and Milligan when you charged them on the morning of the 7th?"

"I charged them in the usual terms."

"Didn't you say 'Come here, you damned rascals, and I'll tell you what you're charged with'? Is that the usual official charge?"

"I certainly did not," Blair said, above, but only just above, a titter of laughter much louder than the judge had raised.

"Didn't you strike Milligan in the cells?"

"I may have corrected him for smoking."

"Is that on the deposition?"

"No, sir—I saw no need."

"Only the adverse evidence appears on the depositions, is that it?"

And so it went on. But whenever Justin felt that the witness's authority was weakening he looked at the jury and thought again. For the jury could see all the time, as he could not, the prisoners in the dock behind him. Even at the height of the Superintendent's admissions he had seen their glances straying towards them, as though asking themselves whether two such farouche and desperate looking men could possibly be innocent. Indeed the moment the last of the Crown witnesses was out of the box he began again to ask himself these questions and saw the persuasive nature of Paget's case, which depended not on one man's word but on many, from the saintly Mr Verney to P.C. Moffat hunting diligently for a trouser button in the snow.

'Our turn now,' he thought, watching Gilmore rise to open the case for the Defence. No array of testimony here. There were only two witnesses in all.

First Kelly's sister, Eliza Jane. Justin knew that this girl had sold almost everything she possessed to help her brother, and there was an intelligence and moral force about her that struck him the moment she appeared and remained in his mind for long afterwards. Perhaps Paget for the Crown recognised this also, for the moment it was his turn he struck at her. "You gave your name as Mrs Piggott, I believe." She had certainly claimed that status for herself. "But isn't your legal name Miss Kelly?"

"I suppose it is, sir."

"You just live with Piggott, is that it?"

"I share with him."

"So it would seem that you have not been frank with us, even in your first words in that box, but have claimed something that is not true. Is all your evidence like that?"

"Like what, sir?"

"Untrue evidence. Lies. Let's look at it. You tell us that your protector, Piggott, never owned the chisel which in his deposition he has sworn is his."

"I never saw it in the house."

"Has Piggott any grudge against Milligan or your brother?"

"I don't think so, sir."

"Is Piggott a deceitful or lying man?"

"Not particularly, sir, not to mention."

There was laughter in court, in which Justin joined rather more loudly than the rest. He was intrigued by this witness who could be cornered and browbeaten and yet managed to emerge foursquare.

"You are not saying, are you," Paget persisted, "that the man you choose to live with is a cheat whose oath can't be relied on?"

"He's a bit old, sir, and stupid like. He's had a hard life."

"Does that answer my question?"

"I don't know, sir. Doesn't it?"

Again that laughter, and this time the judge intervened. "You had best not be pert. I am advising you."

'The damned old Moloch!' thought Justin again. In the last few minutes he had become a convinced partisan, and he was to remember that years later, when other details about the trial had faded.

Mr Paget had rested during the judicial intervention, but now re-entered the fray. "Miss Kelly" ('And he's a damned Moloch too!'), "Miss Kelly, you are not telling us that Piggott swore a false oath in his deposition?"

"I'm saying I never saw the chisel."

"Why should you have seen it? You'd hardly be aware of every tool of trade your man possessed?"

"I'd see them, surely?"

"How should you 'surely' know better than the man who swears he owned the chisel?"

"He's not been here to swear it, sir."

"My lord!"

"Answer the question," the judge directed with a cold disgust that Justin found far more distressing than Paget's histrionics.

"My lord, I'm trying. I never saw the chisel. Can I say more?"

"Or anything that's truthful or pertinent?" Paget said, and forthwith sat down.

A fairly even score. If the Defence had made no headway, it was as certain that the Crown had failed to break this clever and determined witness. But Kelly's fiancée, Amy Dodds, who followed her into the box, was a more vulnerable person and appallingly honest in her answers. Paget handled her with brutal brevity:

"You say you are Kelly's fiancée?"

"Yes, sir."

"Have you an engagement ring?"

"No, no ring."

"You live in the same house as Kelly?"

"Yes, sir."

"You share the same bed?"

"Yes, sir."

"How long have you lived with him?"

"Two year."

"Was he the first man to possess you?"

"Not the first."

"Do you still sleep with other men?"

"Sometimes."

"How old are you?"

"Eighteen."

Now in answer to Gilmore in chief, Amy had declared that of her knowledge neither Milligan nor Kelly had owned a gun, and that the bruising on her lover's body had come about when he had fallen on an icy patch of road some days before. It was testimony of a sort, quite favourable to the accused. Justin could see, however, that no one in such an exposed position as the jury box would believe a word she said once Paget had done with her. In a trice the fact of the real and homely Amy Dodds was blotted out under the licentious image of a naked harlot being subjected—rather forcibly and very pleasurably—to experiences of which the jury had only dreamed. Naturally they would discount her. As for the judge, one could hardly doubt what was passing behind that graven image of a face. He had suffered Amy Dodds and he would suffer the speeches, as the rules of the game demanded. When they were over he was not even in a hurry to begin his part, but arranged himself in his chair, with his robes tucked comfortably around him, like an old gentleman in a shelter at the seaside.

"Members of the jury, let us first look at the indictment."

It was a cogent charge. At times, in a stressed syllable or a turn of phrase, one could judge what weariness had possessed the old man all that day—"justice seen to be done . . . abundant evidence . . . repetitious, as you might think, but the prosecution's duty is to shirk nothing in putting all the facts before you, great and small." That duty was stressed time and again. "You must be *certain*. It is not enough to say 'Here is reason for suspicion: the Defence has not fully explained this or excused that.' You must not place burdens where they do not lie."

Measured and judicious words. The Verneys' evidence called out another such display of them. "Members of the jury, you are the judges of fact. Yet I would be failing in my duty if I did not direct you to consider that evidence with the greatest care, and indeed some caution. Of its honesty you need have no doubt: but you should remember also the conditions in the Rectory that night: the fitful light, the terror and excitement of the moment operating on the minds of Mr Verney and his daughter. Could they have been mistaken? If you are not fully satisfied by the identifications they made, then you should dismiss them from your minds. Turn to the other evidence."

A different note had sounded in the judge's voice, though perhaps only the very alert in court detected it. "Look at the footprints, members of the jury. It is not disputed that the same boots made the casts you have seen in court and the footprints in the lane and on the Deeping Road; and those boots were the property of the accused. How came those footprints there? How came the piece of paper into Kelly's pocket—that missing scrap that fitted into the large sheet found inside the Rectory? Of course it is not for the Defence to prove to you that there are innocent explanations for those footprints and the presence of the piece of paper in that coat. It is for the prosecution to satisfy you beyond reasonable doubt that the evidence adduced is proof of guilt. You are men of the world. You will weigh that evidence and the deposition of the man Piggott with regard to the chisel. Is it not cogent and persuasive evidence? What other explanations can there be? There was, you will remember, some suggestion of Police animus against the accused, though it is for you to say what relevance that could possibly have. On the other side you have heard two Defence witnesses. You have heard them say that they never saw the chisel in Piggott's house; that the accused men never owned a gun; that there was an innocent explanation of the bruising on Kelly's body; that the rabbits were dug up on Bridewell Moor in the exact place where the accused had claimed they lay. Well, what impression did that evidence and the two women themselves make on you? Were you impressed by them? If you are in reasonable doubt, you must give the accused the benefit of that doubt. Such is the law of England—that beneficent system of Justice, perhaps the most perfect the wit of man has ever devised to protect even the poorest and most humble from arbitrary actions, to ensure a fair trial before God and the law."

"Stuff and nonsense!" snapped Justin in a voice that to his horror was audible. Fortunately Mr Rees was rather deaf and so intent on his lordship that he would have missed the Last Trump if anyone had chosen that moment to blow it. In front of them Gilmore sat in an attitude of elegant repose.

"Well, members of the jury, there is your task. You have my directions on the law. That is all I can do to assist you."

When they had gone, and the judge had retired, the tableau of the trial broke up. Paget came hurrying past; the court was emptying; the prisoners had gone from the dock, and attendants were turning down the gas jets above the bench and in the well of the court.

"Could be an omen, though personally I doubt it," Gilmore remarked to Mr Rees, who was gathering up his papers and securing them neatly with tape. "They don't seem to expect the jury back too soon."

"And rightly, rightly. The jury listened to your speech, sir."

"Did they? I wonder."

"Ask young Derry here."

Gilmore looked at him: it was a friendly glance. "Well, Derry?" said he.

"They listened."

"Perhaps they did."

"And wondered about Blair a little."

"Yes."

"But trusted the judge."

"Till death do them part," answered Gilmore, smiling.

Just then there was a stir below them on the left, where the Prosecution witnesses had sat after giving evidence, and the Superintendent's burly form was seen coming towards them on his way out of court. Not even in the witness-box had the man looked more official: his rather bulbous eyes stared straight ahead, he held himself very erect, his chest thrust out aggressively, so that it needed a perceptive eye to see in him something defensive and wounded by the events of the afternoon.

"Nearly over, Superintendent," Gilmore greeted him with his usual urbane politeness. "I expect you'll be glad of it."

"Depends, sir. Depends on the jury."

"Think they'll be out long?"

"Not for me to say, sir."

"Oh, come now," Gilmore urged, "surely you'll chance a guess. Guilty or innocent?"

"I think they'll convict 'em, sir, since you insist."

"You may be right."

"And not take long about it," the Superintendent added in a much firmer and louder voice: "not if they've a grain of sense in 'em. It's plain enough: plain as a pikestaff to any honest man with eyes."

Gilmore let him go, smiling a little at that rigidly retreating back. He forgave the impoliteness and the rancour, though he was surprised to have found them in a man as disciplined as Blair. "Seems I am *not* forgiven," he observed to Rees. "Of course, I asked for it. And I was a little rough on him in court."

"Professionally, as was your duty—he knows that well enough, or should do. No, he was just impudent," said Mr Rees, affronted to the depths of his soul by the breach of class decencies and distinctions he had had to witness. "He forgot himself, forgot himself entirely. Most unlike him."

"You saw that too? He must feel it strongly to take it personally to heart like that. He hates those fellows. Poachers. He remembers he never caught the murderers of P.C. Luke. Will he win this time? We'll know in about an hour, I think."

But three hours had passed and it was close on ten o'clock at night before the jury finally made up its mind and found both prisoners guilty.

V

THE jury's verdict had been given in the judge's lodging, to which Garrowby had retired for the night—an unusual arrangement to say the least. Sentence was reserved for the morning in open court. The prisoners arrived early from the gaol near by, and Justin saw them hurried in by the side door. At ten came Garrowby in his carriage, huddled up in his robes as though he felt the cold. A sleepy and surly old lion he looked as he strode in procession to his room and emerged a few minutes later on to the bench to take his seat in the great chair below the royal arms. Milligan and Kelly came up the steps from the cells as their case was called and stood with their hands gripping the rail, their eyes fixed on him. The court was full. A strong contingent of Police was present, and there were others outside in the corridor. Flutters of rain beat against the windows above the public gallery, and the gas was on in the well and on the bench behind the judge's head. The tableau had recomposed itself, even to the tune of returning Blair into the witness-box to detail the past crimes of the accused—a number of poaching offences of a minor character.

Then Gilmore rose. "My lord."

Perhaps Garrowby had not expected to hear from him again, but he made no particular show of being displeased; merely lowered down at him as he had done throughout the trial.

"You wish to address me in mitigation?"

"I have been asked to," Gilmore said. "By Mr Verney, my lord."

"Indeed? Is he in court?"

Justin glanced behind him, and there, in the last row of seats below the gallery, he saw the old man leaning forward, his hands clasped in front of him as though he were about to lead a prayer.

"My lord, he is," Gilmore said. "But he has desired that in this, my last opportunity of addressing your lordship, I should convey to you his own heartfelt feelings."

"Very well."

Gilmore gave a hitch to his gown, a habit which he only gave way to when he was ill at ease. Obviously he had not liked the discouraging tone of the judge's voice, but he went on in his usual bold, straightforward way: "My lord, these accused are not entirely unknown to him. One, Milligan, was once a parishioner of his. My lord, Mr Verney instructs me that he does not believe these men intended to injure him. He thinks the gun was fired either by accident or out of bravado, to frighten him, when they saw him advancing sword in hand. Mr Verney is an elderly man. In the circumstances of that night he was in the power of these fellows, both much younger and stronger than he. They could have beaten him, killed him with a second shot or by clubbing him. But they did not. He struck out with his sword, and it is his belief still that he wounded or at least touched them, yet no violence was offered him. They sought to escape, not to kill, for neither is a violent man by disposition. There are only minor crimes against them. My lord, Mr Verney is mindful of these things, and because of them he has come to court today to ask for mercy. I ask your lordship for it too."

The judge had listened broodingly, his head slightly on one side, an arm under the scarlet sleeve extended along the bench towards the nosegay of flowers that had been presented at the opening of the Assize. As soon as Gilmore had sat down, he had the Clerk call formally upon the prisoners, and then addressed them:

"Milligan and Kelly, you have been found guilty after a most patient hearing of one of the gravest offences known to the law, and it is only thanks to Providence that you are not charged with murder."

Now as soon as the judge got to Providence Justin knew that it was all up with the prisoners. He glanced at them, but obviously the words meant nothing to them. Kelly's lips were moving, but both stood at attention, indeed like 'drilled men', in Mr Verney's words.

"I have heard with pain, and at the same time with satisfaction," the judge was saying, "the observations made by learned counsel, communicating to me the desire of Mr Verney, and I am sorry to say that I do not think I ought to act upon that recommendation. The offence is one, as I have said, of the highest and gravest character, and I have sought in vain for any redeeming circumstance."

"Twelve years," hazarded one of the Police behind Justin in a whisper. It was not Blair, who was sitting nearer the door among the Smedwick contingent.

"The circumstances were overwhelmingly against you. The verdict was, in my opinion, perfectly correct. Your crime is burglary—breaking into the peaceful abode of a venerable old man and his daughter, with no one, as one of you at all events knew, there to protect them."

"Make it fifteen," the policeman murmured, and indeed Justin was ready to agree with him. Peaceful abode . . . venerable old man . . . unprotected daughter—it only needed Providence to rear its head again. He was filled with awe and almost with admiration at the way the judge had even turned Mr Verney's appeal on behalf of his ex-parishioner into an added argument for severity.

"The offence," the judge continued, "consists of burglary, accompanied by violence, and if ever the law ought to take its course to the extreme, this is the case. Unquestionably, if death had ensued, as it might, both of your lives would have been forfeited. Miss Verney's life was undoubtedly in great danger, and it is almost a miracle that you are not now being condemned to death. I do not hold out any hope, but if the Crown in the exercise of mercy should think it right to act upon the recommendation of Mr Verney, I think that belongs to the Crown and not to me. In order to deter bad characters who break into peaceful homes, and endanger the lives of persons, and steal their property, I must pass upon you the severest sentence, and that is penal servitude for life."

"Well I'm damned!" the policeman said.

THE QUEST
1899

I

ONE January morning, nearly eight years later, Justin was in his office when Harris, his managing clerk, came in to tell him that there was a 'person' outside to see him. Though a kindly man, Harris was prone to such distinctions, probably in an attempt to teach his employer his station, to instil in him a proper understanding of what was expected of a solicitor. It would have been too much to have expected him to relish so easy-going a principal after a lifetime spent in serving a firm of the old school. As well expect such a man to doubt the sanctity of contract or the intrinsic beauty of a conveyance. He never ceased to try to improve on nature.

Now that morning Justin was busy. He had come a long way since he had sat at the trial in Belcastle Moot Hall in the last year of his articles. He had his own practice now, with Mr Harris in the lobby in the glory of a frock-coat. He even had an office boy called Pete, or Spinks, or Mr Spinks, depending upon who was present and how they happened to feel about him—which was usually homicidal, for Pete was an idle and somewhat dissolute youth.

The office near the centre of the town, in the cobbled market-place where it narrows towards the Bolbec Gate, was a thing of beauty which solicitor and clerk would contemplate on arrival and departure with the tender care that is only lavished in the early and very last days of tenancy. 'Is not this Great Babylon that I have builded!' Justin remembered how his younger sister, a girl of lively and astringent mind, would tease him about his feelings for that building and the gold lettering on its windows. It was a second home to him. Inside its doors, in the rather dark ill-shapen room which he had crammed with the oldest deed boxes he could find and cartoons from *Vanity Fair* of judges fat and judges angular in gorgeous scarlet robes, he would feel borne up with the dizzy sense of making his way in the world. In that room he felt fulfilled and triumphant. And it was there that he met Margaret Binns.

She was a small woman, undoubtedly a 'person' within Mr Harris's meaning of the Act, about twenty-eight years old, with a peaked little face from which two dark eyes gazed out in an expression half sullen and half terrified. Probably she had never been in a solicitor's office before and was overwhelmed by the grandeur of the thing and by the presence of Harris looming beside her rather in the style of a warder presenting a criminal in the dock.

"Miss Binns," he announced in a sepulchral and disapproving voice.

Justin rose and offered her a chair facing him across the desk, which he had mounted with a rare assortment of the bulkier legal textbooks. It was a sight calculated to impress, and indeed, flanking him on either side, were bookcases containing even dustier tomes which he had managed to pick up at a knock-down price. Directly behind his head, over the mantelpiece and the fire which Mr Harris's economical soul hated to see lit, was a framed certificate announcing professional competence, in case anyone had any doubt about it. The setting was as nearly perfect a replica of an old-established firm as Justin's savings and Mr Harris's memory of the real thing could make it.

"You want to see me?" he said encouragingly to the girl as soon as they were alone.

He had had a few clients like her before. Sometimes they came into a small—pathetically small—legacy and wanted to know what to do; sometimes their menfolk were in trouble. One had been beaten by her husband and had shown him the bruises with a freedom that scandalised Harris when he came to hear of it. "Really, one cannot be too careful, sir," he had remarked, after making sure that the office boy was out of earshot. Even the hint of a scandal alarmed him. "I have known of a case, sir—not in this town, I am thankful to say—where a professional gentleman was actually threatened with a writ! For an impropriety, sir!" Clearly nothing could possibly be more shocking, and from that time on, whenever Justin had clients of the female sex alone with him, he was aware of the watchdog on guard on the other side of the door.

To have had such thoughts of Miss Binns would have required a real effort of imagination. She was such a sad little thing. And so silent. She was so tiny that Justin could only just see her head and scrawny neck above the piles of books that lay between them. It was hard to establish any kind of contact. She wanted to speak, but obviously she was having second thoughts. 'Perhaps,' he said to himself, 'she has no money to pay me,' and he tried to broach this to her and suggest it was not a matter she need trouble herself about unduly. But she shook her head.

"Is it some trouble you're in, Miss Binns? Some problem you have? Come now, don't be nervous, don't be afraid of me. Do I look the sort of person to be afraid of?"

She looked at him, weighing him up, and assuredly she must have thought that he did not look that sort of man. There was a mildness about him, though it could be deceptive sometimes, and then he was young, with a smile of great charm and kindliness. Suddenly she made up her mind and said out of the blue: "It's about Mr Milligan and Mick Kelly."

She had assumed that he remembered them, and of course he did. The furore of that case had never quite died down in Smedwick, kept alive by an occasional paragraph in the local paper reporting the transfer of the prisoners from one gaol to another; and there was an undercurrent of rumour and resentment that still moved below the sluggish waters of official satisfaction. Besides, Justin had never forgotten his own emotions at the trial. His belief in justice had been put to a test it had not fully overcome, and he was never a man to put an idea aside merely because it was uncomfortable and hard to live with. He was puzzled all the same by this sudden reappearance.

"Are you a relative of theirs?" he asked. It was naturally his first thought. Both prisoners had a quiverful of all sexes and sizes.

"No, sir."

"A friend, perhaps?"

"Not particular. I've met them like."

"Is it some message you have from them?"

"It's something *about* them, sir."

Justin with difficulty restrained his impulse to ask why she had come to *him*. He saw that if he once stopped her or put obstacles in her way she would dry up completely. So he smiled at her encouragingly and said: "So what's your message? You can tell me, you know."

"They're innocent."

He gave a sigh at that, for something about the girl and her air of nervous excitement had roused his curiosity, and yet here she was, repeating gossip eight years stale. "I know there are people who think that," he answered as kindly as he could. "The court didn't, and we can't change that, now can we?"

"Why not, sir?"

"My dear child!" he nearly exclaimed, though they were almost of an age. But a certain suggestiveness in her voice intrigued him, and instead of embarking on a set speech about the immovability of established things, he said: "All right. Suppose you tell me how."

"I'm George Sugden's niece."

Immediately he sat up in his chair, every critical faculty alert. He knew that name. Sugden had been one of the first suspects of the burglary at Massingham.

"Your uncle?" he said, anxious not to frighten her with too much knowledge. "I seem to have heard the name."

"Most people in Smedwick have," she answered surlily. "He's been in the papers, sir."

"Oh?"

"In trouble, as you might say. He poaches, sir."

"Is he in trouble again?"

"He soon will be."

This time there was no mistaking the note of menace in her voice. 'Not exactly a devoted niece,' said Justin to himself. 'Doesn't seem to like uncle much. Now why? And what's it all about? Some family quarrel?'

"Is it on your uncle's behalf you've come?" he said aloud, knowing perfectly well it wasn't. "Is it something he might do that troubles you?"

"Something he's done, sir."

It was a riddle, but he had already begun to guess.

"Some action of his?"

"Yes."

'Some crime?' he wanted very much to add. But at this point his professional rectitude overcame him. It was one thing to encourage the girl to confide in him, but quite another to invite her to make accusations which might lead her and others into trouble. He had no right to ask such questions: he had a duty to listen, that was all.

So for a moment silence fell on the office, behind whose door Harris could be heard announcing his presence and state of watchfulness with sundry coughs and clearings of the throat. Miss Binns looked down at her lap. Justin regarded the wall behind his client's head, on which hung a cartoon of Lord Esher, Master of the Rolls, an inspiring and conscience-encouraging sight. If the silence prolonged itself much longer he felt sure that his clerk would mount some rescue operation and ruin everything, but Lord Esher's gaze, gentle yet restraining, was there as a reminder of the better path. And like most good actions, which are usually wise ones, this silence paid a handsome dividend. Suddenly the client spoke. "You'll remember the night of the crime, sir?"

In Smedwick parlance 'the crime' was the Massingham burglary and had remained so in spite of the fairly constant efforts of the local criminals. So spirited an attempt to despatch a cleric with a blunderbuss had struck a new note, as crimes must do if they are to be remembered; crime being very like *haute couture* in this respect. Justin of course knew this and replied at once: "You mean what happened at Massingham?"

"That I do, sir."

"Yes, I remember it."

"Do you mind that early that morning the Poliss called at where I lived? At Geordie Sugden's place, sir."

"I think I heard of it."

"I mind they called about five o'clock. I lived downstairs with me Grannie—that was Geordie Sugden's mam, sir. And Geordie, he lived upstairs wi' his missus, and still does."

Her voice, once so hesitant, had become quick and light. No need to prompt her now: not even the entry of Mr Harris could have stopped her.

"Well, I heard Poliss go up, sir, and then they come down after a bit, and it got light, and when it got light George Sugden's wife, sir, she come running down and she says to me and me Gran that the Poliss would come back, and when they did we was to say her man had nivver stirred out a step that night."

Justin waited.

"But he *had*, sir," Miss Binns said; "he'd been out a while. It were about four in the mornin' when I heard him come in."

"Did you tell Mrs Sugden what you knew and what you'd heard?" asked Justin, taking up the thread.

"Yes, sir."

"Did you ask why she made you such a request?"

"I did."

"What did she say to that?"

"That blood were thicker than water, sir. That her man was in trouble. That she hoped he hadn't murdered anyone."

"Indeed!"

"And then she come down again, sir—it were mornin' then; it'd be nine or more. And she says to me Grannie and me that Geordie and his mate had been out at Mr Verney's seekin' about the room, and the old man had heard 'em and come downstairs and that they'd fired a gun."

"Who was his 'Mate'?"

"Don't know, sir."

Now Justin was a man who usually got his priorities right. He did not enquire why his client, a niece of Sugden's, had come with this story, since he guessed that some family row had blown up. What was required was to take the evidence formally; so while Harris coughed himself almost into a decline in the outer office he set himself to get the client to make her statement in legal shape, with the sequence correct and her signature at the foot of it. In this way, without pressing the witness, he discovered that on the night before the crime Sugden had been wearing a light grey coat, and that this coat had been destroyed by Sugden and his wife in the small hours. There were also hints of other evidence and certain names were given, including that of a roadman called Green who had lived on the same stairhead as Sugden, though he had since moved.

In retrospect and alone, Justin sat down and thought what he should do about his most recent client. He was no longer excited by what he had heard. It seemed to him probable that the evidence he had so laboriously taken down was no more than a tissue of lies born of some grudge or feud, and he had a horror of such things. Furthermore, though he was a man of wide sympathies and something of a rebel at heart, he was no Crusader; having in him a strong leaven of north-country caution, which is in the last analysis a dread of being made to look foolish.

"Do you know George Sugden?" he enquired of his clerk on the way out to luncheon. "I mean his record and so on?"

"I believe he has a record, sir. I have read of it."

"That was his niece you showed out a while ago."

Mr Harris nodded. It was clear that he had invested her with criminal connections from the start. "Is she a client, sir? Shall I open a file?"

"There's only this statement. You'd better read it yourself and then put it in the safe. I don't want young Spinks to see it."

"Very good, sir."

"And don't be alarmed. I'll probably take no action on it."

He returned an hour later, confident of finding gloom in the outer office and the silence of disapproval. It was Harris's maxim that only long-established firms could afford black sheep among the clients; newcomers must beware of them and discourage all but the 'good-class work'. Wasn't Miss Binns pre-eminently the wrong sort? Justin wondered. He feared very much she was. Yet the clerk's face, instead of being reproachful, was bland and welcoming. Either a miracle of character transformation must have taken place or some outstandingly good news had reached the office during the last hour: a client of the right sort, perhaps, with a deed box fit to stand beside those of Sir Miles Curvis, Mr Freeze-Urquhart and Colonel Deverel, whose names in bold white lettering adorned a corner of the office where the light fell best.

"Miss Deveral called, sir. I showed her in," Harris announced in his most unctuous voice.

So that was it. Justin took fright at once, exclaiming: "My God! Has she been waiting long?"

"Not long, sir. Ten minutes or so. I offered to fetch you, but Miss Deverel said she was quite content to wait."

He gave a sigh of relief, glanced quickly in the mirror to straighten his tie, and went in to his fiancée with what he hoped was the right blend of devotion and professional gravity. "Dearest Georgina . . ."

She was standing by the window: a pale girl of medium height, blessed with the rather Junoesque bust and carriage expected of Victorian young ladies. Good money had been spent on them. Her dress was of mauve brocade, wide at the hips and with a pronounced bustle; she wore a hat tilted at an alarming angle—an equestrian effect—surmounted with a feather sweeping back over her brow; and her hands were hidden in a muff. The effect was charming, expensive, perhaps a little daunting with its suggestion of claims and expenses to come.

Justin began at once to apologise: he was in excellent practice. "Dearest, I've kept you waiting, you can forgive me? If I'd only known. Were you *so* uncomfortable?" Compunction seized him as he saw that this must indeed be true since the ass Harris, that confoundedly economical ass, had all but let the fire go out on this chill winter afternoon. She must be half starved with cold. But the thought and the question gave him his opportunity too and he embraced it eagerly, coming close to her and taking her hand where the grey of a glove projected from the tight curls of the astrakan muff. "What must you think of me?"

"That you're hardly the best of managers," she said, accepting him, but not effusively. "Not very comfort-loving."

"My dear, I know, but in an office . . ."

"Why should an office be so different?" She was looking round the room, and he could see that her gaze was not kind as it lighted on the dusty textbooks in the case whose glass had not been washed these many months, the deed boxes, even the diplomas, which he now observed were hung askew and somewhat off-centre. "Well? Why should it be?" she said with a trace of irritation. "You're the master here."

Justin would never have put it like that; he would never even have thought it in relation to the office boy Spinks, let alone his managing clerk, in whose aura he was endeavouring to improve himself. "I suppose I am," he answered mildly. "Only really we're a team." He liked the phrase and repeated it, feeling that it would appeal to her also, since it was one he had often heard her father use. "Yes, we're a team, that's it, that describes it. I leave the day-to-day arrangements to old Harris. . . ."

"And he decides how warm you feel! Ridiculous. No, it is *not* a small matter. You have too great a tendency to be put upon. Why, I don't know."

She was studying him, standing back a little, her hand still in his, and her determination to change his nature at the first available moment could hardly have been more evident. Somehow it seemed to him that all those close to him, including Harris, were staking out similar claims.

"You're the same at home," she accused him.

"Oh, come now."

"Yes you are. Doesn't Flo dictate to you?" (Flo was his elder sister, who kept house for him.) "And Mamie wheedles you. It's only me you're stubborn with."

At this stage he kissed her—chastely, for she had turned her face away from him, but definitely all the same. Not a sound came from the outer office: Cerberus was not on guard against this particular visitor, the daughter and heiress of the second grandest client the firm possessed.

"What can you be thinking of!" she cried. "You'll ruin the feather, and it is really *very* fashionable. No, you must listen. How do you think I'm here today? Emily came out with me."

"Dear cousin Emily, dear kind Emily," he said.

"Well, you may think that. She had some business of her own at the Assembly Rooms as it happened."

"We must provide more business for her: much, much more."

"Mama would be suspicious. You know how particular she and Papa are about such things. You *should* know. Only you're so lax yourself."

"My dear Georgina!" he cried, appalled at this new line of attack. "Whatever do you mean? Lax? Why it was you who came here today —not that there's the least harm in it," he added hastily and much too late.

"You see! You're sorry that I came."

He glanced up at the ceiling in despair, knowing that once again he had said the wrong thing and that this time there was no hope of restoring the position by gallant actions, for she had moved away from him and her hands were once more tightly tucked into the muff.

"I'd not have come at all," she went on before he could utter a word, "if I'd not had to; if you'd called yesterday as you were bid."

"I was detained in court. Surely you got the note I sent you?"

"But it was Papa who invited you. You see how lax you are, you have no social sense. Don't think it isn't noticed. It makes things difficult for me."

"My dearest, I'm sorry, I'm truly sorry."

The evident distress in his voice seemed to appease her and the expression in her eyes, which were of the same pale blue as her father's, became gentler. "You don't give enough thought to it," she chided him. "To being agreeable to Papa, I mean. You argue with him, which is strange when one thinks how you defer to Flo and to any whim of Mamie's, who is too *free* in my opinion. You could try with Papa to show more understanding of his point of view and to be less *radical* about things. You know how such ideas frighten him."

Justin was startled to find himself a Jacobin; he had always thought of himself as too conservative if anything; and the picture of the hard-bitten Colonel Deverel in terror of his ideas completed the feeling of hallucination that was creeping over him. "I can't think you mean all that," he said lightly. "Radical indeed! I may have spoken up in court for some of his tenants once."

"It's your whole attitude, and Papa notices it. He's sensitive about these things. Of course, if you don't want to listen or to please him . . ."

"I want to please *you*. I want to make *you* happy."

She turned towards him, no longer petulant but radiant, holding out her hand in the beautiful grey glove. "And you *do*, Justin. You *can*—always. By just remembering what I've said."

"I'll try."

"Then you'll be sure to come to dinner on Friday night? And you shall take me to the Assembly Rooms next Wednesday. Giulio is singing, with Miss Campana—and cousin Emily if it comes to that."

From the window, a few minutes later, he was watching her elegant figure cross the market-place between the booths. It looked far too bucolic for her. The correct setting, he recognised, would be a lawn with elms in the background and a marquee from which came music and the sparkle of conversation. The ground would be terraced, falling to a lake fringed with reeds and white with water-lilies in bloom, on whose far shore stood a belvedere with a classical dome. Gardeners might be perceived with besoms sweeping diligently at the paths under the pollarded trees. There would be a lot of servants.

He had reached this point in his picture when she turned the corner between the butcher's shop and the chemist's, where the green and cherry coloured flagons glowed in the afternoon light, and disappeared from view. She would call at the Assembly Rooms for Emily, no doubt, and the carriage would meet them before dark to whisk them home along the Warbury Road. And on Friday he would see her again behind the mahogany at the Deverels' in the darkly panelled room, with the silver candlesticks on the table and old Deverel himself in his white waistcoat and vast expanse of shirt-front, like an ectoplasm in a spirit photograph. What a bore it would be.

The sense of guilt induced by this and similar thoughts sent him back that afternoon much earlier than usual to his home in Laburnum Road. All its houses were tall and gabled in a biliously tinted brick. Trees adorned the street and there were gardens to front and rear planted with shrubs that rustled mournfully in the wind. Here a few professional people still lived, though beyond, in the pleasantly wooded coastal plain, newer 'residences' were springing up, and Laburnum Road, like its neighbours which had once housed the *haute bourgeoisie* of Smedwick, had begun the process of gradual decay that had already overtaken the Georgian houses in Bewley and Pelegate. It would never degenerate into a slum—the bathrooms alone were sufficient to declare it—but it had come to resemble a lady of a certain age whose income has unaccountably shrunk. 'Genteel' was Mamie's word for it and a hurtful one to Flo, who was devoted to the place where her parents had lived and died. Under her anxious care 'The Laurels' had acquired a special gentility: its garden was gloomier and more heavily planted than other gardens, its paint was darker, the curtains more impenetrable, as though the house were trying to make a declaration on behalf of the whole neighbourhood.

Justin, coming through the spiked iron gate, found his heart sinking a little. He might not have to live there much longer, now that he and Georgina had all but settled on a house up the Warbury Road, but for some reason the very sight of 'The Laurels' had made him come to doubt his visions of a new life. That in one bound he could remove from it into the sphere of Colonel Deverel seemed more unlikely every day he trod the gravelled path between the clumps of pampas grass and let himself into the dark, narrow passage that smelt of bees-wax.

In the drawing-room Flo was waiting, tucked into her usual corner of the chesterfield, her small blonde head that reminded him of an angel in a Botticelli painting bowed over her needlework.

"How early you're home, dearest. Such a surprise."

Neat hands stitched at the tambour, unhurriedly, never varying pace. In time some pattern would emerge and go to a bazaar to raise funds for one of the many causes for which the parish of St Bede's was famous. Yet how these pieces of rather joyless needlework raised money, or who purchased them, or what became of them, was always a mystery to him. He sat there glumly waiting for tea, hoping for crumpets. Soon it was time to light the gas, and the room, which had lain in shadow, showed itself in all its determined cosiness. He had only to reach out an arm to encounter a Chinese screen, a music stand, a leather pouffe, two Chinese vases, a workbasket, a rocking-chair, and a paperweight in the form of a dragon's claw. Above the mantelpiece, which was loaded with small squatting idols and lacquer cups, hung a canvas of Highland cattle by a lochside at sunset, the peaks aglow in a fiery orange light.

"Was it a good day, dearest?"

It was normally at this time of the evening, when the gas had been lit and the curtains drawn, that the 'interrogatories' began. Flo never asked indiscreet questions, never expected names or details of cases, showed no interest in the profits of the business. But it was surprising how much she contrived to know about the office which she seldom visited and clients whom she never saw. Her memory was as prodigious as her appetite for news was insatiable. She had to be fed, and he had found that the easiest way to do it was to throw her some more or less indigestible scrap, like the shortcomings of the charwoman or Harris's notorious meanness. Today, however, he had a more generous tit-bit in store:

"Georgina called."

"How nice for you," she cried. "Dearest, now *nice*." She was really pleased for him: she seemed to have been born without jealousy. "How was she looking? Quite well, I hope, the dear girl."

For the next quarter of an hour he laboured to account for his Georgina point by point. The dress—or as much of it as he could remember—was commended highly. The muff was envied. Was it of astrakan? Had it a muff warmer? When Mamie at last descended from her bedroom, sprightly in yellow muslin, her opinion was enlisted and the matter thrashed out between experts who agreed only in blaming him for his imperfect observations of how Georgina had looked and what she had or had not worn. As always he was astonished by this strange ability of theirs to create passionate interests for themselves at second hand. Would they be the same after marriage? Would Georgina?—which was more to the point. What did she in her turn really think of the old-maidish, gossipy Flo and the immodest—or so it seemed to his brotherly gaze—creation in yellow muslin that was flouncing up and down the room? The shape of future quarrels arose like phantoms of horrible aspect between him and these dependants, present and future, who each in her separate way was unintelligible to him. How could he cope with the three of them in harness?

By bedtime, deep in insoluble problems, he had forgotten Miss Binns and Milligan and Kelly; never suspected that a window had opened on his life.

II

"REMEMBER me, sir?"

If only, he thought, old Rees or Featherstone had lived to be burdened with these vexatious people. First Miss Binns with her statement which still lay in his safe in the folder which Harris had provided, complete with reference number and title in beautiful copperplate, and now this other one. He remembered her all right: Miss Kelly, old Piggott's mistress and one of the ill-starred witnesses for the Defence, but she had changed: she had the same intent look that had struck him at the trial, but she had filled out and there was more colour in her cheeks. No doubt one of the reasons for these improvements was to be found in the oafish fellow whom she was edging towards him—"This is my fiancey, sir. Jim Longford, sir. We just got engaged."

Justin smiled and said felicitous things. Beyond the fact that she was rid of Piggott he could see no significance in her remark: that was only to occur to him many years later.

"We come about George Sugden, sir. We seen Miss Binns."

"You have?"

"She telt us about her statement, sir. That she come to you, sir, and telt you about Sugden. That you said you'd take it up, sir."

"My dear Miss Kelly, I'm afraid there's nothing *to* take up."

She was staring at him in bewilderment, her eyes as round and bright as a bird's. "Nowt, sir? But Margaret telt us Geordie Sugden was from hame that night."

"He may have been."

"And that he were at Verneys', sir."

He shook his head decidedly. "No, that's not so. Miss Binns can't possibly say that. She may remember Mrs Sugden saying that he'd been at Mr Verney's, but I'm afraid that isn't evidence."

He thought for a moment that she would query it, and wondered how he could explain the rules of hearsay to that unwavering stare. But instead she went on doggedly: "He burnt his coat, sir."

"There may be evidence for that."

"Isn't it important?"

"In a way. It shows he may have feared arrest, but it could have been arrest for poaching or indeed for anything. Nothing points directly to the burglary. It might be different if anyone had heard Sugden say that he was there."

"I think there were a lad as heard him. Tom Green, sir. Lived on the same landin', but he's moved."

"So Miss Binns suggested, and we could check with him of course. It would be some kind of evidence. Not much, however, I'll be frank with you. The Prosecution called a dozen witnesses, and that was eight years ago and there's a jury's verdict on the issue. To overturn it . . . why, even if Sugden himself confessed . . ."

"Suppose he did, sir?"

"If ifs and ans were pots and pans . . . ," he was beginning with a smile, when she broke in on him insistently:

"No, sir. Suppose he did?"

He stared at her, not knowing whether to be more amused or astonished by that interruption. She was an unpredictable one all right. "Oh, come now," he exclaimed, deciding to make a joke of it, "you can't be seriously suggesting that he'd confess? What would he have to gain? If he's a criminal, as you're telling me . . ."

"But he's changed, sir."

"In what way—changed?"

"Don't know what it is, sir, can't rightly say, but somethin' in 'im's changed. If you was to see 'im, sir—you or his vicar, that's Mr Lumley, sir . . ."

"My dear Miss Kelly," he protested, "you are not asking me to *call* on him, I hope!"

"Why not, sir?"

"Why not!" No really, this had gone too far. "I'm sorry, but let me make this plain. I have every sympathy with you and with your brother and Milligan, because I think there was at least a doubt about their guilt. . . ." She began to protest her brother's innocence, but he held up his hand. "No, listen: you've asked my opinion and I'm telling you that nothing has happened that can help us —nothing. As for the idea that I should force myself on a perfect stranger on the off-chance that he might confess to a crime . . . well, I don't want to be unkind, but you can hardly expect me to take it seriously. And now if you'll please excuse me."

The instant they had gone he went to the safe and took out the file that contained Miss Binns's statement. "You can return this," he instructed Harris who had appeared in answer to his call. "Better draft me a covering letter saying that we regret, etcetera."

"Yes, sir."

"And I do regret it in a way. You've read the statement?"

"Yes, sir."

"Very interesting, don't you think? And disturbing too. If Miss Binns had come forward at the trial. . . . However, she didn't, so that's that and it's too late now; nothing can be done about it. It will just have to be returned."

"A very wise decision, sir," Harris intoned, taking possession of the file which he placed securely under his arm, rather as though he expected it might try to get away from him.

"Yes, I'm sure it is. There's nothing I can usefully do. No good getting mixed up in it."

"That is entirely my opinion, sir."

"And yet. . . . No, look here, it won't do just to send it back like that, it looks rude. After all, Binns took the trouble of coming to see me and in a sense I accepted the thing, so the least I can do is to see her personally to explain why I can't go on with it. Write and ask her to call, there's a good fellow."

Once matters were in Harris's hands they could safely be forgotten. It was an exacting week, with two court sittings and Georgina to be escorted to a subscription concert at the Assembly Rooms, and some days had passed before, going to his safe one morning, he was reminded that Miss Binns's file still lay there.

"I suppose you didn't forget to send that letter?" he enquired of Harris on his way out to lunch. "You didn't hint in any way that I was going to disappoint the lady?"

"Excuse me, sir: you saw the letter. You signed it, sir."

And so of course he had done: he could recall the terms of it. A nuisance that people of her type were so casual, but she would come in her own time.

When another week went by, however, during which a reminder was sent, and still no Miss Binns appeared, he began to be irritated, having a tidy mind and a dislike of loose ends. Could the letters have been misdirected? He took out the statement to read and for a moment thought he had found the answer, for the address she had given was not Sugden's in Bewley Street, as he had somehow imagined, but of a house nearby in Pelegate; and might not Harris have made the same mistake, both addresses being on the file? A word with his clerk soon convinced him that the letters had been sent to Pelegate. Suppose, then, she had moved back to Sugden's house?

Suppose—this seemed the most likely explanation—suppose she had made up her quarrel with her uncle and had returned under his wing, only too anxious to forget that she had ever made a statement or called on a solicitor? The letters could be lying at the house in Pelegate. There at least was something which could be settled, and that evening, ignoring the inner prompting that told him he was making a fuss over matters which did not concern him, he set off to see.

Forty-seven was the number. There were two numbers to each house, an upstairs and a downstairs, which in turn would be subdivided, making a perfect warren of the place. They had not been bad houses once. Someone who had not given particular thought to it, but had been bred in a tradition, had built them and arranged the gentle curve of frontages that followed the line of the street as it led uphill under the moor. There were no gardens. It had been an age that had prized symmetry above everything: ten houses to a row, six rooms to a house: no one had thought of privies, which had proliferated in the yards behind among the rabbit hutches and chicken runs.

Justin approached the house, from the rear of which came the sound of hammering and of a woman berating a child. The whole life of the street seemed to pass out of sight of it in a kind of limbo that the passer-by on the respectable side, the blind side, could never witness. He knocked, hearing the reverberations in the apparently empty building. No lights shone behind the grimed net curtains. A strange sort of desert. He was reminded of tales he had read of explorers along the Amazon seeing no one, conscious of being watched, of a minute surveillance, of life going on around them just out of sight. He looked up. From a window on the top floor the head and shoulders of a man projected like a gargoyle from a battlement, gazing down at him. For a moment he did not know what to say, he was so much taken by surprise and felt so much at a disadvantage, as the watched always feel; then he called out an enquiry whether Miss Binns lived there.

"What do you want?"

He raised his voice. "Does Miss Binns live here? Miss Margaret Binns?"

"In gaol," the voice very laconically replied. "You're Mr Derry, aren't you? The solicitor?"

"That's right."

"I telt her not to see you," the man said.

"What do you mean? What's she done?"

The head was withdrawn; the window came creaking down; but before it shut he caught the last words, uttered in a tone of great contempt and disparagement: "Ask Blair or Geordie Sugden. Divven't bother me."

Justin returned to his office very thoughtful. He made certain enquiries. And when he had the answers he took Miss Binns's folder from his safe and set out to call on the Reverend Walter P. Beaumont Lumley. It was the decisive step of his life.

III

THE Reverend Mr Lumley, Vicar of St Bede's, was a well-known figure in Smedwick at that time, where his compact person with its bouncing step, suggesting one of those rubber balls that are always ricocheting in violent motion from place to place, was often to be seen rushing out from his hideous red-brick vicarage on some errand of mercy or exhortation. Everything about Mr Lumley suggested enthusiasm. His hair was luxuriant, standing up eagerly from his forehead in a quiff above rather staring eyes bright with excellent intentions, and his voice was bell-like, as though he were sounding a constant message of good cheer. Most people liked Mr Lumley, but they preferred to do it at a distance.

Justin bearded him in the vicarage study: a room with Gothic windows looking out over a shrubbery of laurels and a lawn which had once been a croquet lawn but had reverted in nature's vengeful way. Group photographs of whiskered young men in attitudes that had been fashionable in the 'eighties lined the walls, and on the mantelpiece, among an array of tobacco jars in college and club colours, stood a print of Holman Hunt's 'Light of the World' in a steel frame. Books and sermon paper were strewn over the table, which was covered with a red cloth and lit by an oil lamp with a Sheffield plate stem and glass bowl; while on the periphery, ebony tables, whose legs were carved in oriental shapes featuring elephants, were scattered haphazard about the room, loaded with magazines and old clothes for distribution to the poor of the parish. In the heart of this chaos the Vicar himself was to be seen, dressed in a Norfolk jacket and high collar—not a clerical collar, which Mr

Lumley only wore on Sundays and in Lent—suggesting a man of excellent health and appetite, fresh from his daily exercise of wrestling with the Devil.

"My dear Derry, pray come in, come in. What a pleasure! How good of you to call, how very good. You'll take a cup of tea? Rose"—this to the parlour-maid whose cap sat on the top of her head like a halo—"Rose, my dear, will you see to it that Mr Derry has some tea?"

While uttering these words, the Vicar had taken his guest by the arm and urged him towards a very tall chair whose back was covered in a tapestry of St George slaying the dragon or Don Quixote and the windmills—no one had ever been able to determine which.

"Sit down, my dear sir, sit down. If you'll just wait while I remove these papers. Ha! Rose must really clear these away some time. And how are your dear good sisters? Well, I hope. What we should do without them both I can't imagine. You are doubly blessed, my dear sir. And now if you'll tell me what brings you so agreeably?"

So Justin told him of Miss Binns's visit, of Miss Kelly and what had happened since, and Mr Lumley listened. Even when listening he seemed to be the more active of the two: leaning forward in his chair, hands gripping his knees, inclining his trunk forwards and stretching out his neck as though he were about to launch himself on top of the story as a cat pounces on a mouse. At intervals he made clicking noises with his tongue against his teeth, which were not his own and not of very perfect fit. People sometimes found it an ordeal to tell Mr Lumley things. They never had to complain of his zeal or sympathy, however.

"So it comes to this, does it not?" he rushed in as soon as his visitor had finished. "You believe that two innocent men are serving prison sentences at this moment?"

"It seems possible."

"They are not my parishioners, you understand. They are Papists, I believe. Not that it matters in the least, since if they are innocent it is our plain duty to help them, no matter who they are. Are they innocent?"

"It would appear they may be."

The Vicar smiled. It was a pleasant smile, yet oddly enough the wrinkling of the lines around the eyes made him look a much shrewder person. "Now come, Derry, is it your certainty you're bringing me or your doubts?"

"My opinion, for what it's worth."

"How you gentlemen of the law hate to commit yourselves. A good fault, my dear sir, and I could certainly profit from it myself. Your opinion is worth a good deal, and you think an injustice has been done."

"Not only to Milligan and Kelly."

"Ah! You are suggesting that it was *because* she made a statement that poor Miss Binns has been arrested, quite falsely, for importuning in the street. And that your man at the window (who was Mr Green the roadman, also a witness) fears the same treatment from the Police and won't have you in the house?"

"That's what I'm suggesting, certainly."

"I am getting you into a dangerous state of candour, Derry, you must beware of me. Now am I right, are you suggesting that the Police were mistaken in the case they brought eight years ago and are defending their mistake?"

"I have a strong suspicion of it."

"A suspicion, yes. Forgive me examining you in this way, and most incompetently by your standards, I feel sure. But tell me this. Does Miss Binns's statement satisfy you that this man Sugden, my parishioner, was in the Rectory that night?"

"I believe her statement."

"And do you feel that *legally* what she says is strong enough to give you something to work on, some basis of fact?"

"Not without Sugden's help."

"You must mean his confession."

At this point in the discussion there came a knock at the door and Rose entered with a tray on which reposed the enormous silver teapot embossed with scrolls that was usually required to calm the nerves of the parochial church council. Mr Lumley did the honours with hearty benevolence, committing the solecism—and it *was* a solecism in those days—of putting the milk in first: it would not have happened at the Deverels'. While he poured he talked.

"Do you take sugar, Derry? You don't? Neither do I. It has sometimes occurred to me that the decadence of civilisations is not unconnected with what is nowadays called 'the sweet tooth', a patent symbol of decay. I fear I have a tendency to labour the point a little, but to my mind ripeness is not all; it is too much, if I may be permitted an aphorism. We have gone too far from simplicity."

His voice had fallen into the booming cadence which his congregation had known and admired for a decade. Perhaps from long habit he had come to think that all those to whom he handed cups of tea must be parishioners, whose pleasure it was to listen and go away edified. But when he actually handed the cup to his guest he recalled himself.

"You were saying, my dear sir?"

Justin had been saying nothing for some time. But he had taken the measure of his host and replied at once: "My point was that Miss Binns's statement is of only limited importance. One might think of it as a kind of bait, if you'll forgive the term."

"To catch Sugden with, you mean?"

"Not 'catch'," Justin said, detecting the first note of reservation in his host's voice. "'Catch' is quite the wrong word, as I perceive that 'bait' was. I don't want to trap Sugden or do anything improper. But if it should be that he was one of the real criminals of that night, then it follows that two innocent men are suffering because of him—or one at least—and that is wrong."

"Most wickedly wrong," came the resounding chime of Mr Lumley's voice.

"And I think, subject to your judgment, Vicar, that Sugden should be told of this statement and know what is being said. It might affect him. Don't they say confession is good for the soul?"

"Laymen say it, Derry. And priests know it. But it is not a thing to be forced. A layman and his spiritual guide are in a special relationship, you must understand. We are on dangerous ground."

Looking at the zealous face on the other side of the teapot, Justin knew that he was indeed on dangerous ground: if he was not careful the Vicar would remove the whole case into the realm of dogma and ascend with it out of sight. The assumption must be challenged at once. "You will forgive me," he said in his most legal voice, "but I think we are in danger of misunderstanding one another, and that would be a pity."

"A great pity," echoed Mr Lumley, reaching out to refill his guest's cup.

Justin suffered it, though in fact he disliked tea, and the Vicar's Mothers' Meeting brew more than any other. "May I explain my point, Vicar? I would naturally not dream of interfering in any relationship of a confidental kind between you and Sugden. But I used 'confession' in a wider sense as meaning this: that he possesses certain knowledge that may help to right a gross injustice, and I see nothing sacred in that knowledge and nothing wrong in going to him as man to man to question him. I came to you because you know him better than I do; in fact I don't know him at all."

But Mr Lumley was shaking his head. "No, you are wanting *me* to ask the questions," he said. "And then you will be wanting to hear the answers."

"Only if Sugden agrees I should hear them."

"Suppose he refuses? Would you be satisfied with that refusal?"

"In so far as the matter of your enquiries was concerned, I'd accept it."

"And then what would you do?"

"Why, Vicar, I'd go to him and make some enquiries of my own."

Mr Lumley burst into laughter—a loud booming laugh that seemed to originate in the region of his belly and rolled upwards till his face with its pendulous cheeks was shaking with it. Mr Lumley's laugh was famous but a rare effect: many parishioners had never heard it.

"My dear sir, that is most frank," he managed to get out, "most refreshingly frank. What you are proposing seems to me an alliance of a quite novel kind, but pray don't think I'm rejecting it out of hand. Nothing should be allowed to blind us to an injustice. You are on the side of the angels, though you will forgive me if I tell you that your arguments sound quite satanically inspired. Well now: suppose I accept this unholy alliance?"

"That would please me very much."

"You won't ask too much of me? You'll try and understand my position?"

"I'll do my best."

"Well then, Derry, let us seal the bond."

And he poured out two more cups of tea.

IV

SOME days later Justin had a case to prosecute before the magistrates. It was a 'poaching' morning, which had brought a goodly number of gentlemen in tweeds and mutton-chop whiskers on to the bench under the chairmanship of Colonel Deverel. On a table to the left were the remains of three cock pheasants and the ingenious contraption of pole and wire that had been used to charm them off their perches in the night; all in charge of a police constable by the name of Pugh, at whose elbow sat Superintendent Blair, a shade more solid and constabulary, if that were possible, than at the trial in the Moot Hall eight years earlier. Below the bench, facing the clerk who had read the charge and taken the plea, sat the accused man, Peel, in a velveteen jacket with a whisk of hair brushed up on his forehead like a cockatoo's.

When the preliminaries were over and it was his turn to begin, Justin rose to present his case in the concise manner favoured by Rees, who had often practised in that court. He saw the prisoner sitting with bowed head, the Superintendent's glazed appraising stare, Colonel Deverel's darkening countenance as the atrocities committed on the pheasants were outlined.

"Call Joseph Henderson."

Immediately there was a stir in court and the chairman demanded in a troubled voice: "Henderson? Joseph Henderson? Is he a witness for the Prosecution?"

"Yes, sir."

"Is he the . . . ? Oh yes, I see the man."

Justin turned to face the stalwart fellow who was marching into the box. He too had been surprised to learn that the most famous of the Smedwick poachers had turned gamekeeper, and he hoped that the bench would enjoy the experience of listening to him.

"Your name is Joseph Henderson?" he began.

"Aye, sir."

"And I think you are a gamekeeper employed by Mr John Carmichael of High Eals. Forgive my asking you this, but you will not wish to deceive the court: it is true, is it not, that there are convictions against you for poaching offences in the past?"

"Quite a canny few, sir."

"But now you're otherwise employed?"

"And better paid, sir. More regular."

There was laughter in which the magistrates joined, some more heartily than others. What a cool customer the fellow was, thought Justin. It was on him that the Police had called early on the morning of the burglary at Verney's, and there were other things about him, other tales, if only he could remember. . . .

When it was over, after an hour's argument in the course of which he had demolished one of the long and involved alibis beloved of poachers, he hurried out of court almost into the arms of Blair, who appeared suddenly from the vestibule, with P.C. Pugh behind him bearing the remains of the pheasants in a wooden box. Justin made to pass by; then thought better of it and fell into step as they went out into the wintry sunlight gleaming on the bare trees of the park and the castle walls beyond.

"You fettled Peel right, sir," the Superintendent remarked with satisfaction as they went down the steps. "He led us a dance, that chap, and no mistake. But you showed him up, sir."

"I think your witness helped."

"You mean Henderson?" The Superintendent chuckled over the name a great deal more cheerfully than the magistrates had done. "We have to take what comes our way, sir."

"I'm sure you do."

"He made a good witness, sir."

"Almost an expert, wouldn't you say?"

Blair laughed loud and long at that. "Expert? Well, he *was* a poacher, sir, admitted. Beggars can't be choosers, sir. We can't pick all our witnesses."

"I expect not. And how's Miss Binns?" said Justin in the same conversational voice he had been using all along.

"Miss Binns, sir? You mean Margaret Binns? From Pelegate?"

"That's right."

"She's inside, sir; got 'er in the cells. Importuning." The Superintendent gave the word its full flavour, so that one could see respectable gentlemen being affronted in public places. "And attempted larceny from the person. She's a bad one, sir."

"Indeed?"

"One of the worst. One of the sly ones. D'you know her, sir?"

"I do."

"Perhaps you'll call and see her then," the Superintendent said. "She could do with some good advice, sir. Had a bad upbringing that girl. Bein' a niece of Geordie Sugden's. Expect you've heard of him, sir?"

"Yes, I think I have."

"Bad hats the lot of 'em. And as full of tricks as a cage of monkeys. You'd be surprised the mischief a girl like that can do, carryin' tales to folk who might be soft enough to believe 'em. Why, I've seen respectable people—people like you and me, sir—taken in by such tales."

"When can I see her?" interrupted Justin.

"See her? Any time you like."

"This afternoon?"

"That'd do fine. You got those pheasants, Pugh?" the Superintendent called back over his shoulder at the constable who had been following some dozen yards behind.

"Got 'em right here, sir."

"Good lad. Well, back to duty, sir. It was a good turn you did us this morning, a real good turn. Got to stop this poachin': that's been me problem all along." And he marched off with P.C. Pugh.

That afternoon after a hasty lunch, having dodged his Georgina whose elegant figure he had seen on the steps of the Assembly Rooms, Justin made his way to Police headquarters in the Lawnmarket and sent in his card with a request to see Miss Binns. There seemed a long delay in fetching her, and he had begun to stamp his feet with cold when he heard the rattle of a key and the girl was brought into the interview room from the cells, still in the brown woollen dress she had worn at their first meeting.

When the constable had left them he drew up a chair for her and sat down opposite, as he had done across the desk in his office. It was no good rushing things, for he could see that she was afraid and remembered how slowly she had started, but how the confidences had come brimming once she had taken heart and got used to him. Such witnesses were like horses whose trust had to be won by infinite patience, and he was in the mood to give it because she had come to him and he felt responsible for her; she seemed so forlorn and alone.

"How long have they held you, Margaret?"

If he could once start her talking, then the rest would follow. He thought she looked frailer than when he had last seen her, and her rather slanting eyes seemed much larger against the dead whiteness of her cheeks. A strange little face: pear-shaped, with a cleft in the chin, and a certain slyness—yes, the Superintendent had been right in that: a sly little waif from the Smedwick gutters. It was not easy to be patient, with time passing and his questions unanswered. She sat there, shoulders hunched, looking absurdly small, like a child who had strayed into that cheerless place.

Then gradually the responses came.

"Are you guilty, Margaret?"

"Yes, sir."

"You accosted a man and tried to steal from him?"
"Yes."
"Shall I defend you?"
"If you want, sir."
"Have you a defence?"
"Defence, sir?"

He took a turn up and down the room, trying to overcome his irritation. "Have the Police been talking to you, Margaret?"

"Talkin', sir?"

"You never did any importuning, did you? That was a Police invention?"

"I done it, sir."

"What have they promised you? Did they promise they'd speak up for you in court?"

"Don't know, sir. Per'aps they will."

"Why will they speak for you? Must you do something in return?"

"Don't understand, sir."

"You'll remember you made me a statement in my office. Was that the truth?"

"I thought so at the time, sir."

He leaned down towards her, so that she could no longer avoid his eyes. "And now? What do you think now?"

"Don't rightly know, sir."

"Was it all lies?"

"Mostly."

"Very well, Margaret," he said in a gentler voice. He had proved something to himself, but he felt no sense of triumph, only a sadness that embraced the Superintendent in his office as much as the girl before him in the drab, shapeless dress. "You can go back now with the constable, and I hope they'll be kind to you, as indeed I think they will be, and I don't believe you'll go to prison. Don't blame yourself for anything. I know you tried to do right, and perhaps it will come out one day."

Back in his office with the curtains drawn against the chill of the afternoon he settled down to his problem, impervious to Harris, as later he was to his sisters' gossip over the fire. He was in a bad mood, they agreed: 'grumpy' was how Flo expressed it to herself as she lay wakeful in bed afterwards, pondering over God's strange perversity in creating men. And next door to her, in the gaslight which was still shining under his door long after midnight, her brother was remembering Miss Binns, and Blair's jovial words, and reading again the lines in which the Vicar of St Bede's reported on his mission:

> I have been three times to Sugden and he receives me kindly, but I have not thought the time ripe to speak openly of Massingham. You must not hope too much or too soon, but know that repentance ripens slowly like all other fruits of God's goodness and that this has been a sinful man. Yet already he is changing. He is no longer the unregenerate man who broke into Verney's, if he ever *was* that man. We shall know one day, I think.

'I know it now,' thought Justin fiercely and despairingly of the allies whom fate had wished on him. His excellent common sense had deserted him and had left him a prey to impetuous thoughts which would certainly have scared poor Harris out of his wits. Ideas of bearding Sugden alternated with still wilder ones of writing an open letter to the press and even of defending Miss Binns against her will. Next day, of course, these fantasies could be seen for what they were, but an intense, restless curiosity about the case remained, and on his first free afternoon, which happened to be Sunday, he set off across the moor and came down to Massingham as the sun was setting behind Marbury Forest and the gloomy shape of the Rectory on the hill among the trees.

When he came closer he saw what a barrack it was: absurdly large for a village that was little more than a huddle of houses on the slope and a few scattered farms. The main bulk of the Rectory faced south across a river valley crossed by a hump-backed bridge. But there was also a narrower and more formal front looking west to receive those who came in carriages along the drive, and it was through the right-hand of the two windows in this depressingly Victorian façade that the burglars had forced their way on the night of the crime.

He walked over the bridge and up the hill, a little uncertain of why he had come, but as he stood on the high ground where the fields merged into the moorland that ringed the valley he heard the bells sounding for three o'clock evensong, and the thought occurred to him to 'have another look at them'.

He found a church lit by candles. It was a very old church, far older than the Rectory that loured down on it from the hill. Two candles stood on the altar. There was a tall candlestick by the lectern; a few candles for the choir; one for the organist hidden away behind a screen; one for the preacher. The plain glass windows had begun to reflect their light when Mr Verney went up into the pulpit, with the candle in its socket throwing the glow directly into his face. He looked no older than at the Moot Hall. He might have been giving evidence again as he set his hands in their flowing white sleeves on the rim of the wood and leaned forward to give out his text, which was from Jeremiah.

From his seat in an aisle, almost out of the radius of light, Justin watched him and the congregation between them. It was composed mostly of farmers, their wives and children, all soberly dressed and packing as close as they decently could to the rear of the church, where stood an archaic coke-burning monster of a stove that gave at intervals a kind of stealthy rumble, as though meditating some heretical act. One would not have said they were apathetic, for it seemed to Justin that they were listening and extracting from the Prophet's words certain truths that in some mysterious way they believed to be applicable to themselves. He found this engrossing and quite different from the relationship between Mr Lumley and *his* flock of town-bred folk in constant fear of being evangelised and enlisted for some worthy cause, to combat Vivisection or prevent atrocities in Armenia. That Mr Verney and Mr Lumley should be members of the same Church struck him as an odd and at the same time comforting thing, and as the little procession with the Cross went into the vestry he meditated over it and applied the lesson to his problem, which for a moment in that quiet place had ceased to trouble him.

The congregation in the nave began to file out and Justin waited, watching the solid country backs retreating into the semi-darkness by the door. But when he followed them he found that the Rector had come unseen to shake his parishioners by the hand on leaving and to take a tally of them, no doubt. There was no avoiding the man, short of doubling back behind a pillar, though why such a crazy notion should have crossed his mind he could not think, for he had nothing to hide; he had not come to spy on Mr Verney. But just as certainly he had not come to confide in him, and as he arrived abreast of the old man he gave him a formal bow and made to pass on.

He was arrested by a hand, a gnarled hand, scaly as a gardener's, that reached out telescopically and took possession of his own.

"Isn't it Mr Derry? The Solicitor from Smedwick?"

Justin's family had been in the district for generations, far longer than any Verneys, but he was still young enough to be flattered when he was recognised, and besides, 'solicitor of Smedwick' was exactly how he preferred to hear himself described.

"And what brings you to Massingham?" Mr Verney said. "We don't often have the pleasure of seeing our good neighbours from the town at our services. Did you ride across?"

"I walked over the moor."

"Indeed! Most health-giving exercise. A beautiful countryside, don't you agree? I know of none finer in any weather. But remote, I fear. I think very few people know of the beauties of nature to be found in this valley."

While he was speaking the old man glanced round the church, in which a sidesman was going the rounds snuffing the candles till only one burned by the font. "You may leave it, Tom, I will attend to it," he called out, and then in a whisper to his visitor: "Young Merrick from the farm. A most helpful and worthy soul." 'The messenger to Blair on the morning of the crime,' noted Justin to himself, remembering the evidence of the night ride across the moor. "Do you return tonight?" the Rector was saying. "Not on foot, I trust?"

"Why yes, sir."

"In the dark, through this very lonely countryside? My dear boy, is that wise? I speak with some feeling; you may recall the affair, but no matter. If only I could lend you my carriage, but alas! my daughter has it and she is from home."

Justin disclaimed any need of a carriage or of young Merrick's horse, which the Rector was disposed to offer him—"I will see Tom about it. Tom! Oh, he has left, but we could call and soon arrange things. He is my right hand: he and his worthy father. If it had not been for them eight years ago . . ."

The last candle was snuffed and they followed one another out through the darkness lit only by the sulphurous glow of a stove clearly out of its true diabolic element. Mr Verney's hand was again on his as they entered the porch, his voice demanding hospitably: "And now you will sup with me, I trust? At least a glass of wine? Mr Derry, you may *not* refuse. You are surely not in such haste to be home as that."

They started up the hill towards the barrack shape of the Rectory in the starlight. After a hundred yards they came to a gate in the wall leading into an orchard of straggling trees among an undergrowth of couch grass and brambles. Above, surrounding the house, were lawns and flower-beds, and these too, so far as one could see, had a ragged look, as though the place had become too much for its occupants or in some way unloved. But the inside of the house itself still breathed an air of solid comfort, only slightly fallen from the days when the carriages had come rolling up the drive between the laurels, decanting rural deans and their ladies and even a stray bishop. The effect surprised him, for his whole feeling about the Rectory had been conditioned by what he had heard of the crime—as though an act of violence and darkness could have left its mark on the very air! 'A ridiculous notion,' he thought, glancing around in the narrow hall that stretched towards the stairs, flanked on the left by doors leading into the drawing-room and dining-room; and it was then that he found himself staring at a point level with his eyes where part of a door jamb had been hollowed out, as though someone had struck it with an axe, leaving the edges rough with splinters, and then had painted over it.

"Was this where the shot struck?"

"Yes." Mr Verney had moved forward and was touching the place with his hands. "It was fired from inside the dining-room. It was a curious thing, seeing and hearing it in so confined a space—I seemed to be watching the myriad colours of it spreading out like a fan, like a woman's jewelled fan being opened in the light. I wrote a description of it to the *Smedwick Mercury*, you may remember."

Justin *did* remember: and a very ridiculous letter it had seemed to him at the time. But he was in no mood to laugh now, for there was something touching in the old man's earnestness.

"The main charge missed you, of course?" he said.

"Oh yes, and my daughter too, most providentially. If it had been worse than a few pellets that ricocheted we should have been killed without a doubt . . . and then those two unfortunate men . . ."

"I take it, Rector, you've no doubt it *was* those men?"

The old man was gazing at him with astonishment in his very blue short-sighted eyes. "My dear boy, what can you mean? Didn't we see them in this very room? Didn't they leave their footprints in the lane? Why, if young Tom Merrick I was speaking of had only heard them passing and come out he would have caught the pair of them red-handed."

There was a pause and then Justin said slowly: "I thought the Merricks' house was uphill, in the village?"

"So it is, my boy: the farm. But Tom lived in the bothy by the bridge—you must have seen it. That's where my daughter went: straight down Church Lane in their very tracks, the scoundrels!"

"And Tom heard *her*, presumably?"

"Oh yes, thank God for it! He heard her coming—stumbling on the road, he said."

Justin drank his wine and went thoughtfully back to Smedwick by the highway, asking himself a question that kept yielding a surprising answer. It was quite driven out of his mind, however, by the sight of the Reverend Mr Lumley waiting for him in the drawing-room of 'The Laurels'.

V

"He has confessed!" Mr Lumley cried, leaping to his feet in his enthusiasm at sight of his ally. "God be praised for it." Apparently the great event for which he had been working had occurred some hours earlier, after evensong, in St Bede's Vicarage, to which Sugden had been bidden. "And he has agreed that I may tell you everything," the good man confided in high excitement.

Justin had been told 'everything' before in the course of his professional experience and he had come to distrust the word. "You seem very dubious," said Mr Lumley, noticing this.

"Not in the least."

"You expected it, then?"

"Not that either. I congratulate you."

"It is a matter for rejoicing, certainly," the Vicar reproved him, "but you will remember it is God's work, not mine. A sinner has come to repentance."

"If belatedly," murmured the solicitor.

"Yes, my dear sir, but he has come, and there is the point of it. He has come. Let me tell you how it happened. We were in my study. He seemed in a mood to submit to God with humility, acknowledging his sins. Perhaps my sermon had had some part in it. We talked and he said he was a sinful man. So I asked him outright if he had been at Massingham that night. Well, at that the poor fellow turned the most deathly pale, he literally gasped for breath." The

Vicar's moon face seemed to grow even paler and the words came out staccato. "'Oh sir,' he said, 'you've hurt me, you've hurt me, sir,' and he kept repeating it. He asked for a glass of water and I gave it to him, I quite feared for him, he seemed so ill. But his colour came back after a while, so I said to him, 'Is it true you were at Mr Verney's?' and he said, 'Oh sir, but I was not the man who fired the shot.'"

"Yes?" said Justin, and waited.

"Implying that he knew that man. That he had been at Verney's at the time and knew him."

"Quite. Did he have anything more to say?"

"No, he didn't."

Justin never gave way to the sense of disappointment and possibly of outrage that some men might have felt at having their expectations let down with such a bump because he had had no expectations and knew that in the Vicar's shoes he would not have achieved anything at all. "An admirable beginning," he commended him warmly, and meant it.

Mr Lumley looked relieved. "I was afraid that you were going to say something different. I was afraid you were displeased with me."

"However could you think that?"

"Because I should have had it in writing, I suppose. And because it sounds so little when you examine it. Not even a real confession."

"It was a confession right enough."

"Do you truly think so? My dear sir, I can't tell you how much you relieve my mind. It certainly *seemed* what we were wanting. Poor fellow, there was honest contrition there. I sensed a desire to atone, but the flesh is weak. He may draw back."

"Then we must prevent it: we must join forces. Would he see me, do you suppose?"

"I think he might. I will find out tomorrow and send you a note to let you know what he says and where we should meet. Try to be patient."

All next morning Justin sat in his office and applied himself to the conveyances, beautiful in their pink and green ribbons, and to the clients Harris showed in to him. But as the shadows lengthened and the murk of the afternoon invaded the room he became restless and wandered to the window overlooking the square. People were hurrying home, wrapped tightly in their overcoats; he saw someone's hat go flying; and rivulets of rain were dribbling down the panes, making a maze of the points of light that sprang up one by one in the shops across the way.

"Nothing from Mr Lumley?" he asked of Harris, who brought in coffee soon after four o'clock. He had not felt so fidgety since he had been a youth in old Rees's office waiting for six o'clock to strike and release him into the live world outside, which never seemed so adventureful as at the end of the day. He remembered best the winter nights: the ticking of the clock, the scratching of pens in ledgers long closed. There had always seemed to be a wind rattling at the windows, adding its voice to the burble and hiss of the gas, and so it was tonight, with the curtains asway and the fire billowing smoke into the room.

At half-past five, when he had almost given up hope of the message coming that day, a note was handed in asking him to be outside the King's Arms Hotel at six; and precisely to the minute, while the clocks were striking, he heard the rapid sound of footsteps approaching and the figure of the Vicar bounced into the lamplight like a genie.

"Is that you, my dear fellow?"

Not a word of explanation, Justin noted, of why such a meeting-place should have been chosen or why the Vicar had not simply called at his office, which was less than a furlong from the King's Arms. 'It would serve him right if the word went round that he was inside the taproom,' Justin thought, visualising the scene, for the notion of Mr Lumley and strong liquors in the same ring was captivating and opened up prospects he would have liked to explore. But clearly the Vicar was in no mood for badinage, and they had no sooner shaken hands than Justin found himself being marched at speed over the cobbles of the market-place in the direction of Bewley.

Arrived there, in the bleak street down which the wind came howling, driving before it great gusts and pellets of rain, the pace of the advance slowed down a little. It seemed to Justin that the elements alone were not to blame for this, for the grip on his arm had slackened, as though his friend were developing doubts—presumably of a non-theological nature—about the whole enterprise. "Did he ask for me?" he managed to shout into the Vicar's ear as they reached the corner of a tenement out of the worst fury of the gale.

"He agreed you might come," was the cautious answer.

"Oh."

"You must remember he's been distressed and in great confusion of mind. It would be foolish to expect too much."

Justin murmured that he would try to avoid expecting anything, as he had managed to do for some time, but a gust of wind blew the words away; and when they were next in shelter, near Sugden's door, the Vicar was bellowing at him: "He's incalculable. He's afraid of company—a most nervous man, most difficult and confused."

"As who isn't around here?"

But fortunately Mr Lumley did not hear this: he had pushed open the door of the tenement and was leading the way into the stale air of a hall in pitch darkness except for a slat of light under a door directly to their left. "Strike a match, my dear fellow," he urged in a whisper that sounded much louder than the clarion call of his voice in the wild night outside. "We go up a floor."

"So be it."

"Better mind your step. There's a loose board half-way up. The bannisters are *most* untrustworthy. If you'd care to follow me."

Justin struck another match and by its flickering gleam they went up, one behind the other, treading warily, drawing from the boards beneath them a protesting sound like a groan. "These old houses!" the Vicar said as they reached the narrow landing off which two doors opened. "A disgrace to the town. Yet such is the sense of property in our enlightened times. There are landlords drawing a good rent from these"—and he pointed to the walls from which the plaster was flaking in deep blisters like sores.

Justin was looking about him, holding his third match high above his head. They had stopped opposite the right-hand door: to the left was another, no doubt once the abode of the roadman Green: and in the same warren Miss Binns also had existed, and Sugden's mother too. "How many people live here?" he asked.

"A dozen or so. It might provide stabling for four horses if the hunt didn't protest about the overcrowding. But you will see what these worthy folk have made of their pittance."

The Vicar's voice had risen; and suddenly the door they were facing opened, and over his friend's shoulder Justin saw the figure of a man in shirtsleeves without collar or tie: dark eyes, a yellowing, drawn face, clean shaven, with a domed forehead from which the hair receded. "So you heard us, George!" sang out the Vicar in a hearty voice.

The man hesitated. He had one of those tight-skinned faces that are particularly revealing of thoughts, and Justin saw that what he most desired was to slam the door on them. But the parochial smile had already invaded the room; the clerical foot was inside the door. "This is George Sugden. George, this is Mr Derry, the solicitor from Bank Chambers."

"Pleased to meet the gentleman," Sugden said.

"You'll find him a great help to us."

"If you say so, sir, I'm sure."

It was Justin's first experience of the peculiar hazards of parish visiting and he felt a deep embarrassment, but there was nothing he could do about it; he was in the presence of experts.

"A raw night, George." Indeed they could hear the buffets of the gale against the old porous walls of the house, and somewhere a window was rattling with desperate urgency as though someone were forcing his way in. "There'll be snow on the way maybe."

By this time, without even appearing to be trying, the Vicar had succeeded in edging himself into such a position that only force or gross rudeness could have kept him out. But Justin had had no doubt from the start who would win this battle of manœuvre: he entered with the supporting troops and looked around him, finding himself in a room about fifteen feet square, lit by tallow candles and warmed by a wood fire. At the far end from them was an empty bed, the 'marital couch', as the Vicar would certainly have called it, and another and more rudimentary one in which three children lay. The room was scrupulously clean. It looked larger than it was, there was so little furniture, but the walls were hung with Biblical prints and texts, and on the mantelpiece stood a handsomely dressed doll with a mantilla on her head.

"This is Carmen," said the Vicar, introducing them. "A fine young lady, isn't she? If Mary were awake we would hear more about her ancestry, which is Spanish from the look of her. But Robert is awake, I see. We must talk quietly, for it wouldn't do to keep a young fellow from his beauty sleep. How old is Robert now?"

"Nearly nine, sir."

"How they grow." The Vicar had moved close to the bed, looking down at the children huddled together under the blanket, the boy in the centre with eyelids drooping, mouth slightly open to reveal four new buck teeth seemingly many sizes too large. "Master Robert is quite the prize scholar," he said. "Mr Sharp of Sheffield, like our good friend Copperfield before him. Can we talk safely, do you think?"

"Any minute now, sir," Sugden said.

"And your wife's out, it appears. How is she, by the way?"

"Middling. Much as can be expected, sir."

"We must count our blessings, George. It's one obligation of a Christian, and perhaps the one we forget most easily. But there! I didn't come to preach you a sermon. If anything's to be learnt tonight it must come from you, if you understand me."

"I do in a way, sir."

"I hope you'll talk to Mr Derry as you talked to me and think of him as one of us, someone who wants to help us. You can be sure of his discretion."

"You mean nothing will go further, sir? Then I don't quite see. . . . No offence, sir, but *why's* he here? We don't want to waste the gentleman's time."

Mr Lumley's sigh was one of unnatural resignation. 'The meek shall inherit the earth,' his expression seemed to say, 'but let the inheritance come soon.' By nature a missionary, whose impulse in his own words was to 'hit a man in the stomach with a penny loaf and then give him a tract', it was only with difficulty that he had brought himself to this prolonged wrestling with a conscience; it made him feel like Jacob with his angel. But having made the match, he had no intention of giving up until he had subdued Satan and his own unbridled ardour into the bargain. "Mr Derry is here because you agreed he should come," he reasoned patiently. "You told me I might invite him, so I sent him a message and very kindly he came."

"No harm done, sir. I'm glad to see the gentleman."

"But it seems to me, George, that you have developed doubts in this matter and I want to remove them, so that we all know where we stand. You made a verbal statement to me about your part in the affair at Mr Verney's."

"And a great load off my conscience, sir."

A gust of wind swept down the chimney, billowing the smoke out into the room and affecting the Vicar's bronchial tubes to such a degree that he lost track of himself, causing him to splutter to Justin quite crossly: "What was I saying?"

"You were referring to the statement Sugden made."

"Oh yes. Now, George, we've had many a talk about this. I've tried to show you your duty as I see it and as I pray and believe you yourself have come to see it. You know at last you did wrong: a very great wrong in allowing two innocent men to suffer."

"I know it, sir."

"But you are making restitution, George, little by little. If the hardest part, the law's punishment, still lies ahead for you, the great *decision* is made, and that is what matters in the sight of God. All we need now are the means to turn righteous thoughts into the righteous act of self-sacrifice and confession."

There was silence in the room, broken only by one of the children turning on the rusty springs of the bed. Then Sugden murmured: "I don't quite understand that, sir."

"Don't you? Surely it's clear enough. You repent. All well and good. But how does that fact by itself benefit others? No man saves his soul at the expense of his fellows. You must know that from what you've been taught and what your Bible says."

"It says that, sir, no doubt."

"Well then? I don't see any problem."

"Where's this gentleman come into it?"

"He comes into it," replied the Vicar, speaking with an awful slowness, "firstly because we agreed he might come, and secondly because if we are to translate your good intentions into deeds we need his help in the taking of a statement in due legal form which will clear Milligan and Kelly and make your guilt quite plain to everyone. Does that answer your question, George?"

Apparently it did.

"Yes, sir, thank you, sir. I'll not be makin' any statement. I've changed me mind."

VI

As they struggled home through the wind and the sleet, Mr Lumley never ceased to bewail the calamity that had descended like a thunderbolt on his head. The gale was so strong that Justin did not hear everything, but occasional snatches reached him out of the night: ". . . extraordinary decision . . . a soul apparently prepared . . . work wasted . . . not himself . . . powers of Satan. . . ." By the time they had reached the comparative shelter of the market-place the threads of discourse become connected and the Vicar could be heard blaming himself for everything. "It was no fault of yours, my dear fellow. Admittedly he seems to have been nervous of you and terrified of any mention of the law, but it was on *my* urging that you came and you said nothing that could have been misconstrued—*nothing*. I take the blame entirely. What can have changed him? Was it perhaps my reminding him of the harder road ahead?"

For an eternity at the Vicarage, in the cubicle of a study amid the litter of a dedicated life, the good man debated this problem, referring occasional points to his friend before answering them himself. As he talked he regained courage and, his natural buoyancy returning, began to rebuke sin instead of merely suffering it. "It was a wicked act. But the man himself is not wicked at heart, only misguided and afraid. I am confident he can be saved. All we need to do is to keep faith. I will never abandon Sugden."

"And I will *never* desert Mr Micawber," murmured Justin under his breath as he excused himself and went back home. It was well past ten o'clock and 'The Laurels' had settled down for the night, with only a glimmer of gaslight from the drawing-room, where two mantles had been left burning. But the fire was still in behind its screen, and on the round table reposed a decanter of madeira which Flo accepted as a 'gentlemanly' wine on the strength of an old partiality of their father's at Christmas time.

He ate the sandwiches and poured himself a glass, nearly asleep from the warmth of the room after the bitter cold of the night outside. A fearsome draught was whistling in the hall as he lit the candle and glanced around to make sure that he had carried out the various duties Flo expected of him in order to preserve the house from fire and rapine. All gas jets were out and the front door bolted. There was something unexpected in his line of sight, however: something that looked like a square of paper lying on the linoleum under the letter-box which had no cage. He picked it up, shading the flame which was guttering madly, and read what was written in two lines of spindly script:

> Be at the griffin bridge at eight tomorrow night keep N beyond the lamp.

When had it come? He opened the door and peered out, but the snow which had begun to fall in earnest had already covered his own tracks, laying a smooth carpet across the path and garden to the gate into the road. There was nothing to be learnt there and nothing helpful in the message itself, which was unsigned and written on a sheet of ruled paper that might have been torn from a child's exercise book. A very cautious person, apparently, this informant, who preferred to say things and not write them, but that was the hallmark of a class which distrusted the written word and the whole machinery of communication as a kind of witchcraft. That the man (he supposed it was a man) had written at all was remarkable. He must have something worth while to say and feel a pressing need of saying it—unless there were some other reason behind this suggestion of a rendezvous in the darkness, some less agreeable reason.

"Was it a quiet evening? Did anyone call?" he asked his sisters next morning over the breakfast marmalade. While Flo was there he did not press the matter beyond their rather surprised assurance that of course it had been a quiet evening and of course no one had called, for she was an excessively nervous person who had never quite recovered from the news of a burglary that had occurred some years earlier in a neighbouring street, but getting Mamie to himself for a moment, he asked her straight out whether she had heard any suspicious sounds.

"Heard anyone? Where? Inside the house? Do you mean a burglar? How too simply perfect!" Mamie cried. Not for a long time had he engaged her sympathies so deeply, and the disillusionment when it came was proportionately great—"You mean no one broke in! Not even an attempt! I could have sworn I heard someone outside in the snow while we were having supper."

He seized on that. "What time?"

"About eight."

"Did you hear footsteps?"

"It was someone *prowling*. Flo heard him too; she was quite alarmed. She has heard it other nights, she says—like someone who wants to come in but won't."

It was a phrase that kept recurring to him, for on two recent occasions he himself had heard someone walking up and down in the lane by the front gate and had wondered what brought a man out strolling in such bitter weather. He might know very soon; the directions in the message were clear enough: eight o'clock on the north side of the Griffin Bridge, beyond range of the gas lamp, which was the last outrider of the municipal lighting on that side.

At ten minutes to the hour he approached the rendezvous from the Warbury Road, seeing ahead of him the lights in the market-place and to his left the bulk of the castle towering up dimly above the haughs and the griffin on his plinth half-way along the parapet. The night was overcast, with an east wind tearing at the trees and bringing to him, sharp and distinct, the clatter of the southbound express as it raced along the embankment above the estuary, its whistle screaming as it approached the bend by Warbury Halt. Five to eight. One could set one's watch even in winter by that train, whose lighted carriages shone like a glow-worm in the darkness towards the sea.

As the sound of it died away into a distant muttering he stepped off the road into the shelter of the trees and moved down towards the bridge, where a feeble gleam of gaslight illumined the stones against which the snow had drifted. He had reached his chosen point of vantage, about thirty yards from the lamp and close against the hedgerow that followed the highway on its eastern side, when the belfry of the parish church began to strike the hour, followed by the altogether more worldly chimes of the castle clock from directly across the stream. Almost at once he heard a noise in the wood behind him and swung round. Something was there, perhaps a fox or some other wild creature disturbed by his coming, moving very lightly in the undergrowth on a carpet of dead leaves, but he could see nothing in the gloom beyond the dim line of the hedge and after a while it ceased, leaving him in a silence broken only by the moaning of the wind in the trees.

Minutes passed. It was bitterly cold, with a raw dampness that seemed to strike to the marrow of his bones. Even his curiosity had atrophied in the cold, to be replaced by a feeling of unease as the minutes ticked by, and the lights in the castle across the water went out, and that faint rustling began again in the depths of the wood, only nearer to him than before. Suddenly, when all his attention had become centred on the dark terrain to his left, he heard footsteps on the highway to the south.

He drew back further and stooped down, so that there might be no chance of being seen in silhouette before he had made out who his visitor might be. All was quiet now in the wood behind him: and on the bridge the footsteps paced along like laggards behind the beating of his heart. At the far edge of the lamplight a dark shape appeared, then seemed to dissolve in two—two shadows moving as one in the faint aureole of light. He saw their bulk, the tall conical helmets of the Police, then recognised the men themselves: Constables Pugh and Moffat, who had been among the witnesses at the Moot Hall and Blair's particular henchmen.

He remained crouching in the hedge as they went past and along the Warbury Road, walking as one: two police officers on their beat. He thought that now that they had gone his mysterious informant might materialise. But though he waited till nine had struck, no one came.

VII

"WHOEVER he may be, he will have plenty more opportunities of seeing me," reasoned Justin philosophically next day. He could detect a number of reasons, apart from the intrusion of Pugh and Moffat, to keep a timid man from a rendezvous on such a night, and he had no intention of being cast down by one failure of communication. If this 'informant', as he called him in his mind, had failed, the only thing to do was to turn to the other sources, and that meant Sugden first in spite of everything.

When he approached Mr Lumley, however, with a suggestion that they should return together to Bewley Street he was met with a coolness so marked that in another man he might have suspected some ulterior motive, even jealousy. The Vicar did not seem to want to talk about it. He avoided questions. It was only gradually to be got from him that Sugden had taken to his bed where he lay silent and unmoving, refusing to be roused by gifts of food or medicine or the comfort of words. It was something *inside* the man, the Vicar said when he was led at last to express himself about these things. "Some failure of the will. I know very little about it, but I've read somewhere that missionaries in Africa have found the black fellows often die quite unaccountably—from discouragement, it seems, or fear. We could add remorse, and perhaps that's what ails George Sugden."

"Even a dying declaration would be something," mused Justin, "provided it was made in 'settled and hopeless expectation of death' as the jargon has it, and was taken down in writing and signed."

"My dear fellow, isn't that rather callous?" cried Mr Lumley, revolted by the suggestion. "I couldn't think of helping in such a plan . . . unless the man himself desired it. Which, it seems, he won't."

Justin was left with what he had begun to dub in his own mind 'the reserves'. Their form was not encouraging. From young Merrick, by the mouth of Mr Verney, he had received one suggestive piece of information, but of the others, Miss Binns had failed him, the roadman Green refused to see him, and Miss Kelly, for all her fierce devotion to her brother, had been of no practical help.

Then he remembered Kelly's fiancée, Amy Dodds.

"I want young Spinks to take this letter down to Pelegate to Miss Kelly," he instructed Harris on his way out to lunch. "He's to wait for an answer. You might tell him to jolly his ideas along a bit."

He had only asked for Amy's address, and it was a surprise to find on his return a somewhat sheepish Spinks with Miss Kelly herself in tow—a rampant, bridling Miss Kelly hard put to it to contain herself. "I thought fine that you'd be after Geordie Sugden, sir," she burst out the moment they were alone on the private side of the baize door.

"So I have been 'after' him. But the fellow's sick."

"Shamming, sir, more likely, he's that artful. Don't you be took in, sir."

Justin replied that he would do his best not to be taken in. He was amused and at the same time touched by this combative spirit that gave no rest to itself or to anyone else. "Now try and look at it sensibly," he urged. "Sick, shamming, afraid or all three at once, what does it matter? He's dug in his heels for the time being. If it's any comfort to you I believe he was at Massingham."

"Of course he was, sir," she snapped back at him indignantly. She was far too intelligent a woman to be satisfied by empty words.

"Very well, I understand your point of view. Now try and see mine. Presumably you want me to help you?" He saw in her eyes the sudden start of fear that perhaps he was going to throw up the case, and hurried on: "And I *will* help you if you'll give me a chance. But Sugden's only one side of the problem and there are others we shouldn't ignore. That's why I want to see Miss Dodds."

"Just as you say, sir."

"Have you her address?"

"Five Clay Yard. I telled the lad."

"Have you seen her lately?"

"Seen her about, sir. Now and then like."

Justin asked no more questions. Clearly a coldness had developed between the two women, but it was about the last thing to surprise him and in any case it was none of his business. He did not want to be involved in jealousies that had probably been present from the day Kelly had brought his clever, domineering sister and pliant mistress together under the same roof. Even in the witness-box at the Moot Hall when their interests had been identical the difference between them had been striking—Miss Kelly all fire and independence; poor Amy a calamity. He wondered what had become of her. 'On the game', most probably, which would account for the distaste her name seemed to arouse in his formidable and Puritanically minded client.

Yet if Number 5 Clay Yard was a 'gay' house, he thought, then words had lost their meaning. A derelict shack in an alley off Pelegate, it stood between a barn and a stretch of waste land through which meandered a stream choked with rubbish. In the gathering twilight he could see stone steps drunkenly askew, the blank face of a window with drawn blinds, a door with a brass knocker green with age.

Just then he saw movement behind the blinds in the upper room and guessed that someone had heard him and was having a peep. Was the correct response to knock? To take off one's hat? The thought that Mr Lumley would surely have known rebuked him. But after a while he heard sounds upstairs, then footsteps coming down, and the door opened.

His first thought was that she had not changed at all. The same pinched face with big frightened eyes was staring at him from the shadows of the passage, giving him the same oddly pleasurable shock of recognition that he had known when old Verney had gone into the pulpit at Massingham.

Once inside in the parlour in the lamplight he could see that in some ways there had been changes. She had put on weight, which became her, as did the quieter clothes she wore, and her hair was glossier and no longer crimped and curled into a mop. Even the pathetic sticks of furniture had had care lavished on them, though the effect seemed inexpressibly forlorn against the damp patches on the walls and the flaking plaster from the ceiling where the slats showed through. There was a rug whose pattern had all but vanished, a table covered with a cloth on which stood a vase of dried flowers, two devotional pictures, a horsehair sofa with cushions woven in rainbow coloured wools. It was more, he reflected, than 5 Clay Yard deserved; more than the whole community (himself included) deserved that allowed such things to happen.

Very gently, doing his best not to alarm her, he began to explain why he had come, keeping his own expectations of her at a minimum. The most he could look for was that she might have some piece of knowledge, small in itself, which would enlarge the pattern he had been building up or give him a lead to some other witness, perhaps even to the elusive friend who had made the rendezvous at the Griffin Bridge. But there he drew a complete blank. He saw at once that she had no knowledge of any such person. And when he went on to sound her about Sugden's guilt and the identity of the other man who had been at Massingham he sensed in her an immediate distrust, something defensive and resentful, as though after years of waiting she had ceased to hope and didn't want to be bothered any more.

The moment he spotted this he changed tack. Since the future had not drawn her, he would try the past. It made him feel a confidence trickster to be exploiting grief, but he told himself as people do on such occasions that it was for her good. And once they were back beyond the Moot Hall trial into the shadowy world of Piggott's house, with the evening of the crime before them, the sheer fascination of the thing took hold of him and he became engrossed by the tale that only she could tell him—of how Kelly had looked, and what he had said, and how he had gone out to Milligan on the first stage of his journey into darkness.

First, his clothes.

Breeches, boots, a 'newish grey tweed jacket'—his only one. Every detail was in place and vividly recalled. It had been some time after ten when Kelly had gone out with his snares in his pocket saying he was going 'to the Moor', his favourite hunting-ground, clear of the keepers who infested the estates in the plain below. The last she had seen of him that night was at the corner of the street, where Milligan had joined him, and they had turned off into Gilesgate, going north, with Matt the terrier trotting at their heels.

While she had been speaking something had stirred in the back of Justin's mind, just out of reach. It was infuriating being unable to catch hold of it. But he did not like to stop her on the brink of the hour when Kelly had come home for the last time in the grey morning light. "I got 'im into bed, sir. But then these Poliss come, sir, and pulled 'im out, not sayin' what they was wantin' or what 'e done. They got 'is shoes, sir, and the breeches, which was damp but they telt 'im to get into 'em. Then they spots this old coat of 'is, sir—and so I give it 'em."

"But wasn't it a 'newish' coat that he'd been wearing?" said Justin softly, and the wayward thought had clicked into place in his mind. 'A newish grey tweed jacket'—weren't those your words?"

"Was they, sir?"

"How did a newish grey tweed coat manage to turn into that greasy old horror the Police swore to as being Mick Kelly's at the trial?"

She was staring at him wide-eyed. "Don't understand, sir."

"I think you do. Why did you say 'old coat' just now?"

"It were just a word, sir. Just slipped out like."

"Were the Police lying when they produced that hideous old coat as the one you handed them?"

No answer.

"Which coat did you hand them, Amy?"

There was a long silence and then she said: "The old-un. It were one o' Piggott's. I'd burnt the ither."

The intoxicating feeling that he had broken through at last swept over him like a wave. If she had told the truth and the jacket which he had seen in court and in which the compromising scrap of paper had been found by Dr Higson had not been the one Kelly had been wearing on the night of the burglary, then it followed that either the half-blind Piggott had been wearing it at Massingham (which was absurd), or some third party had borrowed it, or else the Police had deliberately torn the large sheet of paper found in the Rectory and planted a piece of it for Higson to find in the lining of what they had believed was Kelly's coat. This last scarifying notion did not alarm him as much as it would have done in Rees's day: he was more hardened to human frailties and thought it was probably the truth. But he could see one great objection to it. Neither Amy nor Miss Kelly had said a word about it at the trial when they had had every reason for speaking out and saying whose coat it was. Could there be an explanation of such silence?

A moment later and he had hit on it himself. They had not spoken because if they had no one would have believed them, even if Piggott had been sane enough to be called or Kelly himself had had the legal right to go into the box. *They had no other coat to produce.* Amy had burnt it.

The wind had got up and for some time the house had been full of those oddly furtive sounds so suggestive of visitors on a winter's night whom one may not wish to see. It was the same at 'The Laurels', where there was a cupboard on the landing with a varied repertoire of groans and loud ejaculations that had scared him out of his wits as a boy and still woke him sometimes with uneasy memories. But this time it sounded different—softer and more purposeful, as though someone had come in through the back door and might be moving in the passageway beyond. He glanced across at Amy, but she seemed to have noticed nothing out of the ordinary.

"Why did you burn the coat?" he said, deciding that he had imagined things. "You can tell me, you know, I'm on your side. You won't remember me, but I was always on your side. I was with Mr Rees the solicitor at the trial."

"I know that," she remarked surprisingly.

"You mean you remember me?"

"'Course I do, sir. There was you and Mr Rees—that was the old gentleman—and a young gentleman in a wig."

"Mr Gilmore."

"I remember all right," she said. "You done your best, all of you. We all done our best."

"The coat," he reminded her gently, touched by her acceptance of him.

"The coat, sir?"

"Yes, listen: I think I know how it happened that you burnt it and never told the court. You knew that Mick had been poaching."

"He telt me, sir."

"So that when the Police came you all thought they wanted him for poaching?"

"That we did, sir. They telt us nothing."

"And did the coat have blood on it?" He saw her trusting smile turn suddenly cold, as though she had glimpsed an enemy and not the friend of Kelly's he had pretended to be. "I meant rabbit's blood of course," he added quickly.

"Don't know, sir."

He shook his head, trying his best to reassure her. "I'm afraid you must have misunderstood me, Amy. Don't you see that if you thought they wanted him for poaching, and you found rabbit's blood on the coat and perhaps rabbit's fur in the pockets, that explains why you burnt it and gave the Police the other jacket? You must see that."

"Should I, sir?"

"And that in turn explains why you couldn't risk telling the court the truth of what you'd done. It would have looked as though you'd burnt it because you thought that Mr Verney's blood was on it or something to connect the coat with Massingham. Don't you see that it explains it all?"

Above the gusts of wind that buffeted the house he thought he heard again the sound of stealthy movement near the back door, something like the raising of a latch, and this time she seemed to have heard it too. She was glancing around her with the closed, hunted look that he remembered from the Moot Hall, but whether there really had been someone in the house who had now gone or whether it was *him* she feared, the hidden enemy who had tried to trap her and Kelly with fair words as they had trapped her long ago with their scrap of paper, that iniquitous lying scrap of paper, he could not tell. He only knew that she had closed up against him. Only at the door, as he was going out into Clay Yard, did it seem to him that her attitude had changed again and that there was something she wanted to tell him, something urgent that concerned him and perhaps the present more than the past. But though he waited she said nothing, and he decided he must have been wrong.

Outside it was a wild night but the visibility was good. He had just turned into Pelegate when he heard footsteps ahead and in a patch of lamplight saw the hurrying figure of a man. There was something vaguely familiar about him, but the distance was too great for him to be sure. He met no one else on the way home.

VIII

THE following afternoon, while he was still puzzling over the problem of Amy and the affair of Piggott's coat, he got word that Sugden's condition had worsened and that Mr Lumley was proposing to make an emergency call that night with food and medicines.

> Most desirable. You can certainly count on me. Will be with you at the Vicarage at six.

he scribbled on a sheet of office paper and sent Spinks off with it at once. It was always as well to present his ally with a *fait accompli* or something that looked like one on such occasions, where otherwise he might go rushing off on his own, forgetful of the gentleman's agreement between them.

He expected some resistance, after what the Vicar had said on the subject of dying declarations. But when at six precisely he rang the Vicarage bell and was shown into the study he found Mr Lumley in one of his most practical moods. "You can help with the parcels," were the words that greeted him.

There were a great number of them. Deeply laden, carrying amongst other impedimenta an oil stove which the Vicar continued to insist was portable, they set off along Gilesgate for the tenement in Bewley Street. Near its door they met two figures hurrying down the hill towards them—a man and a woman remarkably like Miss Kelly and her fiancé Longford, thought Justin, who called out a greeting to them as they passed in the gloom. He got no answer. There was no wind, but it was bitterly cold, and there was no fire in the room where Sugden lay in the double bed with an old quilt drawn up around his scrawny neck. From the other bed the eyes of the children followed them as they came in—the elder girl's bright with fever, bright as Sugden's own—and behind them hovered the figure of a woman dimly seen in the shadows. The man's face was like parchment, a muddy yellow with a scurf of grey bristles; the hands scaly and dry, gripping the coverlet; the mouth open to show broken and discoloured teeth. Justin found himself observing this quite clinically. His compassion was not an inexhaustible well like Mr Lumley's, and though he was sorry for what he saw lying on the bed, his thoughts were with the innocent and with the child Mary a few yards to his left, whose shallow breathing alarmed him far more.

"Now, George, I've news for you," came the Vicar's comforting voice at his ear. "I'm bringing a doctor for you and the little girl, and he'll be coming tonight. You won't be stubborn about it, I'm sure."

"You shouldn't have done it, sir."

"But I have. I know your good wife will see it my way, won't you, Martha?"

"So I will, sir," a small frightened voice responded.

"There you are, George! You surely know better than to quarrel with both of us at once. Besides, we must think of Mary. And you are to have no qualm about payment or anything of the kind, for that will be attended to. Would you care for a little broth? Martha will light the stove. It can't do you any harm if you fancy it."

The Vicar had already begun to unpack his bag, which was seen to contain a variety of articles including three balloons which he solemnly inflated in front of the children's eyes. There was also a bracelet for the further beautification of the doll Carmen, and this the Vicar put in place, having carefully lifted the glass dome under which she lived. He had some difficulty in fastening it and had to call on Mrs Sugden, perhaps for some other purpose also, for Justin heard the anxious murmur of their voices across the room. Glancing down, he saw Sugden's eyes watching him, but whether their expression was of encouragement or fear or some other emotion, he could not tell.

"So you came back, sir?"

Justin replied drily: "As you see."

"It were good of you, sir. Don't know what I done to deserve it, I'm sure. The Vicar—he's a good friend to me, sir, and always has been. He'll say a good word over me when the time comes."

"Should you be talking so much?"

"But you'll be wantin' me to talk, isn't that it? You'll be wantin' it. That's funny that is, sir."

It seemed to Justin that he had at last identified the expression in the eyes, and for so sick a man it was a remarkably ironical one. But at that moment a fit of coughing racked the invalid.

"What's the matter, George?" enquired the Vicar, arriving hot foot at the bedside with a bottle and a spoon which Martha had given him.

"Nothin', sir. Me and Mr Derry's been havin' a little chat like."

"You'd do better to conserve your strength."

"So the gentleman was sayin', but it's all right, sir, I likes company. It was kind bringin' the balloons. You've always been kind, sir."

The Vicar clearly did not know how to reply to this and silence fell, shattered by a sudden banging sound from downstairs and voices raised in dispute.

"You might give them to the bairns, sir," Sugden said, propping himself up on one elbow.

"Isn't it rather late? I don't want to excite them, as I know Martha will agree. They shall have them in the morning. And you yourself can do the honours."

"If I'm here."

"Of course you'll be here," declared the Vicar in a voice that had become decidedly testy, for he was an ardent disciple of Self Help and did not exempt even the dying from keeping cheerful about their prospects. "We'll soon have you up and about. You take a little of this medicine for your cough, and Martha shall make the broth, and when the doctor comes he'll bless me for sure for bringing him out to you on a night like this. That's more like it"—for the ghost of a smile had appeared on the man's gaunt and hollow face. "I never saw such a patient in all my born days—up one minute and down the next. And talkative too."

"You like a good crack yourself, Vicar."

"So I do. It's my job, isn't it? How would it be if I just stood around and gouped at you? You're not all that handsome, eh, Martha?"

She had come to the bedside and Justin saw her properly for the first time: a small woman with a look of defeat about her, as though she had long ceased to hope for anything.

"Martha knows better than that," the Vicar said, seeing that she was not going to respond. "And so should you, George Sugden. Not be here indeed! If I'd thought you'd talk that way, bless me if I'd have come. Is that broth ready yet?"

"Be a while yet, sir."

"We'll get it into him and then he can sleep till the doctor comes."

"When you've asked me the questions like," said George.

"What questions?"

Justin found it hard not to smile, the Vicar's voice had sounded so surprised and indignant at the idea that anyone should think him capable of baiting a trap with gifts or fair words. Certainly if he was manœuvring his quarry into the right frame of mind for confession he was doing it by instinct and not with any conscious intention; but then perhaps he was not manœuvring at all but had merely been overcome by his scruples, as seemed to happen fairly regularly. Justin waited and wondered which way the cat would jump. He soon knew.

"I'll not ask you any questions, George. My concern is that you should get well. But of course if you were feeling that you *wanted* to say something to me. . . ."

"And to this gentleman?" Sugden said.

"And to Mr Derry, of course."

"I thought that might be it, sir. I telt him it were funny like: he'll see it one day, sir."

He had closed his eyes, and Justin, glancing across at his friend, saw the quick shake of the head, like a signal of disengagement.

"George," said the Vicar.

The shutters of the eyelids came slowly up and Justin found that it was at him that the man was looking, with a strange and questioning alertness.

"George, can you hear me?"

"Yes, sir"—but he had not turned his head.

"You are to rest. Mr Derry is going now, and I will go too if that is what you want. I'd like to stay. I'll ask you no questions, and you shall say nothing unless you wish, and I will take nothing down. It shall be between us and God who made us."

'Damned if I go!' thought Justin rebelliously at these words. If he could still recognise the Vicar's innate goodness of heart, this latest expression of it struck him as sanctimonious nonsense, and unfair nonsense too, which took no account of Justice or the claims of the living. He was still feeling indignant about it when Sugden spoke.

"What was that?" demanded the Vicar sharply, for he had turned away from the bedside.

"I said I wanted to tell you about it. It's on my conscience, sir, and has been these years now. I can't forget it. I'd like to confess, sir. If I should die . . ."

At the word 'confess' an expression of radiant and tender joy had passed across the Vicar's face, but that he was simultaneously aware of the practical issues involved was made clear by the little gesture he made to his ally, as though inviting him to advance the legal battalions into the fray, and by the very words he uttered: "Thank God for it! And here's Mr Derry to get it down."

"I'd like to have it wrote, sir, and yet I durstn't," Sugden said.

"Come now!"

"I just durstn't. This other man, sir. . . ."

"You don't need to give his name."

"He'd find out, wouldn't he?" Sugden had struggled up in bed, so that Justin was reminded of an illustration of a death-bed scene from Dickens that had greatly impressed him as a boy. "How'd we keep it from him, sir?"

"He'd not harm you."

"He'd *kill* me. You don't know him, sir. I just durstn't."

And then, when Justin thought all was lost, it began, and he was writing hard on the folio sheets in the candlelight, while the children stirred restlessly and the paraffin stove hissed in the corner.

IX

I, GEORGE SUGDEN, being of sound mind, make the following statement of my own free will without fear or favour, declaring it to be true:

On the night of the 6th/7th February 1891 I and another man went poaching in Hirsley Wood. There was no game to be had, so, being in the neighbourhood of Massingham, it was agreed between us that we should break into Mr Verney's and see what we could get.

We went to the window on the west side and opened it. The other man went in first. There was a lady's small gold watch on a kind of tripod on the mantelpiece. It had a gold chain with a seal at the end of it shaped like a bird, an eagle with its wings spread and a red stone like a ruby in its claws. The other man took them and put them in his pocket. The room was pretty full of furniture, and there was a table in the middle of it; at least it appeared like a table by the light of the candle we had lighted. On the other side of the room there was a desk and another table with drawers in it. I remember the other man ransacked the drawers. He opened the desk, which was locked, and turned all the papers out. The papers in the desk seemed to be letters and suchlike and all we got were a few coppers.

The other man then tried the door and found it locked. I saw him put something in it, like a chisel, and at last he managed to force the lock. We got into a passage and tried another door. The foot of the stairs was opposite this door, and when standing in the room you can see up the stairs for some distance.

We had got into the room, leaving the door open behind us, when I noticed a light on the stairs. It was a candle, I think. I noticed it was carried by Mr Verney. The other man was alongside me, having the gun in one hand and a candle in the other. I whispered to the man to get out of the house as quickly as we could; but he said afterwards he misunderstood me. He said he thought I told him to fire and frighten the old man. He put the muzzle of the gun through the door and it went off. It kind of exploded. I made off for the other room by which we got into the house. Just as I got into the passage I met a man and a woman just beside the door. The woman caught me by the head with both her hands but she could not keep hold, my hair was so short.

I easily got away from her. I got out through the window and made down to the burn over a little wooden bridge, then bounded across the road in three or four strides on to the heather till I got to the Three Linns. I kept to the moor all the way, and so to Smedwick about three o'clock.

I saw the other man next day. I asked him about a chisel the papers said he had found and he said he must have accidentally left it there. He told me afterwards that he had taken the watch to Belcastle but could neither sell it nor pawn it and at last he had thrown it off the bridge. This may be true. I never knew what came of the chain and eagle seal.

All the above is true to my knowledge.

(signed) George Sugden

"If only you weren't so busy, dearest," Flo complained from the chesterfield which was gay with a spectrum of threads of coloured silk. "Do you know you've hardly spoken a word to me all evening?"

"Haven't I? I'm sorry."

"Is your work so pressing? I mean, I don't want to interrupt you if it is. You must tell me."

"It's work, that's all."

"But you seem so *intent* on it: I declare I hardly dare to speak to you: indeed it is becoming quite a habit. You have not been very approachable or even agreeable lately, Justin."

"I'm sorry."

She glanced fondly up at him over the spectacles she wore for her embroidery. "What is it, dearest? Don't think I'm prying. But something is troubling you."

"Perhaps."

"I know you can't confide in me, which makes me feel so useless. If only I could help you. You have so little time to spare and I have so much, though of course there is the house to look after and the sewing for dear Mr Lumley, who is always so full of great schemes for everyone. If only women weren't so useless."

"No one could possibly say that of you, Flo," he assured her, one eye on Sugden's statement which he had spread out on a reading-rest across his knees.

"A compliment, I do declare! I have extracted that from you at least: you have not quite forgotten how to be gallant. I must tell Georgina. When did you see her last?"

"Last week," he said. "I think it was Tuesday."

"You think!" She was properly scandalised. "There is nothing gallant about *that*. Really you are becoming too casual and it simply will not do. You should be ashamed of yourself. The truth is that you are working much too hard. Isn't it true that he works too hard and brings far too much home at night?" she demanded of Mamie, who had paraded into the room in a new dress of magenta and gold bombazine which she and her dressmaker had created for the general confounding and ravishment of suitors.

"He behaves detestably," Mamie said, whirling up behind him and enclosing the top half of him in a close and fond embrace. "Who's I-George-Sugden-being-of-sound-mind?" she enquired, peering over him. She had none of Flo's inhibitions and was always eager to discover what she could about his mysterious goings-on. "Is that wee Geordie Sugden?"

He struggled free—not without difficulty, for she was a vigorous girl—and got hold of the statement which she had all but snatched from him.

"Really, Mamie!" Flo exclaimed from the chesterfield, but her eyes were bright and she had quite forgotten her embroidery. "It's his work, you know."

"Yes, the provoking thing, always making mysteries. Is wee Geordie a client?"

"That's none of your business," he replied severely, smoothing the pages which had got decidedly crumpled in the struggle. "What do you know of Sugden anyway?"

"That he's a poacher: one of the best in Smedwick."

"Best! My dear!" wailed Flo.

"Well, he is. Bill says so. He was on Bill's land one night and they had a rare old game going after him, dodging from tree to tree, but he got away. He's artful, Bill says. An artful dodger. Is he a client?"

"He is not," said her brother very firmly.

"Then you're prosecuting him. I should look out if I were you. Bill says . . ."

"I don't care what Bill says. Who is he anyway? And I am not prosecuting, if that answers you."

"Then what *are* you doing? Is it deathly secret?" She gave a delicious shudder. "Are we all *menaced?*"

At such moments, if at no other, Justin thanked providence for his Georgina. Her dislike of his work might pain him, but at least she never asked questions about it; and when next evening he presented himself at Warbury Hall, the Deverel home, formally arrayed for a *soirée musicale*, with Flo on one side of him and Mamie on the other, he had no other fear than of being cross-examined about his constancy.

That indeed began the very instant he and Georgina found themselves alone in an alcove of the drawing-room:

"Where *have* you been? How provoking you are—really quite heartless. You've left me alone all week without a word, not even a letter—too cruel. Anyone would think you lived a hundred miles away; you have no thought for me."

She was due to sing, and fear of the ordeal had made her overwrought and very unlike her usual confident self. His heart warmed to her.

"You are quite callous," she accused him.

"My dearest!"

"How can you even use the word when I am the very *last* person to be thought of? I suppose you'll tell me that you've been busy every night. Have you found time for Flo?"

"I've hardly seen her."

"Or Mamie either, I suppose. What a *dress* she is wearing! I declare it would be quite in fashion if this were a ball in London. Does no one advise her?"

Catching sight of his younger sister across the room, Justin was disposed to agree: he had ventured a few words himself about the dress before setting out, and it certainly went remarkably badly with the décor of a room which had not been designed to accommodate anything even remotely primrose in shade. 'Like a butterfly,' he thought bitterly. The other gentlemen, however, had not been afflicted with such critical thoughts. They clustered: it was all too evident. In one half of the room stood the piano, with a few upright female figures near it waiting for the music to begin, and in the other his sister presided at the centre of a group in which Colonel Deverel could be discerned in his white waistcoat, looking, as Lord Holland had once looked, 'like a turbot standing on its tail'. A pretty start to the evening. No wonder Georgina was outraged. Before it was over the old man would be bound to ask Mamie to sing, and she would oblige too, and the fat would be properly in the fire.

Notes came from the piano. Mrs Deverel was sounding the recall to duty. Justin took another look at the room as it began to settle down to the serious business of the evening. A fashionable gathering. The duke could not quite be aspired to—he was understood in any case to dislike music very much—but several other gentlemen of rank were present with their ladies and the town was quite excluded, unless one counted Mr Lumley, Vicar of St Bede's, an unexpected figure much encumbered with music sheets. The atmosphere was one of dutiful attention proper to a gathering about to be subjected to ballads of a cultural nature.

At this moment a polite tinkle of applause broke out and the vocalist was seen at her station. Cousin Emily was no stranger to such occasions: she clutched in her hands a scroll and could even be seen to be consulting it, but it was not left to her audience to feel that this was anything but an act of modesty or perhaps a declaration of amateur status.

"A little song of Claribel's," Mrs Deveral announced.

Cousin Emily's bosom heaved and her face assumed a decidedly reproachful expression.

"You are not what you were, Robin" (the loud accusing voice rang out)

> "Why so sad and strange?
> You were once blithe and gay, Robin,
> What has made you change?
> You never come to see me now
> As once you used to do,
> I miss you at the wicket gate
> You always let me thro'.
> It's very hard to open
> But you never come and try:
> Won't you tell me why, Robin,
> Won't you tell me why?"

'Devil take the woman!' thought Justin as the sense of the words gradually crept up on him. It could be coincidence, of course, for with a few jolly exceptions all the ballads he had heard seemed to be either morbid or concerned with the complaints the sexes had against one another (in this respect being remarkably true to life), and Claribel's 'little song' was not much more wan than its competitors. It was uncomfortably near the knuckle all the same. Cousin Emily must have known it. Cousin Emily, he decided, watching that swelling bust embark on the second verse, must have intended it, the venomous hag. To his horror he found himself blushing and wondered desperately whether anyone would notice him or the thunderous expression on Georgina's face.

"Capital fellow, Claribel," a voice boomed in his ear above the applause and cries of 'Encore!' from the gentlemen of Mamie's circle. "Georgina, my dear, you should take up Claribel. *Janet's Choice*—now there's a song for you."

"If one happens to like Claribel, Papa."

Justin made way for his host: he was very happy to welcome a contestant better fitted than himself to cope with the evening.

"Don't you? What are you singing, my dear?" the Colonel asked. *"Du bist wie eine Blume."*

"Do I know it?"

"You should. It is familiar to most people. Schumann's setting of Heine's words."

"Of course. Such a charming song. So suitable. I shall enjoy it so very much. And dear Mamie if she will consent to sing," added the Colonel, undoing all his good work. "Has she brought her music?"

"You should ask Justin."

"I am asking Justin. Well, it's no matter, we shall find something for her, never fear. Such a pure and natural talent. Yet Miss Derry does not sing, I think?"

"She admits to choruses."

"And you not even to that, my boy? You mustn't let the law dry you up completely. By the way, while on the subject, there's a little matter I wished to speak to you about. Something Superintendent Blair was telling me. Disturbed me: can't pretend it didn't. Oh, here's this fellow Lumley now," he broke off gloomily as the Vicar of St Bede's was seen advancing on the piano with the unmistakable look of a baritone about to harrow his audience.

"Invocation, from *Faust: Even Bravest Heart,"* Mrs Deverel announced over her shoulder.

Colonel Deverel subsided, grumbling. He professed an admiration for Gounod's oratorio *Redemption,* which he had never heard, but *Faust* (which he had never heard either) had for long excited his contempt as 'tinkly French stuff' that had somehow got through the Customs. Nor was he reassured by the sight of one of the Vicar's cloth attempting a song which was identifiably a soldier's farewell to civilian life. It smacked too much of sacrilege.

"D'you know the feller?" he muttered to Justin through the applause that greeted the end of the aria. "What d'you make of him? Pretty radical johnny, isn't he? Wants to see everyone equal. Bit of a republican too, if I know anything about it. Old Bishop Knowles appointed him, and it was Gladstone appointed *him*. Birds of a feather. Can you understand the feller's sermons?"

"Perhaps not always."

"That's honest, at any rate. Neither can I. In my day we had the Tractarians and high-flyin' Oxford fellers like Newman and so on, but that was *doctrine,* and no one was expected to make much of it. No revivalism about it. No socialism such as he preaches—does it from the pulpit. Of course he's a good enough feller in his way."

"I must get my music, Justin," Georgina said.

He escaped with her across the room, past Mamie at the centre of a group in a state of perpetual agitation with people fetching and carrying things, and Flo wedged on an ottoman between two elderly ladies in black taffeta and bangles. Beyond them, all by himself in an alcove, Mr Lumley was sorting his music, his face flushed and beads of sweat standing on his forehead which he dabbed with a silk handkerchief rolled up into a ball.

Justin regarded this dangerous firebrand with affection. "You might have sung *The Lincolnshire Poacher* while you were about it," he chided him as he came up, leaving Georgina to go on ahead. "Well, why not? What are you looking so shocked about? Was it bad taste? Is Sugden worse? Or the child?"

"Both much better as it happens. Thank God for it."

"Somehow I always thought he was a surviving type. An artful dodger, so Mamie says. I've been re-reading his statement, by the way."

"I don't want to stop you, but shouldn't you be looking after Miss Deverel?" enquired his friend.

She was leaning over the piano, her elegant blonde head very close to Mrs Deverel's immense coiffure, and Justin watched them, fascinated by the contrast and the likeness that he saw there. "Oh, Georgina's all right. She was a bit on edge, but she's got over it. Besides, I'd only be in the way up there. Now about that statement."

The Vicar sighed resignedly. "Very well: go on, my dear fellow, if you really think you should. Is the statement what we require?"

"Up to a point. It contains some significant and important things. But there are grave omissions. The Other Man isn't named. Miss Verney's watch and seal aren't properly accounted for. In fact, there's very little in the statement that you can really get your teeth into; that can be put up against known facts and checked. And without definite proof . . ."

"People won't listen."

"They won't listen; they'll think the man's a crank or up to some dodge. When I say 'people', I mean of course official people, those in the ministries whom we'll have to move if we're to get the case re-opened. But there are others who might listen."

"Go on."

"The Verneys, to begin with. If they saw that confession they might help. If they were to think again about their evidence in the light of what Sugden says, then we'd be on altogether firmer ground, with something really good to show the Lord Chancellor or the Queen herself. Are you a Radical?"

"What's that you're saying, my dear fellow?" exclaimed the Vicar in astonishment.

"Just a passing thought. I don't suppose we're going to be exactly loved for this . . . by the powers that be, I mean. Subversive: is that the word?"

"Our host would say so, certainly."

"Why our host particularly?"

"Didn't you know? Because he was the committing magistrate: it was he who sent Milligan and Kelly to the Assizes," the Vicar said.

X

Snow lay over the countryside. As they crested the hill they saw the valley below them, piebald where the ribs of walls and rocks showed through, but further north the fall had been heavier and the flanks of The Heriot looked as smooth as a crystal globe. In the foreground lay the village: castle and church by the stream; the zig-zag of road climbing the hill past the rambling bulk of the Rectory, more piebald than the rest in its grove of trees. "It would do for a bishopric," Justin found himself murmuring aloud. "Let us hope that Verney has a stipend to match. Has he?"

"I believe Massingham is a good enough living."

"One you'd fancy for yourself?"

"My dear chap!" Mr Lumley's expression was one of dismay as he gazed over the pony's ears at the hamlet and scattered farms. Where were the souls to be saved? Where were the parishioners to be dragooned into good works? In such a place, after a few dinners with the gentry, the poor man would have died of discouragement or started an agrarian revolution.

On foot, leaving the trap at Merrick's bothy at the bottom of the hill, they reached the Rectory gates and came immediately on Mr Verney shovelling snow. Flakes glistened in his beard and in his long white hair; he had on mittens, and goloshes so thick with slush that he seemed to be wearing a pair of enormous clogs; and in his wake the fruits of his toil showed in a beaten track from the gates to the front door along which the Vicar of St Bede's advanced, hand outstretched, rather like the explorer Stanley on a similar occasion.

"My dear Mr Verney!" He seemed to be finding it an affecting moment. "Mr Verney, will you forgive this intrusion into your labours? I hope you are not overstraining yourself. You know Mr Derry, I believe?"

"I do, sir."

The old man leading, they went into the hall, having the drawing-room on their left, from which came the sulky crackle of a wood fire. Ahead of them a baize door opened. "My dear, we have visitors," Mr Verney called out into the gloom. "You know Mr Lumley, of course. And Mr Derry: but I don't think you've met Mr Derry."

It was a narrow hall, not suited to social occasions. Justin, who had only seen her once, at the Moot Hall, could barely see her now, but he could hear her—the rustle of whalebone and satin coming towards him over the linoleum.

"I fear we have intruded," he heard his ally say.

"Not at all. If you'd go into the drawing-room."

A scrimmage developed of the kind usual where several people are urging one another to go through a door, and at the end of it they found themselves, as the Massingham burglars had done, in a pleasant squarish room, much beset by furniture which projected at unlikely angles, forming a kind of obstacle course. There was the table in the middle of the room, and the desk the 'man' had rifled, and on the mantelpiece the tripod on which Miss Verney's watch and seal had hung. It was all as Sugden had described it: so exactly, that the critic in Justin's mind awoke and began to ask questions. Was the statement in his pocket really the memory of something seen across a gap of eight years, or had Sugden seen the Rectory more recently? Was it possible that the Verneys never moved their furniture? They had certainly not carried out repairs to the dining-room door where the shot had struck; which might argue poverty, or carelessness, or even a perverse kind of sentiment, for the burglary had, after all, been a great event, perhaps the most memorable of Mr Verney's life.

He was suddenly aware that his friend, with no such speculations to comfort him, had found himself in an exposed position between the Rector of Massingham and Miss Verney, both breathing an intimidating hospitality.

"A glass of wine?"

Mr Lumley did not drink: he had been known to describe strong liquor as an abomination.

"Will you not take some refreshment? You have come a long way in this hard weather."

"And there will be more snow coming," her father said, wagging his beard at them with lugubrious relish.

"Papa!"

"My dear, there will be. Tom was saying so this morning and you know what a nose for weather he has. This winter reminds him a little, as it reminds me, of the beginning of . . . my dear, you won't remember what year it was when even the mail could not get through?"

"If as you say it is to snow . . . ," Mr Lumley tried to interrupt with a kind of desperation.

"It has begun already."

Indeed a white cloud had swept down over the moor, and flakes like small hailstones were whirling against the window panes.

"Then we must hasten our business, I fear, if you will forgive my abruptness, seeing that we have such a long journey in front of us."

"Your business. Most certainly."

"It concerns something that happened a long time ago. The Massingham burglary in fact."

"The Burglary!" exclaimed Mr Verney, clearly astonished by this remark. "But how can the Burglary concern . . . ? I don't understand."

"Perhaps if you were to let Mr Lumley explain, Papa."

"Gladly, gladly. I was not aware that he was involved in any way, that's all."

"Then he will tell us."

Mr Lumley suffered this colloquy and then said in a diplomatic voice: "I was not concerned at the time at all, except that of course

I shared the general sense of outrage that you should have been subjected to so dastardly an act."

"But that was eight years ago," Miss Verney said. "We have had time to forgive and forget."

He turned towards her. "Could we say the same of the two men who have served those years in penal servitude? A life sentence—very disproportionate to the crime, bad though it was, as your father in his goodness of heart saw at the time, even *had* Milligan and Kelly committed it."

"But there can be no question that they committed it," said Mr Verney, looking around in perplexity. "The jury found them guilty; and how just that verdict was both my daughter and I know well, seeing that we both saw the men at work, most flagrantly at work in this very house. Is that not so, my dear?"

"Let him explain, Papa."

"Thank you," Mr Lumley said. "I beg you not to think me impertinent: there is too much at stake. It's no easy thing to come here and say what I must. But I have read the reports of the trial, and I have had the invaluable benefit of Mr Derry's recollection of it, and it is clear enough that in your anxiety to be fair you never claimed on oath or at any other time to have seen the faces of the accused."

"We saw them—those men themselves."

"No, Miss Verney, forgive me, you did *not*. You never saw Milligan and Kelly for the simple reason that they were miles away on Bridewell Moor. You saw two fellows very like them in the semi-darkness and excitement of the moment."

"It is kind of you," came the supercilious, cutting voice, "to tell us what we saw. We are obliged to you."

"Must you take it like that, Miss Verney?"

"How would you have me take it? You come here—for no clearly disclosed reason that I can see—and you tell us that my father and I went into court and perjured ourselves."

"No, I never said that. No." There was distress in Mr Lumley's voice; his face had gone very pale and his eyes stared out from it, bright with appeal to tender and compassionate emotions. "It was the very last thought in my mind. If I had thought it for a moment I would never have come here, never, I beg you to believe that. You told the court what you *believed* you saw."

She gave a shrug of the shoulders, infinitely contemptuous, and replied: "If you can see a distinction there, you have a truly ingenious mind. You are saying our evidence was false."

"Mistaken, my dear young lady—no more than that."

"How can you even voice such an opinion? How are you qualified to do it?"

"I am qualified," said Mr Lumley very slowly, "because I have seen, and we have here with us, a confession signed by one of the two men who were in your house that night."

"What next! A confession indeed!"

"My colleague has it in his pocket. If you will produce it, Derry."

Justin did so, unfolding the folio sheets and holding them out towards their host, who showed some inclination to accept them until arrested by an imperious movement of his daughter's hand.

"It is a perfectly genuine confession," explained Mr Lumley in his most conciliatory voice. "If you will look at it you will see the man's name, which I ask you to treat as confidential for the time being."

"We don't wish to see it."

"And you will find there a full and meticulous description of everything that happened, from the moment the men broke in to the time of their return to Smedwick."

"I said we didn't wish to see it."

Mr Lumley took a step towards her, his hands clasped in appeal as Justin had often seen him in the pulpit of St Bede's. "Miss Verney, I have been unkind; I have not prepared you as a wiser man would have done. I recalled to you a very terrible moment, and I did it clumsily, with too little thought for you both. It has come as too great a shock and I beg your pardon for it."

She did not answer, but stood watching him: a small withdrawn figure in a satin dress that matched the dark hair drawn across her brow. In the background the old man was moving uneasily but she paid no attention to him.

"Will you not say you forgive me, dear young lady, now that I acknowledge my fault? I have no desire to prolong something which is so distressing to you. We could leave the statement with you, and perhaps later . . ."

"No," she interrupted him, "no, you must take it."

Surprise was on Mr Lumley's face and sounded in his voice as he said: "But Miss Verney, you will surely not dismiss it quite in that way? Here is a statement which in my opinion, and that of my colleague who has experience of such things, is a true and detailed confession to a crime for which two other men are suffering at this moment. We have examined it closely and it bears every mark of truth. At the very least it surely deserves to be examined attentively and with an open mind—not now perhaps, not at this instant, but later, when the shock I so misguidedly forced upon you has passed. That is why I ask you to accept it."

"We shall do nothing of the kind."

"Do you distrust our interference so much?" said Mr Lumley sadly. "You have every reason to complain of the way I have carried out my mission."

"That is certainly part of it."

"But the statement itself? You surely cannot refuse to read it?"

"I do."

"And you, sir?"

He had swung away from her towards the old man, but she came between them and he saw the light of passionate resentment in her eyes. "Nor will you trouble my father with such things. You have no right."

"I have the right to expect justice," said Mr Lumley, not without dignity.

"Justice for what? For some lying scrawl! No, Papa, I will speak out"—for he had tried to restrain her. "A tissue of falsehoods, made up for what reason? I am sorry to say it in my father's house, but you should not have come, you should not have listened to lies so credulously. For lies they are. We *know* it. We don't need to read that paper—which you may put away, you'll find no use for it." Her voice had risen and rang out shrilly in the high-ceilinged room. "For we will never read it. You will *never* persuade us we were wrong."

XI

THE Verneys had failed them and he must try another line. Yet no problem of detection, reasoned Justin in the privacy of his own room, ought to be very hard. Something either exists or it is chimerical. If it exists in human shape it leaves traces of itself, has friends. If one could deduce a man's character from the company he kept, one could equally deduce that company from the man: indeed, so far from existing in a vacuum, Sugden's 'Other Man', whom it now behoved him to find, must have certain characteristics that were individual and unlike anything to be expected of the average Smedwick citizen. Suppose, to begin with, a friend of Sugden's but with more violent inclinations: the kind of man who would use a gun; which in its turn supposed a person who had already used one. In the background of his mind was the memory of a crime earlier than the Massingham affair. Miss Kelly might remember it; she or Longford; he could look to them for help because they were the most directly interested of the Pelegate folk and perhaps the nearest approach to clients he possessed in '*In Re Milligan*', as the case had been listed in his files.

They made a quaint pair as they sat facing him in the tall-backed chairs: the thin, rather pretty but fading woman and the loutish man in his shapeless breeches and tweed coat. He felt sorry for them both, and grateful too, because they had not vexed him lately with endless visits and questions. They had their curiosity, however:

"What happens next, sir?"

He began to explain as discreetly as he could, choosing each word with scrupulous care. "Nothing's settled. There's still a lot to be done. But certain facts have come to light which will be passed to the authorities, and if a certain view is taken of those facts we may expect some kind of enquiry and perhaps the arrival of a Commissioner to take evidence—from you among others, I expect."

"And from George Sugden, sir?" she asked.

"If he gets well, as I think he will. If he'll oblige and give it."

"Why shouldn't he give it? He give it you, sir."

Justin sighed and answered as soothingly as possible: "I'm sure he'll be helpful. But as to what he said or didn't say to me, that's something I'm not free to tell you."

"Though I'm Mick Kelly's sister, sir?"

She had begun to bridle; her cheeks were flushed and her eyes were bright, as though she had sensed an enemy. A brave, quick, determined young woman. He felt a real admiration for her.

"Now see here," he said gently. "I have to keep faith with people who trust and confide in me, you must see that. But don't be anxious. Things are moving at last. I feel quite sure that he's in the mood to be helpful if only he doesn't get frightened by the thought of punishment, of prison."

"He deserves worse, sir. He might get it too."

"What do you mean, Miss Kelly?"

She hesitated and then turned to him, trembling with the force of her emotions. "What do I mean, sir? That some of us have waited and waited and we want something, sir—justice—and we want it done: but there are others, sir, that don't want it and they might take steps, sir."

"You mean the 'Other Man'?" said Justin softly. "His companion at Massingham that night. Because of course there *was* another man." She seemed to hesitate, and suddenly a forgotten name recurred to him and he said out of the blue: "Wasn't there a crime at Hannington some years back? Wasn't some policeman killed?"

He had no sooner spoken than he saw his mistake, for she had swung round and he saw in her eyes the glint of fear. "I mind there was, sir," she said in a defensive voice.

"There was a gun used, wasn't there?"

"Aye."

"And it seemed to me that perhaps the same man might have used it that shot at Mr Verney."

But he could see from her face that he would get no further. Perhaps she had good reason to be afraid, as Sugden had been afraid at the mere mention of his companion. He had no right to press her further, or Longford, who was her shadow and might be in the same danger. For that matter, the unwelcome idea had come to him that he himself might be treading on perilous ground—not that he had any intention of being deterred by such thoughts, which his sturdy common sense rejected out of hand as a piece of imagination very much out of keeping with the spirit of the age. He had a problem to solve and he would approach it rationally, making use of the best material to hand. Miss Kelly had failed him, and since Blair still ruled in the Lawnmarket it seemed wiser to avoid the Police, to whom he would otherwise have gone, and rely instead on the *Smedwick Mercury*, in whose filing room, among the back numbers of the paper, he felt sure he would encounter Sugden's past and his associates among the Bewley and Pelegate poachers.

He found it hard going at first—wading back through the dust-laden pages. But after a while, as he began to get his bearings, the fascination of the search grew on him. Events he had forgotten suddenly re-surfaced, but quaintly, in reverse: the conviction before the crime, the inquest leading the death. Some of his own cases were there, in somewhat obscure corners. Mr Lumley was there too, his earnest face peering from the background of wedding groups, and at prize givings, holding out tomes of enormous and discouraging size. Gilmore was there: and Blair in uniform. Deaths, elections, fires, robberies, seductions, marriages passed before him in a quickening stream, making of the world an even more remarkably sinful and exciting place than he had remembered it to be. And as he went back, the landmarks of the Massingham affair began to show. Here was the departure of the convicts on their way to gaol; Mr Justice Garrowby in his robes, regarding the camera with awful severity; the trial report from Belcastle; a picture of the Rectory; Mr Verney's letter in which he had described the impressions received by a man at the wrong end of a gun:

> I was right in front of the gun and yet saw no flash. What I did see was a meteor of transcendent brilliance, so that I exclaimed to myself, 'I never saw so beautiful a meteor as that in my life,' and added mentally, 'And I believe very few people have and lived to talk of it.'

Justin began to smile: he had not remembered the letter as being quite so fascinating or so odd.

> I knew the meteor was somehow connected with the gun; it changed colour far more rapidly than I expected, from whitish red to deep red, and finally to purple. In looking down the barrel for some distance of its length, I saw the gunpowder exploding within the breech as well as the train of fire without, and both foreshortened into a kind of exceeding brilliant ball of fire.

To have known so much, seen so much, and to have identified the wrong burglars at the end of it! It seemed incredible.

Soon, going back, he had reached the burglary itself and the brief but exclamatory remarks with which the *Mercury* had announced this new atrocity to the world. He read it through closely, as one in need of enlightenment, but of course there was nothing to be learnt from it; and turning back into the journal's deserving past, he was out in the open country beyond the crime among a generation that knew not Massingham. A more serious matter had perturbed it: the Hannington murder whose echoes he had already caught, which also had arisen out of a poaching expedition, though its end had not been a gunshot ricocheting off a wall giving interesting pictorial effects on the way, but one that struck a man and blasted the life out of him.

THE QUEST: 1899

A most foul and brutal crime is reported from Hannington. P.C. Luke, one of the Force's most respected officers, has been done to death. The weapon was a shot-gun, the crime occurring in the small hours of last Monday on the fells above the village, hard by the wall of Mr Chevely's estate, on a patch of open ground near a stream known locally as the Carrick Burn.

The officer was unarmed. He had been brutally and treacherously shot down at point-blank range. Great indignation is being expressed in the locality at this latest outrage, which follows numerous complaints of poaching and of marauding parties of armed men in the countryside around the village. No doubt is felt that this gallant and well-loved officer had happened that night on such a party and had been in the course of apprehending them when he was struck down from behind, without a chance of defending himself or even of seeing his murderer.

There are clues in the possession of the Police. An arrest is confidently anticipated. Certain persons have been seen by the officers in charge of the enquiries. A statement has been made by one George Henry Sugden of Bewley Street, Smedwick. . . .

"The devil it has!" Justin exclaimed aloud. He read on further in an increasingly thoughtful mood and then went downstairs to the Editor to ask him what he remembered about the murder. "Very little," was the answer, "except that it was a bad business and they never got to the bottom of it or charged anyone. Hicks would know more. He covered it."

Hicks was the senior reporter: a dusty gnome with a battery of pencils sticking out of his pocket and one behind his ear. "Here's Mr Derry," the Editor said, when the man had been produced from the bowels of the *Mercury* building, "and he's asking about Hannington, the crime, you know."

"The murder, sir?"

"That's right, Willie." The Editor kept one eye on his subordinate, the other on his copy, for he was writing an impassioned leader on the subject of the Smedwick rates. "You were on the spot, I seem to remember. Just fire away, Derry, and Hicks will do what he can. You won't mind if I get on with this?"

"Won't we disturb you?"

"Not a bit; I like background noises. Just fire away."

So Justin 'fired away', beginning with Sugden; and Hicks remembered him at once. "That's right, sir: the Police thought Sugden was mixed up in it."

"Was he?"

"In a small way, I expect. They were poachers who did it, and poor Luke copped 'em and someone shot him. That wouldn't be Sugden, not wee Geordie, though he may have been around. They never proved it."

"Who do you think shot Luke?"

Hicks considered, feeling behind his free ear as though he had mislaid something. "There was talk of a chap called Longford," he remarked at last.

The effect of this name on Justin was prodigious. It was about the last he had expected; it conflicted with all his thinking, for if Longford were his 'Other Man' it made Miss Kelly's part in the Massingham case enigmatical to say the least. She had certainly shown fear at mention of Hannington, and perhaps there was some connection that the reporter would know. "Isn't Longford the chap who's just got himself engaged to Mick Kelly's sister?" he enquired.

"I wouldn't know about that, sir." Indeed Mr Hicks did not look well equipped by nature to enjoy life's happier occasions: it was acknowledged on the *Mercury* that he was at his best at funerals. "But to my mind they were wrong about it, sir. He never shot Luke; he was only a lad at the time, a bit lad."

"Who *did* shoot him, then?" demanded the Editor, scribbling away for dear life.

"It's hard to tell. Some older man, more likely—one of the Pelegate tykes, and there are enough of 'em. Green . . ."

"You mean the roadman?"

"He works a bit that way. Or Henderson—he's turned respectable. Piggott, O'Malley and some others of the Irish set. Ah, there's a wheen of 'em. Has something turned up about Hannington, sir?" he asked, changing tune quite suddenly.

"Not that I know of."

"I thought it was Massingham you were interested in—you and the Reverend Gentleman. People seem to think so. You got something for us, sir?"

"Not a thing."

"I've got something for *you,* sir, right up your street," said Mr Hicks with gloomy satisfaction. "One of your witnesses passed on. Lass by the name of Amy Dodds down Pelegate. They just fished her body from the pool below the weir."

XII

It was a mild evening, with a sudden thaw out of the west bringing quite a springlike air to the gardens where a few snowdrops were raising their heads. He passed the vicarage of St Bede's and the castle, whose sprawling mass receded into darkness, pricked by points of light from the windows of the bailey. Further west, where the last of the afterglow still lingered, he could see the crest of the moor where the road swept up the hill, and below it the amorphous shapes of streets hiding in its shadow.

In Pelegate and Bewley, in this sad quarter of the town, lay the answer to his problem, if indeed the whole thing did not turn out to be a hoax or the fantasy of a sick mind. There had been times when he had thought that this might be the truth of it, remembering the scene at Sugden's bedside, the man's strange humour, as though he had been enjoying a joke at his expense. But there was nothing humorous about the fate of Amy Dodds. Whether she had committed suicide, as Hicks seemed to accept, or whether there was some more natural explanation, the fact of her disappearance from the scene and the timing of it, so soon after his visit to Clay Yard, filled him with a profound disquiet; he even felt a kind of responsibility, though he knew this to be absurd.

As he argued it over in his mind he reached the foot of the hill and began the climb between the old stone-built houses of the quarter. The town ended abruptly on that side: it was not the polite suburban world you found along the Warbury Road where the moneyed folk were building streets of new 'residences' for themselves. He felt the need of a walk and went striding up the hill, beyond the last of the gaslight, till he was in the open country where the fields were lapped by the moor. It was good to be out there with the wind moist against his face. From the ridge he could look right across Smedwick, but no stranger would have guessed there was a sizable town down there, so thinly spread and faint was the lighting under the clouds that had rolled in from the west. There was not a sound to be heard except the distant rumble of a train on its way up the coast and a dog howling in a Bewley yard as though its heart would break. Old Matt, perhaps.

After a while he turned back down the hill. The first houses appeared, their curtains drawn close, hardly a chink of light showing. Here the day had already ended, but there were still a few people abroad, for he could see someone ahead of him in a patch of light near the entrance to Gilesgate, and nearer at hand a door had opened to disgorge a cat which came racing out almost under his feet. The dog was still howling, and now he could place the sound to within a few yards of Sugden's tenement, the shape of which he could just make out from the darkness some distance to his right, and he crossed towards it, suddenly taken with a desire to see his penitent again.

Footsteps sounded to his left, quite close—no doubt the man he had seen in the lamplight—and there might be company behind him too, for he heard a sudden stirring, as though someone had moved in the deep shadows under the wall of the house. He halted and swung round, a little surprised, for he had passed no one and had heard no door opening on that side: and in that same instant it seemed to him that a sheet of flame reached out towards him, moving with paralysing speed across his line of sight. He saw no meteor, no change of colour such as Mr Verney had described; just an impression of fire swallowed up by the shattering roar of the explosion.

An instant of silence fell, during which he stood quite still, uncertain whether he had been hit or indeed still lived, for all was darkness around him. Then the night was rent by the pounding of feet and a voice crying out something, though he could not catch the words; and he found himself leaning against the rough stone of a wall, hearing the waves of sound receding into the distance like the disembodied noises in a dream.

"Mr Derry, sir, Mr Derry!" he heard a voice exclaim almost in his ear. Immediately in front of him a small dumpish figure, apparently in a state of great excitement, seemed to be bouncing up and down as though it or the pavement beneath it were made of indiarubber. "Mr Derry, are you hurt, sir?"

"All in one piece, I think," he answered, trying to focus on this apparition, whose gnomic shape made him fear the worst until he recognised the *Mercury's* Mr Hicks peering solicitously up at him. "What happened, anyway?"

"Well, what happened, sir," said the reporter in a voice not entirely free of satisfaction, "is that someone took a pot shot at you. Are you sure he missed?"

"Feels like it. No bones broken. No holes in me to speak of."

"If you'd let me look, sir."

A match was struck, and by its light Justin saw the inquisitive eyes darting over him. "That set your mind at rest?" he asked as the flame died and they were back in darkness.

"Seems like he missed you, sir. Providential, I'd say. Very providential. Almost uncanny. Was he close?"

"I'm not sure."

"How d'you mean you're not sure, sir? You were nearer to him than me—much nearer."

Around them the quiet streets had begun to come to life. Across the way the curtains in an upstairs room were drawn back and a face could be seen at the window, while further down towards the market-place a door opened and someone came out into the road, calling over his shoulder to those inside the house. "Wonder who it is and if he saw much?" Hicks said, watching these signs with interest. "A proper *cause célèbre* he'd have here and no mistake. Smedwick Solicitor Fired On. Make a good headline, sir."

Justin put his hand on the reporter's shoulder and said with great earnestness: "Don't use it. If you do, you'll lose a story, a far bigger one than this."

"Oh, I see that, sir," Hicks agreed.

"I knew you would. You'll be discreet about it?"

"Of course, sir. That's if the others will. If no one saw him and they don't tell on him to Blair."

There was a moment of silence and then Justin demanded plaintively: "Tell on whom?"

"On young Longford, sir. I saw him go haring off, as plain as plain, as I came up and found you by the wall."

XIII

THE more Justin thought the matter out, tossing and turning in bed that night, the more incomprehensible it became. If Longford were his attacker, then Longford must surely be the 'Other Man' and Sugden's partner in the burglary. Granted that, however, why should the fellow have tried to kill him, when Sugden looked so much the more likely and indicated victim? It was Sugden who was making statements and knew the dangerous facts that could send a man to penal servitude. Where was the point in attacking the agent, who had a mere confession which was of limited value, rather than the man himself who could give the evidence on oath? Perhaps it had been meant as a warning, to frighten, not to kill, which would account for the fact that the shot had missed; or might he have been chosen as a kind of 'second best' because Sugden had a healthier regard for his own skin and was too fly to be caught in the dark? That made some kind of sense. But if Longford were the 'Other Man', how could one account for the role this apparently stupid and guileless fellow was playing as Miss Kelly's fiancé and one of the advocates of Sugden's guilt?

Next morning, on his way to work, he went by the main shopping street, loitering in his tobacconist's which was a clearing house for gossip, but everything seemed normal and he noticed no curious glances from the passers-by. Indeed all seemed so quiet, that it came as quite a surprise to Justin when in mid-morning a note was delivered asking him to call at the police office in the Lawnmarket.

He found Blair sitting at a large mahogany desk, on which lay a number of files and a pair of handcuffs which the Superintendent politely removed and put in his tunic. Behind him on the wall hung a map of the district, broken up into coloured segments, flanked by a pair of gilt-scrolled truncheons which had retired from active service and were now exhibits of an earlier heroic age. Three chairs, a cupboard full of photographs, a pipe rack, a daguerreotype of heavily whiskered constables on the beat, a helmet and a police whistle completed the furnishings of the room, which was austere and covered in brown paint.

"Now, Mr Derry." The Superintendent had cleared his throat and was tapping his desk where lay a sheet of paper, in a way very reminiscent of a schoolmaster Justin had encountered in the sinful days of his youth. "I've a report here, sir. Report of a disturbance occasioned last night in Bewley Street and involving the use of firearms. Have you any comments you'd care to make, sir?"

"Hadn't you better read me the contents first?"

The Superintendent smiled a frosty smile at this piece of professional caginess and replied: "Just as you like, sir. I want to be quite frank about this. I'll give my help freely, sir, just as I'm hoping for yours."

It was a constable's report from one P.C. Buchan who had been on duty in Gilesgate the previous evening. Buchan had heard a shot and had 'proceeded' towards it at the double, encountering a householder from whom he had learnt of Justin's and Hicks's presence at the scene. No cartridge case had been recovered or trace of a weapon found; there were no reports of casualties, and no other witnesses had come forward.

"Were you in Bewley, sir?" Blair asked.

There was no point in denying it.

"So you heard the shot. Were you close to it?"

"I was some distance off: it's hard to estimate how far in the dark."

"You must forgive this upset in our positions, sir," remarked the Superintendent pleasantly. "Very unfamiliar ground for you, sir, I expect. It's usually you who asks the questions."

"You deserve a turn."

"So I do, sir. Now then: did you observe anyone in the street?"

Justin replied that he had seen someone coming from his left, from Gilesgate; he thought that would be Hicks. And he had sensed someone behind him in the shadows.

"So you think this someone fired the shot?"

"It looks like it."

"At you, sir?"

"Why should anyone fire at me?" he answered as lightly as he could.

"That's what we must find out. But someone fired, that's evident, and it looks as if you were the target. Will you be making a complaint?"

"Why should I?"

"Why, Mr Derry. Don't you want to discover your assailant?"

"He wasn't my assailant as you call it."

There was a pause while the Superintendent got up and walked to the window overlooking the Lawnmarket, clasping his hands behind him. When he swung round into the room again Justin saw what he had not seen before: the hard, alert face of the man whom Milligan and Kelly and countless others no doubt had met in that room.

"Now see here, sir," the Superintendent resumed briskly. "Here's a crime been committed and it seems to me you were a witness. If you'd just give me more details of what happened?"

"Haven't I already done so?"

"Well hardly. Here was a shot fired, and fairly near you from all I hear, yet you went straight off home without telling anyone about it and you don't seem anxious now to make a case of it. That's not what I expected. It's not the frankness or quite the attitude I'd looked for from a gentleman in your position."

"What's my position got to do with it?"

"Now really, sir!" exclaimed the Superintendent, managing a smile, though it was an extremely laboured one. "I mean to say! A man of law, sir! You wouldn't expect such a person to conceal a felony, now would you?"

"There wasn't any felony to conceal. It was probably an accident and the gun just went off."

"Of its own accord, no doubt! Perhaps you'll tell me it was poachers shooting at pheasants in Bewley Street."

"You should know all about those fellows," replied Justin wickedly.

Blair's eyes narrowed, but he said with the same jocular air: "Might I say the same of you, sir? Been doing some visiting down there, I understand. On Sugden, sir."

"Suppose I have?"

"Bit off your beat, isn't it? Of course, I've no call to be asking what you were doing there those other times—but last night, now that's different. Why *were* you there, sir?"

"I was out walking."

"Do people usually shoot at you on such occasions?" demanded the Superintendent with ponderous irony. "Why did it happen at that particular spot, near Geordie's house? Would you call that coincidence?"

"What else?"

"Don't like coincidences myself, never believed in 'em. Cause and effect: that's more my line. Now I know you, sir, and very fair you've always been in our little encounters. But *someone,* some other fellow, whoever he is . . . he hasn't the same faith in you. Thinks you're interfering in something; that might be the way of it. I should watch out if I were you."

Once out in the Lawnmarket in the sunshine of the afternoon, Justin drew a deep breath. He did not think that Blair would pursue this particular matter any further for the time being, but what he himself should now do was far from clear. Should he warn Sugden? It seemed unnecessary, seeing that the shot had been fired almost under the man's window and the whole district must be buzzing like a hive. To see Longford might be a more rewarding experience; so, making up his mind on the spot, he set off along the road he had taken the previous night and knocked at Miss Kelly's door.

No one answered.

He knocked again, glancing around him at the deserted street which seemed little less secretive in the daylight than in the dark. He was about to give up and go away, when the door was opened very slowly and a small figure appeared: a girl of about seven wearing a black knitted smock and a pair of clogs several sizes too large for her.

"Now, who are you?" enquired Justin of this apparition, which stood with several fingers in its mouth regarding him with lively apprehension.

"I'm Ethel," the child replied.

"Well, Ethel, we've not met before, but don't be frightened, I'll not eat you. Would you like a sweet, Ethel?"

She put her hands behind her back.

"Quite right," he said, feeling rebuked and replacing in his pocket the bag of toffee he had bought that morning. "Do you live here, my dear?"

"With me Auntie," she replied.

"Is that Miss Kelly—the one who's to marry Mr Longford? Ah, I see it is. Well, look here, Ethel. You be a good girl and run and tell her that Mr Derry's called, and then come back with her and we'll see about that toffee then."

"Auntie's not in," replied the child, beginning to close the door against him.

"Oh. Is Mr Longford? Jim. Will you give a message?"

There was no answer; only a small crack remained open, through which he could see an eye still watching him and part of one of her enormous clogs. He felt sure that both the people he had called to see were inside but he did not like the idea of going on and frightening the child, who had looked nervous enough in all conscience. The circle of fear, he thought, was perceptibly widening around them. First Sugden had felt it; then poor Amy; now it had spread to this house. Why was it happening? He had set out to help free two men from the burden of a crime, but he had the strangest feeling that in doing it he had stirred up something that had lain in the background even before the burglary at Massingham—something unexplained, of which he was seeing only a part, yet of which the murder of P.C. Luke at Hannington was also part.

For the rest of the day he pondered on the problem in the intervals of coping with Harris in the office and Flo over the tea-cups—a Flo still mercifully ignorant of how near she had come to being bereaved. All her talk was of a bazaar shortly to be held in Smedwick to raise funds for some worthy cause, the details of which escaped him, though his own part in it as escort to his elder sister and Georgina seemed already to have been settled. When he tried to back out he was met with the inflexibility that Flo always showed in the cause of charity: "Of course you must go. Mrs Deverel is a patroness and the Duchess will be there. Really I should have thought you would have heard of it already, dearest, if you didn't bury your head in that office and think of nothing else. Don't you realise there are unfortunates in the world who need your help? Mr Gilmore is speaking."

At that, he pricked up his ears. "Gilmore?"

"Yes, he is coming up from London specially: a Q.C. and a Member too, and busy though he is. I suppose his family connections with Smedwick bring him—and naturally the Cause."

"Naturally," said her brother, thinking hard.

"And if *he* can spare the time to come, how can you excuse yourself?"

"Oh quite, I can't."

"You mean you'll take us?" Flo exclaimed, astonished by the ease of her victory.

"Yes, if you and Georgina wish it."

"Naturally we wish it but I thought . . . I didn't quite expect . . . Really, dearest, you have made me *very* happy. It would have pleased Papa and Mama so much. Dearest, you are *so* good to us."

Justin had the grace to blush, and this sense of shame and the knowledge that he was deceiving natures in every way superior to his own persisted on the day of the bazaar as he handed Flo into the hired carriage and set off up the Warbury Road for his Georgina. It was an atrocious morning with the rain teeming down, so that his fiancée's beautiful blue taffeta dress suffered some damage before he even got her inside on the plush cushions, chill with the damp of a coach house, and at the hall there was a delay while grander carriages were directed to the door ahead of them. By the time they had arrived in the auditorium among the cane chairs Georgina's emotions had reached a very high pitch, and they broke out the second they were separated in the crush from Flo—

"I might have known it. Really you are not to be trusted to arrange anything nowadays. That awful cab! There was damp everywhere. It had run down on the seat, and that is what you must choose for me—*me,* if you please! You have quite ruined my dress."

Always solicitous, he began to search anxiously for the proofs of damage, murmuring condolences which were interrupted by a far fiercer whisper: "Stop it! You are making me ridiculous. Have you no sense at all? Sometimes I think you take pleasure in humiliating me in public, and my family too. You have greatly displeased Papa."

"Displeased him? How?" cried Justin, appalled by this news.

"Something you've done, something interfering and unprofessional; you can hardly expect me to know the details."

Fortunately at this moment Flo joined them and there was a stirring up on the platform, which was suddenly filled with people of importance, ranging from the Duchess to Mr Lumley in the wings, wedged between a piano and an alderman of intimidating size.

Then Gilmore rose. He had the practised air. He congratulated the audience on its good fortune in having achieved a platform so distinguished. He would except himself. (Laughter.) But he would except no one—*no one*—from the charitable duty that had brought them all together that morning. Let them consult their consciences and turn out their pockets. (Laughter.) He himself had done so. (Renewed laughter.) He had found little in them, but in his experience that was habitual. Were wives to blame? (Much laughter.) The money went somewhere. On worthy objects, no doubt. And what worthier object—or Cause, as it would be more happily described—than the one for which they were all gathered together in that place? He would commend it and sit down.

During the applause that followed, Justin sat groaning inwardly and commending all charities and politicians to the Devil. Of the success of the speech, however, there could be no doubt. Collection boxes were being handed out and a subscription list in a book bound in calf and tooled in gold was being flourished under his nose by a rampagious matron in a hat with feathers that soared heavenwards. "You will be generous, dearest?" he heard Flo murmur as he looked round for rescue, seeing far off the figure of Mr Lumley moving down from the platform through the throng, a sliver of white starched linen around his neck, for he had put on his dog collar for the occasion. "Where's Georgina?" he demanded, searching for her too.

"She has her box, dearest. I've mine here."

He pressed a sovereign into the slot. Over her shoulder as she turned away Mr Lumley was seen approaching. "A ghastly scrimmage," muttered Justin, scowling rather horribly around him as his friend came up mopping the sweat which the least exertion brought out on him. "Do you really have to run charities this way?"

"People seem to like it."

"They like their own importance."

"Of course, my dear chap. Don't you? How severe you've become all of a sudden. I hope you've signed the book."

Justin laughed and most of his ill temper vanished. "Where's Gilmore?" he asked.

"Our worthy opener? With Her Grace, presumably." It was by now impossible to see into the centre of the hall, where a solid block of humanity had got itself wedged like bees in a hive. "How they crowd around to be sure; such enviable enthusiasm. She is a very good and patient lady. And our Q.C. spoke well, don't you think?"

"Most professionally. Was he your selection?"

"In a sense," replied the Vicar, smiling. "I suppose I can claim some part of him."

"Then do so. Show him Sugden's statement. I have it here."

The Vicar glanced hastily around, fearing an imprudence, but the tide had receded from them and they were now alone, out of earshot of anyone. "If you think it wise," he answered slowly.

"I do indeed. He's the very man for us. He knows the case and he believed those men were innocent. Besides, I'm sure he resented that verdict, resented it personally. Even after all these years he might give something to overturn it and pay Garrowby out."

"Hardly a very estimable wish," objected the Vicar.

"But human, surely, if he still is human, which remains to be seen. Will you have a shot at him?"

There was a pause and then the Vicar answered: "Perhaps you'd better do it, my dear chap. He might listen to you better. Don't think I'm dodging anything."

"I'll be the one doing the dodging," replied Justin with a conviction that could be felt. "I've Flo here, and Georgina for that matter. Will you keep your eye on them?"

"My dear fellow, a most enviable task, but don't you think . . . I mean, is it quite wise? A weak vessel."

But Justin had already detached himself and was working his way through the crush. Collection boxes were rattled at him, people stopped him to remark on the success of the bazaar or the heat inside the hall which was stupendous, and, as fast as he advanced towards it, the official party kept pace with him in its retreat towards the doors and a mercifully early lunch. Behind him he saw the Vicar hovering solicitously on the outskirts of a mêlée containing Flo and a blue taffeta dress, but he had no time to do more than regret these dependents as he elbowed his way into the street in the wake of the Duchess and Gilmore, Q.C., who was now sporting a top hat of almost supernatural glossiness. He could see it like a beacon above the heads of the crowd that had jostled forward to catch a glimpse of the great lady as she drove off, and tracking purposefully he came up with it just as its owner was about to step into a hansom cab on his way to the station.

"Mr Gilmore."

The man who swung round towards him had a decidedly testy look. No doubt he was in a hurry and anxious to escape, but the bony, patrician face was covered with a network of lines radiating downwards from the eyes and corners of the mouth in a way that suggested that this was now its natural expression.

"Probably you don't remember me," Justin ventured, feeling regretful, for he had liked and admired Gilmore.

"Remember you? Why yes I do. Didn't we meet some years ago? But you'll excuse me. Train to catch," he added, climbing into the cab and raising his hat the bare minimum of inches from his handsome greying hair.

"It was at the Moot Hall," Justin reminded him, getting a good hold of the handle to prevent the cab door from closing. He had never required much converting to a belief in firm measures.

"I remember. Those poachin' fellers."

"It's about them I'm here."

"Interesting. But train won't wait, you know. Most regrettable. Some other time perhaps," Gilmore replied, and knocked with the knob of his cane on the partition in front of him.

"Would you mind if I came along with you?"

"Well really, sir!" the Q.C. exclaimed, lifting his saturnine eyebrows in astonishment, though even he had no conception of the full scandalous nature of that remark.

"Shall I whip 'er up, sir?" came the cabby's voice from above them.

"Just a moment. Better let this gentleman in. He seems to insist on it."

The solicitor in fact, lost to every social decency, was half-way in already, and subsided on to the cracked leather seat as the cab started off with a fearful jolt and began to clatter through the streets. "Very kind of you," he murmured, reaching for Sugden's confession in his breast pocket. 'I might from the look of it be serving a writ on him,' he thought as he got it out. The idea amused him and it was all he could do to prevent himself from slipping the thing into Gilmore's hand in the lubricated manner perfected by generations of writ-servers, who are born, not made.

"Now will you tell me what it's all about?" Gilmore enquired in a suffering voice.

"Gladly. Those poaching fellows, as you said."

"But wasn't Rees their solicitor?"

"Mr Rees is dead."

"Oh. Have you inherited?"

"I've this, if you'll look at it."

Gilmore took the confession from him and Justin waited, glancing out of the window at the rain that was still falling in torrents, sending rivulets down the dirty glass. He heard the crackle of the sheets, the occasional grunt of approval or disapproval—he could not tell which—and then he saw the Q.C. glancing up at him, head slightly on one side, speculatively.

"What is this—a Dying Declaration?"

"The man may have thought he was dying," he replied.

"But you knew better, eh? Was it made voluntarily?"

"I don't say we didn't have to fish for it a bit at first, but yes, it's voluntary."

"We?"

"I was working with the man's vicar—Mr Lumley, you may know him."

"Indeed I know him. Who doesn't? Can you tell me how the statement came to be made?"

"Sugden's bad conscience, I suppose."

"No threats or inducements?"

"You might call them exhortations. There were a few of *those*."

Gilmore allowed a bleak smile to appear on his face as he answered: "Exhortations—yes, that has a definite sound of Mr Lumley. Have you checked the statements made here?"

"Yes, and the result's impressive. The interior of the Rectory is still exactly like he says. You see he even describes Miss Verney's seal—the little gilt eagle with the ruby in its claws—though that was never mentioned in detail at the Moot Hall; it was just called 'a seal'. Significant, I feel."

"Most interesting," Gilmore said, handing back the confession and taking out his watch, which was a very handsome hunter in a gold case worn thin with age. "Most interesting," he repeated, glancing out of the window to see how near to the station they had got.

"I'm glad you think so."

"Oh, I do, most certainly. If I'd had that evidence eight years ago . . ."

"You have it now."

"In a sense that's true."

"Then you'll take up the case?"

"Now, my dear Derry, whatever are you talking about?" Gilmore said, "What case? I know of none. You have shown me a statement, and very interesting it is. It is always interesting to see how people try to incriminate themselves, but as to why they do it . . . ?" He shrugged his elegant shoulders. "How should I know? Perhaps he's mad. People often are: far more than the public realises or the Lunacy Commissioners can take to their bosoms. Perhaps he has a rage to impress himself on the folklore of the district, or just be anxious to please. What he says may even conceivably be true, but suppose it is, what can one make of it after all these years?" He broke off and remarked as he replaced his watch in its chamois-leather pouch: "He's made excellent time, this fellow."

They got down. The train was already standing at the platform, belching its importance in clouds of steam. The stationmaster bustled up in a top hat noticeably less glossy than Gilmore's to conduct the great man to his seat, while Justin followed, suppressing a desire to commit some memorable atrocity. He had not given up, however, and as the Q.C. turned in the doorway of the carriage and held out his hand, he said to him: "It's true, you know. I'll prove it one day. I'll find this other man."

"That might be helpful," Gilmore said.

The engine gave a hoot, and far down the platform the guard was brandishing his flag. Justin came to the window, looking up into the face above him which in these last moments had seemed much more like that of the junior in the stuff gown who had fought Garrowby on that distant afternoon. "You mean you'd take it then?" he said.

"I might. Your lunacy is quite infectious. Faith. Hope. Don't expect Charity from your neighbours, by the way, as I expect Mr Lumley's told you. You're a bold fellow."

The train had begun to move, and though Gilmore was still speaking Justin could hear no more above the hiss of steam and the clanking of couplings. He felt bold no longer. He had just remembered his Georgina marooned with a collecting box in a rapidly emptying hall.

He returned as fast as he could to town—not to his office, for he rather imagined that Georgina might be there, but to St Bede's Vicarage, in the hopes of finding a cleric more or less in one piece. Nor was he disappointed. The Vicar had survived the morning, if hardly in his usual state of health, to report on his stewardship:

"My dear fellow, your dear sister was kindness itself to me, but I fear Miss Deverel was not pleased. It was not easy to explain why you should have dashed off like that without warning, and then of course there was the carriage."

"What about the carriage? I know it leaked."

"My dear fellow, it did not *come*. We were left waiting at the door, and the weather being most inclement, we were marooned there until Mrs Deverel, who must have guessed our plight, came back in *her* carriage to take us off."

"Never!"

"Well, that is what happened," said the Vicar mildly. "I won't pretend that Miss Deverel was as grateful as I was. Apparently she had been asked originally to accompany her mother but had chosen to go with you instead, and I fear she found me inadequate as a substitute for either of you."

"Was anything said?"

"Well, yes," admitted the Vicar truthfully. "Things were said, though I don't think they were intended. In the throes of disappointment I find people often say things they don't really mean, and that would even be true of young ladies. A peace offering, however, might not come amiss."

Justin had already thought of that. 'Flowers. Masses of them,' he said to himself, remembering successes in that line at other fateful moments in his relationship with Georgina. There was a flower shop in the market-place not far from his office, and with a few heartfelt words of thanks to encourage his ally, he hurried off through the rain.

Facing him at the entrance to the market-place was Coates's jeweller's shop.

He walked past it; stopped; walked on a few paces; then gave a sigh as he recognised the need to think extravagantly, and turned back to gaze through the window at the rings in their satin- and plush-lined boxes. Coates's was the most fashionable jeweller's shop in Smedwick. Georgian teapots stood armorially inside the door. Small silver porringers awaited the arrival of godparents bidden to Christenings. There was an array of coffee-spoons, salvers, clocks, necklaces, tiepins, brooches, watches and chains with sinuous, richly glistening links, worth £20, some of them, though surely there was a limit to what bad conscience could do to a man. A locket? That was more his weight. There was one in the glass display-case directly ahead of him as he went in. The ticket said £5. And next to it was a ruby in a gold clasp beneath a tiny gilt bird with outstretched wings.

XIV

"You mean it has been there all this time!" cried the Vicar in amazement.

"Since '93. It was brought in about two years after the crime. Coates had no means of knowing it was stolen. Perhaps he didn't enquire as closely as he ought. It was in the window for some months —yes, actually in the window, where Miss Verney must have passed it dozens of times—but no one bought it, and Coates was thinking of having it reset and wearing it on his chain."

"Astonishing! Quite astonishing! What a strange Providence led you there. And the person who brought it?"

"Coates can't recall who it was. Thinks it may have been a woman. He's trying to remember."

The Vicar was standing by the window turning the seal over and over in his hand. "A pretty thing," he observed over his shoulder. "A very pretty thing. Who is the owner of this very pretty . . . ?"

"We know that, fortunately."

"So we do, my dear fellow. How happy she will be to have it back again."

That was on the Wednesday. Justin had a court for the following morning which would be bound to last for hours, but on the Friday, as soon as he had dealt with his appointments, he hurried to the livery stables and rode over the moor to Massingham.

A glow of satisfaction warmed his heart through the chill of the winter afternoon as he thought first of Sugden and then of this new pointer to his theory. The log jam of doubt was breaking up at last, allowing him to feel the sweep of the current bearing him along towards the truth, and there seemed such a pleasing irony in the thought that the girl who had dashed his hopes over the confession must help him now, that it was with affection that he saw her come into the Rectory drawing-room and held out to her the little trinket he had found.

"Pray where did you get this?" she demanded, holding it uncertainly in her hand.

For some reason he had expected with Mr Lumley that she would be pleased, and the grudging way his prized exhibit was accepted disconcerted him.

"You say it was in Coates's window?"

"Actually in one of the showcases," he replied.

"Then someone has treated it very badly. Do you see the way the wings are bent? And some of the links are missing from the chain. It was kind of you to restore it, however. We are obliged to you. I know my father would wish to join me in that thought."

She had glided towards the bell-pull which hung beside the mantelpiece, with the evident intention of ringing for the parlourmaid to show him out. How to frustrate such a manœuvre? It was in no book of etiquette. No gentleman would even wish to know how to force his attentions on a lady. The lack of practical counsel in such important matters and the thoroughly unfair balance of the sexes, which had never troubled him much before, affected Justin with a sense of grievance and injustice too hard to bear. "Miss Verney . . . ," he burst out.

"Yes?" she enquired, looking at him in surprise.

"I know you must regard this as an importunity."

"Certainly not," she interrupted him severely. "We are under an obligation to you, as I said."

"But coming so soon after our last visit . . . which was so unfortunate and ill-timed. My dear Miss Verney, you can't surely have thought that we relished saying what we did?"

"No gentleman would do that."

"Oh, I agree," he said earnestly. "No man of feeling would deliberately hurt the feelings of another, particularly of someone of your father's age. Mr Lumley was most deeply distressed about it: he can't forgive himself for coming."

"So you ventured all alone this time."

'Bless me if she doesn't think of me as Daniel in the lions' den,' thought Justin, seeing the hint of amusement in her eyes and astonished by it, for a sense of humour was the last thing he had allowed her. When she looked like that she was decidedly attractive. Indeed, if only her hair wasn't dragged down over her ears, and if she would smile oftener and wear more dashing clothes to display her small but most seductive figure, there was no knowing what ideas a man might not get of her. "Quite alone," he said. "On my head be it."

"You are excused, as it happens, seeing you brought the seal."

"*Timeo Danaos*, Miss Verney. Shouldn't you fear the Greeks when they come bearing gifts? After all, we're on opposite sides, however regrettable that may be—and I for one regret it deeply."

"Not more than I."

They were the first encouraging words she had used to him and their effect was all the more intense. The small objectives with which he had come were submerged under a wave of feeling far more emotional and disturbing than he had ever bargained for. "My dear Miss Verney . . ." He had come much closer to her, looking down into eyes that had become clouded and uncertain. "You are generous . . . too generous. I have done nothing to deserve it—only caused you pain by questioning your story. . . ."

"But you *still* question it."

"Dear Miss Verney, don't you question mine? We have this division between us—though it's not of our choosing and you have just shown me by example how little it should count when both of us are really only wanting to get the truth. Couldn't we help one another there?"

"You didn't see those men," she said, "as I did."

"Just as you never heard Sugden or Miss Binns. One of us is wrong —from the best of motives, but wrong. It could be me, and I admit it freely. I only ask you to consider . . ."

"Whether *I* am wrong?"

He shook his head. "To consider the *evidence*, Miss Verney. On the one side yours and your father's . . ."

"And all those others," she broke in.

"Yes. Including Sugden and Miss Binns. And now this seal."

"How does my seal come into it?"

"Because Sugden described it in his statement, though that was never done in court or in the newspapers, as far as I remember. Doesn't that suggest that he was here that night and saw it stolen?"

She thought for a while, smoothing her finger against the eagle's damaged wings, and then replied: "He could have got his facts from someone: oh, from Mrs Milligan or a dozen others—they'd all be in it. They could have described the seal to him."

"Why should they describe it? Why should Sugden listen if they had, much less put it down in a confession?"

"I don't know. He'll have some reason."

Soon afterwards he took his leave, accepting failure. Yet he felt no resentment as he mounted his horse and rode off past Merrick's bothy at the bridge. Respect, compassion, understanding and something warmer—they were very strange feelings to have towards one who for the second time had wrecked his hopes. He had a sudden impulse to turn back; and the thought of what Georgina would have said to this notion and to the excitement passing through his mind was the last thing that weighed with him as he rode off through the deepening twilight. 'I might almost be in love with her,' he thought desperately. 'The whole thing's a lot of witchery. She's probably sailing past me on a broomstick at this moment to make up a coven down at Sugden's and laughing fit to burst.'

In fact, the wind had risen and the night around him was full of sound and movement not altogether reassuring to a townsman's ear. Some beast was roaring in the valley down by the ruined castle and the noise of it pursued him as he galloped along the grass verge of the highway, going rather faster than he need and half expecting some uncouth shape to manifest itself over his shoulder. At the top of the hill he stopped and glanced back. He could see the pinpoints of the Rectory lights in the darkness, but there was no other sign of habitation in that cold, desolate world over which the wind came tearing, rustling the bent-grass of the moor. Some Scots pines appeared ahead in silhouette against the sky. He had admired them under snow from the dogcart when he had last come to Massingham, but by night, with the gale moving in their branches, they took on shapes from which it was pleasanter to avert the mind. Beyond them lay the flat top of the moor, and he crossed it at a smart canter, the wind behind him billowing his cloak around him till he felt that he was on some airborne and forbidden journey.

The pace quickened. He sensed the slope of the ground away from him and knew himself on the Smedwick side of the divide, where a belt of woods closed in towards the road before it began the long descent into the town. Soon he would see its lights below him. About a quarter of a mile ahead a bridle track came in from the left, and he reined in his horse, remembering that the road was bad hereabouts, with potholes on which he had remarked from the dog-cart when he had last passed that way. Leaning forward in his saddle, patting the mare's neck companionably, he rode on. He was accustomed to the darkness now. He saw the white blur of the signpost at the entrance to the bridle track, and beside it a shorter, bulkier shape—a shape that moved towards him across his path.

XV

It was too late to turn. He had no more than a sudden awareness of danger very close. And in the same instant a voice spoke urgently out of the darkness:

"Mr Derry? Is that you, sir?"

He felt a wild desire to laugh, curse, drive his horse forward at the shadow confronting him as it took shape and he recognised the solid figure of P.C. Pugh, which he had first seen at the Moot Hall and, more recently, following in Blair's steps like King Wenceslaus's page with a brace of stinking pheasants.

"Mr Derry, sir," the voice repeated. It was no illusion. The man was indisputably there. He could see the Minerva shape of the helmet and the truncheon hanging from the fellow's belt. "What the deuce! Scaring the wits out of me!" he grumbled, approaching the apparition which grew more solid with every moment.

"Beg pardon, sir."

"And well you might! What the devil d'you mean by it? Did Blair send you after me?"

"The Super? No, sir."

"Then *why*? And how did you know I'd come this way?"

"Just guessed it, sir. I knew you was at Verneys', sir."

Justin came closer to him, leaning forward in the saddle. The possibility that there might be others waiting for him in the darkness of the bridle path had not escaped him, but he had become excited by the man's voice and manner which suggested something that had been dimly in his mind for days. "So you've been watching me," he said. "Was it you who left a note for me at my house one night by any chance?"

"That's right, sir."

"Telling me to meet you by the Griffin Bridge?"

"Right again, sir. But P.C. Moffat come up on the beat—wantin' company, he said—and I durstn't shake him off."

"Now see here," said Justin, "let's get this straight. You want to see me for some reason—very well—though I must say you choose some quaint spots to do it: on that bridge and this blasted heath. What are you up to?"

"Been wantin' to tell you somethin', sir."

"Go on."

"About the burglary at Massingham. Remember Piggott?"

"The old man Kelly and his sister lived with?" Justin said, containing his excitement. He remembered Piggott well.

"Right, sir. He's in the workhouse now."

"It's coming back. Didn't the Police find a chisel in the Rectory after the crime? Didn't they call on Piggott to show it him, and he identified it as one he'd owned?"

"No, sir."

"Surely that was the way it went in evidence," said Justin in his official voice. "It was in Piggott's deposition!"

"It was in his deposition right enough. But what *happened* was this. Some days after the crime the Super sent for us—for me and Inspector Mathieson. He shows us that chisel from the Rectory. And he tells us to go down to Piggott's house and plant it on him."

"Plant it?"

"That's right, sir—only of course he put it different. Workin' a ruse, he called it. So Inspector Mathieson and me goes down there. Piggott, he'd been a receiver, sir—done a bit of it in his time, but he was gettin' old and almost blind by then. 'Let's see your tools, Piggott,' the Inspector says, Piggott bein' a carpenter by trade. So we turns out the cupboards, and Mathieson slips in the chisel with the rest, then hauls it out and says to him: 'Piggott, is this yer chisel? There's been a burglary done at Stope and a man claims he lost a chisel the spittin' image o' this. Is this yer chisel, Piggott? If it is, it can't be stole from Stope, now can it?' And Piggott, bein' nervous of us like, thinkin' otherwise we'd fix a burglary on him, identifies the chisel right away. 'It's mine,' he says. 'Been mine for years that chisel has.'"

There was a long silence, and then Justin murmured almost to himself: "And you lent yourself to *that!*"

"It's been on me conscience, sir," Pugh said. "I've been wantin' to tell someone. And then you come along, sir, makin' enquiries about Massingham, so I heard. 'There's me man,' thinks I. 'There's the man I can go to if I can get him alone like when no one's watchin'.' It wouldn't do if they *was*, sir."

He was glancing around uneasily in the darkness, and the mare, as though aware of this, began a series of small restless movements, raising and lowering her head.

"What do you mean? Wouldn't do if *who* was here? Blair?"

"Best be off, sir," the constable said. "It's a bit outby, like, but you get folk around sometimes."

"Will you make a statement? Here, come back!"

But he got no answer. Pugh had turned away into the gloom, and a few seconds later the clatter of hooves sounded along the bridle path that led downhill in an arc towards the town by Benton Moor.

XVI

NEXT morning the inquest on Amy Dodds opened in the Lawnmarket. It was surprising what little furore the death had caused, even among the Bewley and Pelegate folk. Apart from officials and a handful of spectators, among whom he recognised Miss Kelly, Inspector Mathieson and Mr Hicks from the *Mercury*, the court was empty when Justin went in soon after ten o'clock, to see the jury of seven reluctant citizens herded into their places, coughing and spluttering in the fog-laden air that had crept in from the streets. Only Mr Hicks seemed to have much stomach for the occasion. "You interested in this case too, sir?" he enquired, twisting round to greet the new arrival. "Pretty universal taste for crime you seem to have. Will the Reverend Gentleman be coming?"

The first evidence went to identification and was given by a neighbour of the deceased called Adams, who had last seen her alive on the late afternoon of 18th February, five days after Justin's visit to Clay Yard. It had been bitter weather, and as she had set out towards town she had been 'arl muffled up', with 'a bit scarf like' round her head and wearing clogs.

From that moment she had disappeared from view, though one of the girls in Preston's bakery in Hewitt Street believed she had caught a distant glimpse of her at dusk, headed towards the Bewshaugh meadows and the river. Next morning a forester employed by Sir Miles Curvis of High Crags had been cutting timber near the Red Mill pool when his attention had been drawn to something in the river below the weir—he had thought it was a small tree-trunk with some pink material attached, till he had come down on to the path and seen the half-submerged body entangled in driftwood and rushes about six yards from the bank.

There the Police had seen it later that morning. Afterwards they had searched the bank for footprints or any signs of a struggle, but the frost was iron hard and they had found nothing. Nor had Dr Higson discovered any bruising on the corpse beyond what might be expected from a sudden fall. "I think she went into the water some time between four and nine o'clock," he told the court. "From the general condition, and in particular from the mud under the finger nails, I incline to the view that she made a determined effort to reach the bank. That of course is consistent with her having fallen in by accident. But it is also consistent with the act of suicide. That is a crime people sometimes have second thoughts about," he added grimly.

Last into the box came a retired pitman by the name of Snell, who at dusk on the day of Amy's disappearance had been exercising his whippets in the fields at Bewshaugh. He had just turned for home, he said, and had whistled up his dogs, when he had heard voices in the woods near the Red Mill pool. There was a man's voice and a woman's and they had seemed to be arguing. No, he had not recognised them or caught any definite words—they had been too far away from him: perhaps two hundred yards. Nor had he seen anyone in the gathering darkness. But he felt sure they had been angry voices: 'the lass's much the louder'. His dogs had heard them too and had run towards the sound till he had called them back. They were obedient dogs.

"No doubt," the Coroner remarked tersely at this point. "The fact is, isn't it, that you were coursing them?"

"On Bewshaugh, sir!" It appeared from Mr Snell's virtuous disclaimers that there were no hares left in that somewhat over-hunted meadow at Pelegate's back door.

"At all events," the Coroner persisted, "the attention you paid these voices that you say you heard was cursory. You didn't investigate them or report them?"

Mr Snell had 'nivver thowt on it'.

"Quite. The impression that they made on you was simply of a quarrel, not the first you have heard perhaps. You had no cause to apprehend that any criminal or homicidal act was likely."

"They was just arguin'."

"So you called your dogs off and went home?"

"That's right, sir. To me tea."

When the Coroner came to address the jury he dealt caustically with this evidence. "How much it may be expected to help you is most debatable," he remarked with a sour glance at Mr Snell. "Whether the man was coursing game or not—and you may have formed your own opinions as to *that*—what is certain is that he paid only the vaguest attention to anything else that afternoon. That two people were talking in the wood we may accept, but beyond that all is surmise. Gentlemen, I must tell you that there is not a scintilla of evidence to show that it was the deceased's voice in the woods. Of course it may have been. That the body was found next day near the spot is suggestive, but no more than that. Still more definitely must I direct you that the fact that an unknown man's voice was heard in argument with an unknown woman is no indication whatsoever that anyone murdered Amy Dodds, whom no one, so far as we have heard, had cause to fear or threaten. You might just as well accept the obedient activities of those dogs of Mr Snell's as being probative and helpful; and indeed one can be a great deal more certain of what *they* and their master were about that evening.

"Now, gentlemen, free of these beguiling but quite misleading thoughts . . ."

Of course, the Coroner was perfectly right, and by the standards of proof demanded by the law there could be no question of the jury finding anything but Misadventure or, perhaps more appropriately, an Open Verdict. But as he went back to his office, leaving them still deliberating, Justin was remembering Mr Snell and the raised voices in the twilight by the weir. He felt quite sure that one of those voices had been Amy's. What had taken her through the

Red Mill woods? The riverside path, which had been used as a right-of-way by Smedwick folk for generations, was a notorious place for lovers, and though Amy had not put on her best clothes, and the weather had been arctic, the possibility of some rendezvous must be the most likely explanation of what had drawn her there.

But the Red Mill path was also a convenient short-cut between Pelegate and the streets on the Warbury side of the town—including for that matter Laburnum Road. 'If she had been coming to "The Laurels" to see *me*,' he thought, 'she might well have come that way' —and checked suddenly as an idea obtruded itself into his mind: certainly the most unpleasant he had had to live with since the beginning of the Massingham affair. Amy's words to him in Clay Yard, the furtive sounds behind the walls and the hurrying figure in the lamplight all seemed to merge with the voices in the wood to form a pattern, part of a wider pattern which he began to glimpse. It might not be true to say, as the Coroner had said, that no one had had cause to fear or threaten the dead girl. It might be the very reverse of the truth. Her evidence about Piggott's coat could have become a very pressing danger to some people. Her willingness to talk, and perhaps to say far more than she had done already, need only have been overheard that night by someone who felt threatened by it, for a powerful motive of fear to have arisen. And who better than the Police to have had such a motive? Far more directly than the guilty men who had broken in at Massingham, Blair and his subordinates had been threatened by Amy's words with an exposure which if proved would ruin all of them. Now it could be proved no longer— unless Miss Kelly had also known about the switch of the coats, or Piggott himself could be winkled out of his shell in the municipal workhouse.

See Miss K—Piggott—statutory declaration in both cases, he scribbled on his memo pad, having dodged guiltily into his office through the private door in the irrational hope that Harris would imagine he had been there for some time. He had no sooner opened the nearest file in sight, however, than there came the faint rap at the door and his clerk entered with the expression which only Flo had developed to a more poignant pitch of suffering.

"Colonel Deverel is in my office, sir."

He shot up from the desk, appreciating from the tone in which these words had been uttered that Harris was not reproaching him, and that in itself was alarming.

"Has he been here long? Why didn't you show him in? Did you tell him where I was?"

"Viewing the *locus in quo,* sir—of a conveyance, sir."

Justin began to breathe more easily. "Miss Georgina isn't with him?"

"No, sir."

"It'll be about a codicil, perhaps. I thought last time he had a mind to add one."

One glance at his client, however, and this particular illusion took flight and was seen no more. A formidably belted and tweeded knickerbocker suit intruded itself into his view—the most rural thing in Smedwick according to the Duke, who was privileged to joke about such things. Justin felt no desire to emulate him, however. There were positions from which everything could appear absurd, and positions from which absurd things had frightening aspects, and he was now occupying just such a viewpoint, in the presence of an irascible magistrate who was also likely to be his father-in-law.

"What the devil do you mean by it?" the Colonel exploded the instant they were alone.

The field of guilt, when one looked at it, was wide. Could it be anything apropos of Sugden? Or of Miss Verney? Abandonment of Georgina? The affair of the carriage? Association with Mr Lumley and the radical interest? None of these things seemed capable in themselves of causing such a turkey-cock hue in the Colonel's cheeks or such a splutter in his voice, only apparent in the presence of the most heinous and depraved criminals.

"Suborning a police officer," the Colonel shouted with the virulence of a man who has kept something pent-up far too long.

The victim could hardly have been more astonished: it was the one crime of which he knew himself to be innocent. "Suborning? Excuse *me,* sir," he was beginning in an aggrieved voice when the Colonel swept ahead of him:

"I will *not* excuse you. You are the very last person one can excuse. A man of the law with professional knowledge! What can have made you do it?"

"Do what, sir?"

"Suborn Pugh. Are you telling me you didn't? Do you deny you saw the man?"

"We met: that's true."

"So you admit it?"

"Of course I admit it."

"And you pressed him to say—for what reason I can't imagine—that he took part in a conspiracy with other officers to pervert the course of Justice in the case of those poachin' fellers at Massingham who shot at Verney."

"Poor Pugh."

"What's that?" demanded the Colonel, whose hearing had begun to fail a little.

"I was thinking aloud, sir. May I see Pugh?"

"Naturally you cannot see him. A most improper suggestion."

"But if I'm accused . . ."

"You are *not* accused. No action will be taken. Do you want this bruited abroad? Superintendent Blair, though as mystified as I am about the whole business, agrees with me that this is not a matter that should be aired publicly and that the best course will be to transfer Pugh to another place, as has been done already, and forget the whole distressing incident. He has seen the Chief Constable about it."

"A very tidy and agreeable solution, I must say. Very typical of Blair."

"What *I* do not find agreeable," the Colonel said, "is your attitude to this affair, which has come as a most profound shock to me. You will of course apologise."

"I do to you, sir. I am most deeply sorry to have distressed you."

"You will apologise to the Superintendent, which will be more to the point."

"I'm afraid I can't do that."

Colonel Deverel listened in silence to what followed. This was because after the first few words his emotions began to choke him, and by the time they had got to Blair's part in the affair of Piggott's chisel he had become so painfully apoplectic that Justin began to fear for him. 'Just like that old cock,' he thought, remembering a salmon he had landed the previous summer. A too squeamish fisherman, he had felt sorry for the salmon then and he felt sorry for the Colonel now and would have liked to return him to his own element. The gaff was in, however, and the victim lashing out in convulsive movement:

"I'll not believe a word of it. A Police conspiracy indeed! Those men were guilty, and who should know it better than me? I committed them."

"On the evidence before you, sir."

"Conclusive evidence. Do you imagine I've forgotten it? Conclusive of guilt. The footprints: they were enough in themselves. The paper in Kelly's pocket. There was a trouser button too. Then the Verneys' evidence. Are you suggesting *they* conspired?"

"I think they were mistaken."

"My boy, it is *you* who have been mistaken; you have been misled," the Colonel said with deep earnestness, moved by the pit he saw opening before a young man whom he liked. "You have listened to gossip and been deceived by a worthless scoundrel, for that is what Sugden is. That you meant well I have no doubt, but you have been used by unscrupulous people whose only aim is to cause trouble and embarrass the Police. There is no great harm done, however, apart from your approach to Pugh, and I put that down to a misguided enthusiasm which in the circumstances Blair must overlook. I ask for one thing only: your promise that you will forget this . . . this folly. Will you do that?"

"I can't. I'm sorry."

"I too am sorry," the Colonel said. "You are a young man and impulsive, and there is time to recognise it and mend your ways. But not much time. Do you understand me?"

"I think I do, sir."

"I think you do too, but let me make it quite plain. If you persist in a course which I regard as mischievous, then you do it with your eyes open. I can't help you any longer. Nor will you be allowed to see my daughter. The engagement will be at an end."

XVII

'DAMNED if I'll let him dictate to us!' thought Justin. It was a long time since he had felt so warmly and companionably of Georgina. The memories of the old rapturous days of country walks and balls at the Assembly Rooms had seemed very distant lately, and though he had not supposed that this was anything more than happened to other couples caught in a long engagement once the delirium of first love was over, he had been aware of a feeling of void and a vague longing and regret which had disturbed him greatly. Now it had gone. 'I'll see her,' he thought. 'They'll never stop me. But I must make it easy for her and not embarrass her. I must catch her alone.'

For the next two days, in every moment he could spare from his office, he haunted the Warbury Road. Showers of sleet raged across the plain from hills whose crests were white in fugitive gleams of sunshine, and the roads were ankle deep in slush which the traffic churned up into a mess of the consistency of glue. He remained buoyed up with a feeling of excitement. He had written her and hoped for some sign. It would surely be possible for even the most obedient daughter to go out unchaperoned in the pony chaise, say to Cousin Emily's, which more than once had been used as a *pied à terre* from which visits could be launched on his office. But nothing happened. He might have been a tramp out there in the bitter weather watching the social round go by—the phaetons in the drive, the lighted windows in the dusk.

On the third afternoon he returned home much earlier than usual, and as he came up the path between the laurels he had a vision which he had not had for years, of a small boy hurrying home from school with a satchel on his back, and Flo's pigtails as she stood under the mistletoe.

"Is that you, dearest?" he heard her call out.

In the drawing-room she had rung for tea. "You look quite exhausted, dearest," she remarked compassionately. "I know one must say nothing against Mr Harris, who is above criticism and can do no wrong, but in my opinion he is much to blame. You have a bad colour."

"Are you blaming the poor chap for that?"

"Someone is to blame. You're surely not still worrying about that man—what was his name? Sugden?—and that attempt on poor dear Mr Verney?"

"I've not seen Sugden for ages."

"You quite relieve me. Really I was distressed to think of you in such a company of desperadoes. How Mr Harris permitted it . . ."

"Harris is my clerk."

"True, but he has great influence on you, as anyone can see, and if he had wished to stop it . . ." She broke off and added breathlessly: "It's not some trouble with Georgina?"

Once Flo had got on to a problem there was really no point in trying to dislodge her, and resignedly he waited for the lamentations to begin—'Your poor father! . . . And such a perfect match! . . . so well bred . . . so ladylike . . . a dear good girl.' To his astonishment she said nothing, but continued to stare at him, her eyes very round and bright with an anxiety which he found unnerving. "Now you're not to worry," he tried to reassure her. "Her father and I . . . have had a disagreement, that's all."

"My dear!"

"Nothing that can't be mended. However, it makes it a bit awkward for me to call on her just now."

"Can I help? Suppose I ask her here, dearest?"

He could have embraced her. "The very thing," he agreed happily. "It seems a bit steep on you, that's all, dragging you in. You see they may have told her things at home . . . about this Massingham business—that I'm stubborn and interfering . . . and a Radical and so on."

Flo let out the beginning of a wail at this last horrific notion, but stifled it and responded loyally, even passionately: "I'm sure you're *not*."

"Well it doesn't matter if it's only what they think. But we must find out what Georgina thinks. I'm hoping that she'll see my side of it."

"I know she will."

"And if she sees it . . . well, they'll listen to *her*, Flo."

"Of course."

"Just as they did over that business of the engagement. Remember how to begin with they wouldn't hear of it? Yes, if you could only in some way manage to get her to come here. . . ."

The very next afternoon at three she was in the drawing-room at 'The Laurels', splendid in royal blue serge trimmed with fur, with fur hat and muff, the most elegant and eligible young woman in Smedwick. He only wished he could have been at ease with her. All the way from the office, out of which he had been prised by an urgent note from home, he had been reminding himself of his past neglect and wondering about the future, yet somehow neither bad conscience nor the problem of Colonel Deverel seemed quite at the root of the anxiety with which he watched her seat herself in one of the tall rosewood chairs and saw Flo slip tactfully out 'to make tea'.

"It's your father," he plunged in directly they were alone. "Of course, you've heard what happened. I tried for two whole days to see you. I didn't like to call, couldn't make any kind of contact until I hit on the idea of Flo—or rather Flo hit on it herself. Thank goodness you've come. I was so afraid you wouldn't. I thought you'd still be furious with me over that bazaar affair."

"Oh, but I am. Quite furious."

He came up close to her and took her hand. "Dearest Georgina, you are so good to me and I haven't deserved it one bit. I've been so shamefully offhand."

"I know," she said, withdrawing it.

"And inattentive."

"So you have. And quite cruel and vexing to poor Papa. Aren't you ashamed of that?"

But he could see that far from being really angry with him and taking her own line in the old peremptory way, she was playing a game, uncertain how to treat him. He found it encouraging. "I'm ashamed of hurting *you*," he corrected her, getting possession of her hand again without much difficulty.

"And not Papa?"

"That's different."

"Why? Why did you have to quarrel with him? Surely you could have put things tactfully?"

"I tried."

"Or not have bothered him at all with it. You can't imagine the trouble you made for me. He even talked of ending our engagement. It's all nonsense, of course, and already he's beginning to come round. But you must give up these adventures of yours around the town."

There was a pause and then he repeated, "Adventures?" not really understanding.

"Isn't that the word? I'm sorry. This Massingham business. Anyway you must give it up."

He said slowly: "I'm afraid I can't do that."

"Why ever not?"

"I just can't, dearest, that's all."

He was looking at her unhappily, wondering how he could explain without using words like 'principle' and 'duty' which were smug and which she might be in no mood to understand. He had not, he reflected sadly, had much experience in refusing her things.

"But it's perverse," she berated him. "You must have *some* reason for preferring strangers, *criminals* to us. Papa says that these men you're worrying about aren't even clients."

"That's quite true."

"And that you're just stirring up the mud for notoriety's sake and to make trouble for everyone. I don't believe that." Her hand was still in his and he felt its warm pressure against his own. "I said I knew you better. That however mistaken you might be you'd never act spitefully or out of mischief or do anything to hurt me."

"You know I wouldn't."

"Then why so perverse? You must see what you're doing by being so stubborn—that Papa will never consent to our marriage as things are. He's quite determined."

"But if I'm determined, that's wrong? Haven't I a right to an opinion?"

"Not to a foolish opinion," she burst out impatiently. "You are making yourself ridiculous with these enquiries in every hole and corner."

"I can't help that."

"But you are making *us* ridiculous too, and I won't have it, it's not to be borne. Papa is right: if this goes on we shall become a laughing stock in Smedwick, and you surely can't want that?"

"Of course not. And it won't happen if you'll only believe in me."

"I used to believe in you," she said, and suddenly she was leaning forward, almost in his arms, and he could see the charming curve of her neck and the lips very slightly parted as he remembered from earlier and gentler days. "I believed you loved me. I never thought that you'd refuse me anything that I really wished for. How can you be so cruel to me?"

He gazed at her, unable to put into words what it was he held by and must continue to hold if there was to be any respect and love between them.

"Because, Justin, it's a straight choice, you see. Either you love me . . ." Her lips brushed against his cheek and he could feel the warmth of her body close against him. "We could be married. We could be married quite soon and I'll never ask another thing of you, *never*, you shall have it your own way always. Shall it be that?"

He didn't answer, and suddenly she had started back, thrusting him away, her voice rising in a wail of incredulity like a child deprived of some greatly prized possession. "Why, I believe you've chosen! You'll let me go!"

As he trudged forlornly back to his office in the twilight under a sky heavy and ominous with snow he was still trying to take in what had happened. The break had come so bewilderingly at the very time when he had imagined that her natural impatience with him was giving way to kinder thoughts, but if he understood it at all he blamed himself for having failed her. He saw that he had expected too much and given too little. And he had explained nothing. His own deeply felt conviction that no one should accept dictation from another on a matter of principle had never been put to her at all, and it was with shame that he remembered how he had simply assumed she would be indifferent to such arguments and indeed to the idea that there was anything more at stake than the chance that people might find them ridiculous and laugh at them.

The impulse was strong to turn back, to find her again and say all the things he should have said—to say also that he loved her, which was the greatest omission of all. The stubbornness that had been one of the factors in driving them apart was acting now on the other side, to make him hold to the agreeably ordered world he had made for himself, in which Georgina had been the 'bright particular star'. He did not come of a race that relinquished things easily.

But he did not turn back, and with every second the possibility of doing so receded. At first his reasoning was very practical. Enough had been said for one day. He must give her time for second thoughts. Only gradually, as he climbed the office stairs and sat himself down in the familiar chair, did the knowledge come to him that there was no point in going back because the positions they had taken up were utterly irreconcilable. And he was glad. He could hardly credit that this ending of all he had hoped for with Georgina should bring him nothing but relief, but that was what he began to feel with increasing certainty as the first flurries of snow beat against the panes. No feelings of guilt were proof against it. He went to the window and looked out across the market-place to the lights in the shops and offices across the way, small beacons in the dusk through which the snowflakes were whirling, and he felt an extraordinary sense of release, as though some intolerable weight had been lifted from his shoulders and he was a free man again.

It was about five when he heard voices in the outer office. He rose from his desk and went towards the door, only a step or two at first, for to go nearer was to eavesdrop on his clerk, a crime only committed by very young solicitors in great despair of clients. Mr Rees's training had been explicit on this point, but as a fiercer flurry of sleet lashed up against the panes he forgot it. "I'll not can see 'im then?" a voice demanded. He had not heard it above twice before, but he recognised it; had perhaps recognised it some moments back when he had first realised he had a client. Longford. There was no mistaking the vernacular, far broader than Sugden's quick and canny speech. And Miss Kelly presumably. The inseparables.

But when he opened the door he found only Longford, loutish in velveteens, standing by the clerk's desk like a big lad hauled up to the master for a thrashing. Not that it wouldn't be deserved, he thought, remembering the explosion of light and thunder in the darkness of the street, but he had too much curiosity to send him packing, no matter what Harris might think. "Come in if you wish," he said, leading the way into his room.

Seen at close quarters there was something different about the man: a kind of suppressed excitement that had not been there on those other occasions when Miss Kelly had been spokesman. It was like watching a wax model that had suddenly acquired a life of its own together with certain intentions and desires, though exactly what they might prove to be was not clear, and perhaps it was just as well.

He glanced quickly about him. Close to his right hand lay a bronze paperweight which he found himself regarding in an altogether new light, and in the hearth was a poker, but that was some distance off and only to be reached by turning his back on his client. Though by no means of a nervous nature, he could not fail to see that Mr Harris's advice to stick to the 'better-class work' had a great deal to recommend it, but it was rather late to think of that with the man only a couple of yards off, one hand reaching into the flap pocket of his coat with a gesture like that of a conjurer about to produce some surprising object.

In fact it was an envelope.

Justin gazed at it, feeling more foolish than he had ever felt in his life before. He realised that only a blessed inability to act had prevented him from shouting for his clerk or bombarding a client with a paperweight. Visions of headlines in the *Mercury* flashed before his eyes, each more horrific than the last. What an ass he had been. There on the desk in front of him lay the envelope, fat, dog-eared and dirty with thumbmarks like so many other papers brought to him by clients of this kind; and there was Longford watching him with a puzzled expression, as well he might.

"My good man, what's this?" he managed to stammer out. "I mean, why bring it me?"

Once he had spoken he felt better. After all, he had not actually done anything scandalous, only imagined it, and the habits of professional life were quick to reassert themselves and very comforting. What did the fellow want? That he should keep the envelope, apparently, and put it in a safe place, which seemed reasonable. But on the heels of this there followed a suggestion that Longford should return to the office that night to tell him something . . . something of mysterious importance.

"Is it about Massingham?" he asked, all his doubts returning with a rush.

A nod of the head.

"What could you have to tell me that you can't tell me now?"

No answer.

"I shall certainly not be here. The office will be shut."

Silence again.

"Do you understand? I shan't be here. Devil take it, man, haven't you a tongue in your head? And come to think of it, what would I be doing trusting you after the way you took a pot shot at me the other night?"

"That I nivver," he heard Longford say.

"Of course it was you. Someone saw you go haring off just after the shot was fired. You must be quite handy with a gun. Weren't you at Hannington the night poor Luke was killed?"

This time there was no doubt that the blow had gone home. 'He was there!' he thought with a thrill of triumph and expectancy, recognising at last the kind of man he had to deal with—either the murderer of Luke or one of those who had stood by and seen the deed done. It was strange how the crime at Hannington kept cropping up as though related to his problem in some way.

"Where's Miss Kelly?" he demanded suddenly, as he put the envelope in the safe.

"Be 'ere t'night, sir. She said nine, sir, if that suits. Might be bringin' someone else, sir."

"You're wasting your time. I don't make appointments out of hours." He had not the slightest intention of walking into a trap at the call of such devious customers.

He let eight o'clock go by that night. But by half-past, in the silence of the drawing-room broken only by the rhythmic click of Flo's needles, he had become anxious about the safety of his files. The office faced the market-place where people might always be passing, but there was a back way up an alley rejoicing in the name of Slipper's Lane, from which it would not be difficult for an enterprising man to break in. Admittedly it was hard to see why Longford should have advertised such an intention, if indeed he had one, but the idea of that night rendezvous was so challenging that he knew he would never rest till he had found out what lay behind it.

"Where are you going, dearest?" he heard Flo call as he was putting on his overcoat in the passage.

"Just off to see Lumley," he shouted back.

"At this hour? How thoughtless men are. Have you got your goloshes on?"

But he heard no more, for he had closed the door behind him and was out in the snow whose glistening whiteness he could see by the gaslight at the corner of the street. He felt his spirits rising. The fall was over; there was a bite in the air and the flakes were crisp under his feet, reminders of the magic world of childhood that had been often in his thoughts these last days. Ahead of him a light went out, then another, as the lamplighter came down towards him with his long pole in his hand, and in the market-place all was dark under a sky in which a few stars appeared beyond the wastes of cloud.

He drew into the doorway of the chemist's shop that faced his office across the square, and from this vantage point he could just make out the line of buildings on the other side, with one light high up in the attic of the newsagent's shop at Number 24. The silence was uncanny, as though the town were muffled in crêpe, and he nearly jumped out of his skin when a whirring sound came out of the air and a clock began to strike nine.

As the last reverberations died away he slipped from his hiding-place and hurried across the square. He saw no one, heard nothing but the crunch of his footsteps in the snow. In his own doorway he turned and took out his key. The chemist's shop seemed closer than he had expected, as if it had followed him a few paces on the way, and looking up he saw the moon almost free of the cloudbank with a retinue of stars glowing frostily in a pool of ice-blue sky.

Inside, all was as black as pitch, and he felt in his pocket for a match. The stairs seemed strangely unfamiliar in the flickering light; and his room, which he was used to seeing in a mellow glow, was filled with shadows that flitted along the walls like fugitives. He was about to light the gas when the thought struck him that he could play the watchdog—if watchdog were needed—better from the clerk's office beyond the green baize door, where it was warmer too, and the embers of a fire still glowed.

Time passed as he sat half dozing in Harris's chair. Ten o'clock struck from across the square. It was getting colder, and with the chill came a growing sense of the absurdity of his vigil. He would give it another half-hour at the outside. He had just decided this and had risen, matches in hand, to light the gas, when there came out of the darkness below a small sharp sound.

He stood quite still, listening. An occasional mouse had been known to disturb the office calm; indeed one morning he had come upon an invader actually browsing off the papers on his desk; but Harris, in a campaign of traps and poison, had won a fairly well accredited victory over the tribe. Besides, it was too loud a noise; unless one postulated rats.

Just then he heard it again, and this time identified it for what it was. Someone was coming up the stairs, moving with infinite caution. Now it was almost abreast of him in the passage, close against the private door that led from the landing directly into his office. He heard that door open and close; and he stood there, uncertain what to do, while around him he could sense the stillness and loneliness of the night under its blanket of snow.

From his office a small flurry of activity broke out: faint and exploratory at first, like the tapping of fingers against some hard surface, and then much louder. As he crossed on tiptoe to the green baize door he began to identify each sound: the tap of an instrument against metal, the grating of a key in a lock—till at last, with a very queer sensation, he heard the door of his office safe grind open and the rustle of parchment under someone's hand.

Then there was only silence. It was the eeriest thing that had happened to him that night: the sudden stillness and feeling of void that seemed to spread until he might almost have doubted there really was a man crouching there by the open safe, not a dozen yards from him, but for the acrid, tell-tale smell of a blown-out candle from the room beyond.

'I'll count up to twenty,' he told himself, striking a balance between elation and downright funk. But he had got no further than eleven when there came a scurrying sound from inside the room and he was through the door, colliding with a body that seemed to fall towards him as a badly loaded sack might do, except that he could feel the embrace of arms twisting themselves around him.

He went down, submerged under that weight like a drowning man. There was a humming sound in his ears and he thought he saw a light start up on the threshold by the private door, outlining the shape of a head pressed close to his own; then the picture was reversed and there was someone under him, thrashing this way and that with legs and arms. The scene steadied and he saw everything clearly: the open safe, the papers strewn over the floor, the guttering candle in Longford's hand. Beneath him, blood gushing from a cut above the eye, lay his ex-witness, the gamekeeper Henderson, and on the boards beside him a lady's gold watch with deep incisions where something, probably initials, had been erased.

XVIII

"My dear fellow," the Vicar said, "my *dear*, dear fellow, let me try and understand what it is you are telling me. Forgive me, are you quite well?"

"Perfectly."

"But you are saying that it was this man Henderson who was Sugden's companion in the burglary at Verney's."

"Exactly. His accomplice. And our Other Man."

"You seem very sure of it. You're not jumping to conclusions out of a natural sense of outrage at having found the fellow trying to burgle you?"

"I'm not jumping at anything. Henderson has made me a very full confession admitting that he was at Massingham that night; that it was he who scuffled with Verney and carried off the seal and this watch, which he was in the act of taking from my safe. Longford had put it there."

The Vicar had been awoken from his slumbers in the small hours and his understanding was so ill attuned to news of this kind that he put his head in his hands and groaned quite loudly.

"Why, whatever's the matter?" said Justin, somewhat light-headed himself from his exertions. "Haven't I been making myself clear?"

"My dear fellow, I won't deceive you, you have not. Say it all over very slowly. There was a watch . . ."

"Certainly—which Henderson took from Verney's that night and never disposed of. Longford and Miss Kelly found out about it, so they managed to steal it from Henderson's house, put it in an envelope and lodged it with me in my safe, allowing Henderson to know what they had done."

"You mean they had laid a trap for him?" the Vicar cried, clutching with a good deal of desperation at this idea.

"Exactly."

"Hoping that Henderson would dash straight off to get the watch as soon as everything was quiet and that you'd be there to catch him? Yes, I know you told me that's how it happened, and in my opinion it was *most* providential. Now let me get it clear in my mind why Henderson should have thought it necessary to recover the watch at such risk to himself."

"Because it was valuable, to begin with. Besides, he may have feared it would be dangerous evidence against him in our hands."

"But how was Longford to know that you'd arrive to catch the burglar so conveniently in the act? And why should Henderson have obliged you with a confession?"

"I don't see how it matters, seeing that he *has* confessed and I have the result in my pocket. I suppose he felt trapped. He may have thought we had more against him than we had. Or perhaps his conscience over shooting at me the other night had something to do with it."

"Shooting at you!" cried the Vicar, discovering with horror a new obscurity in the story.

"Didn't I tell you? I thought it best at the time to keep it dark, but someone took a pot shot at me near George's house about a fortnight back. I thought Longford had done it, since he was thereabouts at the time. But it was Henderson; he makes no bones about it; says he just fired 'a bit close like' to frighten me off Wee Geordie and the case in general. Seems to have frightened Longford the worse of the pair of us as it turned out. Poor chap. Suppose *he'd* been hit by accident?"

"At least the outrage would have been reported to the Police," returned the Vicar with some asperity. "You are becoming altogether careless of your own safety and of ordinary rules and regulations, or so it seems to me. This burglary of your office, now—have you reported *that?*"

"Well, no, as it happens."

"You haven't had Henderson arrested or charged?"

"For burgling me! Good heavens no."

At these shameless words the Vicar's severity, which never set very hard, melted completely and he began to shake all over with one of his most awesome effects of laughter. "For a legal man you have the most w . . . wonderfully anarchic notions," he managed to blurt out. "Aren't you compounding a felony by failing to report this crime?"

"I may be misprising one, if you want to be technical about it."

"Then suppose it was a trap laid to catch you? Suppose this burglary was arranged *in the hope* that you'd cover up and compromise yourself?"

The possibility in fact had already occurred to Justin. He remembered how he had just handed Longford back his envelope—without the watch of course—and was sitting down at his desk to begin the questioning which was to lead to the confession, with Henderson to his right on a chair between him and the window, and Longford standing on guard near the rifled safe, when, looking up, he had caught a glance pass between them. From all he had seen he felt sure that the interests of these two men were widely, even desperately conflicting. Yet something had passed: some threat, or warning, or perhaps a promise. It was only a small mystery to set against the reality of the confession that lay in his pocket, yet it troubled him, like a piece of a jig-saw that obstinately refused to fit. There was no point in bothering the Vicar with it, though. It would fall into place in time, no doubt, and meanwhile there were more important things to do.

Soon after half-past eight he let himself into the deserted office. A smell of candle grease and none too clean bodies met him, so he opened the windows and lit the fire, which was soon spluttering its evil-smelling coal dust over everything. He heard Spinks arrive, the brisker step of Harris moving on his rounds and then a sudden exclamation, followed by a knock at the door, around which the clerk's face appeared with the expression of one whose most cherished images have been profaned.

"I know: don't tell me: we've been burgled," Justin greeted him irritably. "What have you found? The broken window catch downstairs?"

"The mud, sir—mud everywhere."

"Has Spinks noticed it? He's not a very noticing lad, but better get rid of him on some errand just in case. Then get Billings to mend the catch and we'll sponge off the worst."

"But the Police, sir!" Harris objected, aghast at this. "Surely the footprints, sir . . . ? Won't they want . . . ?"

"Bother the Police. Just do as I say and I'll explain later."

Now that he had burnt his boats he felt much calmer, for though he was in no doubt of the seriousness of what he was doing in shielding Henderson, he knew he simply dared not trust the man to Blair's custody until some independent person had interviewed him and taken a more official statement; otherwise there might be a recantation and everything would be lost. 'Must pacify Harris, though,' he thought. 'Mustn't breathe a word about Misprision—too awful! Suppose I merely tell him there were burglars here but nothing was taken and there's no case for the Police?' The rattle of a bucket and the smell of soap and carbolic from the landing apprised him of the fact that by his orders proofs of a crime were in the very act of being removed; and still wondering how on earth he could explain it away, he opened the private door almost on top of his reproachful clerk (who was down on his knees on the landing carpet) to see rising into view behind him on the stairs the top half of the *Mercury's* Mr Hicks looking more gnome-like than ever in an ulster about three sizes too large for him.

It was a bad moment.

"Cleaning up, sir?" their visitor remarked, taking in Harris and his bucket with polite surprise. "What's become of young Spinks? Too arthritic for this job? Or have you sent him out snowballing?" He had approached nearer, where the trail of half-dried mud was plainly visible in the sunlight flooding through the office window and the open door. "Disgustingly careless people are," he lamented. "Quite beastly habits, some of 'em. If you'd had a squad of burglars, sir, at work all night they could hardly have made a nastier mess of it, now could they?"

He seemed much spryer than usual, his eyes darting here and there, from the safe to the footmarks and Harris's anguished face. Once inside the office proper, however, all this playfulness seemed to fall from him and he gazed at Justin with the rather constipated stare so familiar to his colleagues.

"Now then, sir . . ." There was reproach in the voice. This man had been hurt and disenchanted beyond even the common experience of the Press. "You know why I'm here, I expect?"

Justin replied guardedly that he thought he had some notion.

"I think you have, sir. You had visitors last night."

"Indeed?"

"No need to deny it, for I saw 'em. I saw *you*. Anything you'd care to say, sir?"

"Only that you must have had a devilish cold and miserable time out there and I hope it was worth it."

"Oh, don't worry, it will be worth it," Hicks said, turning up the corners of his mouth in a little mirthless grin. "There's a story here, sir. Make some nice copy, as I seem to remember saying once before at the time of that little contretemps of yours in Bewley. Not that we want to print anything about *that,* though."

"I'm sure you don't."

"Seeing that what we're after is another story, the biggest that's hit Smedwick since the Scots came down and massacred half the population in 1308. Now there's a story worth having."

"You shall have it too."

And he tossed Henderson's confession across the desk.

The effect of this manœuvre was immediate. Mr Hicks, as a good journalist, was prepared for most things—catastrophe for choice—but even his professional aplomb was not quite equal to the occasion. He stared at the thing wide-eyed; then, as he began to read, broke into a prolonged whistle of astonishment.

I, Joseph Henderson, declare as follows:

I remember the night of the Massingham burglary. I was out poaching over the moor with George Sugden. I had my gun with me. We got no game, so Sugden said: "Let's try the priest's." We went through Hirsley Wood to Mr Verney's house. We had with us a bag made of old poke, and this we tore up and tied round our boots. In an outhouse we found a chisel, and with it we forced a window and climbed into a room. We lit a candle and searched around for what we could get. There was a lady's gold watch on the mantelpiece: it is the same as the one now shown me. There was a kind of seal too in the shape of a bird which I sold some years ago.

We then went into the dining-room next door. We heard footsteps and voices above and we saw a light on the stairs. We blew out our candle. I saw Mr Verney coming down towards us with a candle in his hand and I believe his daughter was with him. I had the gun in my hand. Sugden pushed against me to get to the door, and this accidentally set off the gun. Mr Verney's candle went out. Sugden had run out. The old man came into the dining-room and went after me in the darkness. I was dodging about. I then ran into the passage, through the other room, and dived into the flower-beds. I did not see Sugden anywhere. I ran across the garden, over the wall into the fields, and followed the burn uphill. At the quarry near Mellow's Ford I pulled the old poke sacking off my feet and threw it away. I had dropped the chisel somewhere in the house. I got home about three and burnt my boots, stockings and breeches which were soaking wet. The Police came about two hours later.

"My God, but this is dynamite!" Hicks cried as he laid it down. "Beautiful! Beautiful! How the devil did you get it? Have you been after Henderson all this time?"

"Longford has. I owe everything to Longford."

"Including the confession?"

"In a way. Henderson just folded up."

"And told the truth, the whole truth and nothing but the truth?"

Justin thought for a while and then said slowly: "No one tells that. There are discrepancies between the two confessions; for I must tell you I have Sugden's too. But I think this is the truth all right, or as near as makes no matter. You see he mentions one particular piece of evidence that explains what was never explained before: something quite striking and new. . . ."

"You mean the bit about the sacking, the 'old poke'?"

"You've spotted it. This means the end of Blair."

"Fortunately it's just the beginning of the Story," said Mr Hicks with reverence in his voice.

XIX

FEW of our readers (declared the *Mercury* in a leader which Justin preserved among the papers young Mr Jobling found) can have forgotten the sense of shock and outrage that followed the infamous attack upon the Reverend Mr Verney and his daughter at Massingham in February 1891 or the subsequent trial at which two Smedwick men, MILLIGAN and KELLY, were adjudged guilty and sentenced to Penal Servitude for Life. When the convicts were committed to durance vile it was our belief, and that of most of our fellow citizens, that crime had been punished and the district rid of two worthless scoundrels.

Is it permissible to believe this any longer? The *Mercury*, which conceived it its public duty to record all the details of an odious crime and the condign punishment that followed it, now feels impelled to ask whether justice was done or INJUSTICE; whether it was not the INNOCENT who were punished rather than the guilty. The *Mercury*, fully aware of the gravity of its questions, but aware also of its duty as an organ of public CONSCIENCE, asks now whether the jury that found Milligan and Kelly guilty was not misled; whether the judge who sentenced them was not an unwitting agent of oppression; whether the police officers who brought the case against the accused men performed their duty?

That suspicions such as we voice of infamies more to be expected in barbarous lands, among Turks and heathen, could even arise in our own enlightened state and time, under a Government (whatever its political complexion) owing allegiance to our most gracious QUEEN, is a matter for wonder and dismay. Fortunately the force of evil does not go unchallenged. Where the voice of the appointed guardians of peace and public welfare have been mute, two ordinary citizens (whom we are proud to claim as *fellow* citizens), obeying only their sense of Christian duty, have raised the questions that we ask in the most cogent form in Whitehall and Westminster itself, adducing evidence which may be of an unparalleled and startling kind.

And even Government must hearken when the PEOPLE speaks. The need for a ministerial enquiry is quite plain. The *Mercury* urges it. The common weal requires it. Let the Government act *now*.

Unknown to the author of this heartfelt call, a Commissioner from the Treasury, charged to investigate the whole affair, had reached Smedwick before the paper was in the press. Respect for its wishes could hardly have been prompter—and much credit was claimed afterwards in the editorial offices. Justin, busy at his desk with a spate of conveyances, was the first to be alerted by the sudden appearance of the Commissioner, a razor-sharp, intent gentleman in a frock-coat who would have served for the model of what Harris never ceased to hope his employer would become. "Mr Wilcox—from the Treasury, sir," he had intoned with deep satisfaction.

No one had announced the Commissioner's presence or purpose in Smedwick; he had simply descended from Olympus with his black gloves and his black bag; but local intelligence was omniscient, and long before the day was out news of his activities had begun to filter back to the office in the market-place. Apparently not a moment had been wasted. Miss Kelly had been the first witness to be seen; then Longford; then the men who claimed to have seen Kelly and Milligan at dawn near the Duke's Wall, six miles across the moor from Massingham. It was a formidable beginning.

On the next day, a Wednesday, the Commissioner saw Bulwer

the tailor, who had been a witness of the affair of Milligan's trouser button, though he had not been called in court. Dr Higson followed —he who had found the scrap of newspaper in the lining of Kelly's coat—and later that afternoon the news was all round Smedwick that Wilcox and his bag had been seen disappearing into the workhouse in search of Piggott. If this was a sensation—and it now required only the slightest movement on Wilcox's part to rate as one—it was soon overtaken by another, as the news flew from house to house that Geordie Sugden himself, 'pale as a bogle', had gone at supper-time to the King's Arms where he had been closeted for two hours with the Commissioner.

After the fevered activity of the two previous days the town seemed almost morbidly quiet next morning, for Wilcox had been detected at an early hour driving west along the moor road in a hired trap and his destination had been settled for him without much difficulty. 'He's ganned awa' tae Verney's', the word had gone round amidst general approval. The sight of the trap returning down the hill from the moor drew perhaps the largest audience Pelegate and Bewley Street had known since Milligan and Kelly had passed that way after the famous confrontation scene, but the Commissioner would hardly have been aware of it or have seen the faces peering at him from behind the curtains in the dusk. He had other calls to make—one, most vital, upon Henderson—and these were noted too; until the darkness closed in and the watchers saw only the dim glow of the trap's lamps and heard the clip-clop of hooves in the Lawnmarket near Police headquarters.

Justin heard them on the cobbles of the market-place, then the man's footsteps on his office stairs: the evidence of an activity he had called up but controlled no longer. He longed to know how the Commissioner had been impressed by the witnesses he had seen, particularly Blair, whose punishment now appeared as the great necessity in the case, apart from the release of the wrongfully accused men. But when he broached the matter he could see at once that Mr Wilcox was not to be drawn beyond his strict terms of reference—"Punishment of the Police, sir? My dear Mr Derry, is not that premature? The possibility exists, of course, as do other possibilities; I think I should say no more. It is all in my report."

"Which you are publishing?"

"Well, naturally that will be a matter for the Minister," Mr Wilcox said, raising his voice on the word as though invoking some more than mortal power. "The Minister could if he desired make public the results of a Treasury enquiry, but it has not in my experience been a very frequent practice to do so. You will appreciate the highly confidential nature of this business."

"I ought to, seeing that I have been handling it myself for weeks."

"And most vigorously," Mr Wilcox commended him. "Your initiative in this matter has been most marked and I shall acknowledge it in my report. Of course, I don't pretend to understand exactly how it came about that you happened on all this and first became interested in Sugden. . . ."

"But surely you've seen the man and heard his story. And Henderson's."

The Commissioner had cleared his throat ominously at the name. "I have seen Henderson," he said. "I owe it to you to say that I have seen Henderson and that he has made a statement which in material particulars seems to me significant. Perhaps, sir, seeing that the subject has been raised, you will now elucidate certain matters arising out of it. Firstly"—here Mr Wilcox began to unfasten his portfolio—"firstly will you explain how it came about that a certain watch, highly important to these enquiries, was taken from the man's house and lodged with you? Secondly, will you be so good as to inform me when and in what place the man's confession came to be made. Take your time, sir. These are matters vital to this enquiry—and perhaps to you."

XX

On the 3rd of March Gilmore put down a Question in the House in terms which he had communicated in advance to his allies in Smedwick:

> To ask the Home Secretary whether an enquiry has been made on behalf of the Solicitor to the Treasury in regard to the confessions of two men who allege that they committed a burglary at Massingham Rectory for which two other men were convicted in 1891 and sentenced to Penal Servitude for Life, and whether any report has been made by the Solicitor to the Treasury with respect to these said confessions, and if so whether such report does not show the truth of the said confessions and the innocence of the said prisoners, in which event . . .

"Does it have to go on like that—interminably?" cried the Reverend Mr Lumley as he reached this point. "Surely it is possible to put things more simply?"

"On the order paper of the House of Commons!"

"Well, my dear fellow, perhaps I am being naïve about it and Gilmore should certainly know his business, though it sounds more like a conundrum to me. Do you understand it?"

"In parts."

"Then let us hope the Home Secretary shares your enviable discernment when it comes up today. At what time exactly?"

"I imagine about three."

It was then two on a murky afternoon with a thin drizzle falling on the square, in which half the booths were already down and the cheapjacks resignedly loading their carts, leaving behind them a scurf of refuse no dirtier than the slush among which the cats and dogs of the vicinity were scavenging. He stood at the window looking down, trying to imagine the scene in Westminster, but somehow there seemed no connection between it and the little grey disconsolate town under the rain. He tried to think of Milligan and Kelly far off in their prison cells, but their images were fainter still—no more than the memory of faces glimpsed in a crowd. Since the coming of the Commissioner to Smedwick the whole case, which had once been so close and personal, had receded from him in the strangest way, leaving him like some watcher in the shadows who sees the passing of distant and mysterious events. Only the sense of excitement remained: greater than ever now that he had no controlling part to play. It was almost unbearable to have to sit and wait for the news Gilmore had promised him that day.

Soon after four he gave up all pretence of working and went out into the town through which the last of the market folk were straggling, some on foot, some on horseback, some in carts that jolted and slithered over the snow. Its first whiteness when every roof had glistened like crystal had long since gone and the whole place had a grubby look, like a stage set by daylight. In the Dene, the open grassy space behind Queen's Row, the ground was a piebald of white and grimy yellow, pitted with the tracks of dogs and humans and toboggans which has worn a shiny run down the slope of the hill on the Pelegate side. Shrill voices reached him from across it as the children came out of school and he could see their small grey figures flitting over the landscape under the trees where a few crocuses showed their heads with the forlorn look of castaways on some unwelcoming shore. What a laggard of a spring it was. Out there in the mist and drizzle with the wind off the sea it was hard to believe that there would ever be warmth again, or birdsong, where now a flock of starlings settled with a whirring of wings and rooks prospected in the branches.

By six he was back in his office, hopeful that a telegram might have come. He poked the fire, which was nearly out, lit the gas behind the desk, and settled down with the best will he could muster to a dispute about the ownership of a tea-service which had convulsed two households and threatened to spread to the collaterals. Rain beat against the panes. He heard Spinks decamp and the portentous steps of Harris as he made the premises secure against any recurrence of unspeakable events. A kind of murmuring was rising around him. For a moment he thought he must have late clients in the waiting-room and his mind flew back to that other evening when he had heard Longford's voice on the far side of the baize door, but it grew louder, and he understood that it was from the street and that a number of people must be out there in the darkness. Yet all the market stalls were down.

He went to the window and drew back the curtains. There were lights down there, torches made of straw and sacking from the debris of the market, in whose flickering gleam he saw the crowd of dark figures on the cobbles and faces raised towards the window at which he stood. Mr Harris was behind him, and as he threw up the sash and leaned out he heard a great cry go up, saw the torches waving like fireflies in the darkness, and in front of them, directly below him, a small figure capering with a piece of paper in its hand. The cold sleet-laden air was beating against his face, tinged with the smell of fire; he caught the voices calling up to him, laughter, words tossed here and there, a confused mêlée of sound dying into silence around the figure of Mr Hicks below. Only then, at third hand via the *Mercury* office and the wildly excited crowd, did Justin learn that Milligan and Kelly would be free.

The first train into Smedwick from the south next morning was the 'milk' from King's Cross which arrived at 6.50 on a good day. It was not a train that commanded a large or enthusiastic following, and the surprise of its crew on coming to rest at Number Two platform to discover a reception committee of about two score excited people was extreme. "What's awa'? Have ye all ganned daft?" shouted the driver, a Lowlander from Dunbar, as folk came running alongside through the steam. Cries of "Worr are the lads? Worr's Mick?" exploded around him while the milk churns were noisily unloaded from the guard's van. "Who's Mick?" "Mick Kelly. Man, have ye nee *hoard* of the Smedwick mortars?"

By two, when the northbound express from London went wailing through the station like a banshee, the crowd had grown to over a hundred strong, watched by a detachment of Police under an Inspector. "Worr's Blair?" voices called out to them. "Fetch the Suporr." The burly figure had been glimpsed that morning on the steps of his headquarters looking, as one observer had it, "like a muckle black de'il", and the Pelegate folk were not in a forgiving mood. "Has he catched Wee Geordie yet?" people wanted to know. "And Muckle Joe? Man but he's aafu' slow. He didna want to have catched 'em forbye."

In fact both Henderson and Sugden were already on their way to Belcastle gaol, having been hustled aboard the southbound 12.15 under the noses of the crowd that watched the horizon for every puff of smoke coming north across the snow-covered plain. A tall rushing pillar soon after four presaged the arrival of the *Flying Scotsman*, its whistle shrilling, whirling a debris of paper contemptuously in its wake as it rushed through on its way to Edinburgh. Mothers clutched their children; cries went up, "It's the Fleein' Scot. Worr's our Willie? Can ye no bide near to mither, ye gomeril!" A few eyes had already seen another column of smoke far off down the line, and as it approached and was identified as 'The Bomb', a notorious 'slow' that haunted every forlorn platform between York and Berwick, the crowd surged forward to the edge of the track, returning the astonished stares of driver and fireman with wild shouts for 'Mick' and the 'Smedwick mortars'. "They're not aboard," an authoritative voice called out from the rear, armed with the superior intelligence of the *Mercury* reporting staff. Lamentations broke out against the Government and the Great Northern, and as 'The Bomb' clanked and puffed its way on to the loop line to make way for the next express derisive boos and catcalls followed it.

Just before six the arrival of the editor of the *Mercury* and a reinforcement of police indicated to the observant that the great hour was approaching. Justin was there, at the back of the crowd that may have numbered a thousand, and near him the rotund figure of the Vicar of St Bede's in knickerbockers and Norfolk jacket gave the scene an individual flavour. A plume of smoke like a red serpent uncoiling could be made out through the gathering darkness, and now for the first time the crowd fell silent, so that the approaching rumble mingling with the voice of a child crying to its mother to go home could be distinctly heard.

As the train pulled in and the people saw the line of carriages and faces pressed to the panes their energies were released. A babel of shouting broke out down the length of the platform. Doors were wrenched open and the startled eyes of passengers stared out into the gleam of lamps and home-made torches waving as though in the course of some fantastic dance. Suddenly a great cheer went up. From his position near the ticket office Justin saw the crowd in front of him sway like some living thing with tentacles and a central core that swelled and heaved. "Open the barriers," someone shouted close to him, and he heard the rattle of iron being swung back before the struggling mass that rolled towards him. As he was engulfed he heard a whistle shrilling, the hiss of steam, stentorian bellows from police officers, the sobbing of children, voices that called to one another wonderingly across an expanse of time—"Is it ye, hinney? My but ye've growed so. Worr's wor Jennie, me wee lass?"

The pace of the retreat was slowing as the Police, with linked arms, shepherded the mob past the gates into the forecourt; and close at hand, not more than a few feet away, he saw the bearded figure and the much younger one that had haunted his waking hours for so long. He looked around for his friend to share the triumph with him, for suddenly his detachment had gone and he was able to feel the joy and pity of all those who wept and laughed and embraced one another after a long parting. But Mr Lumley was nowhere to be seen. On the far edge of the crowd he was busily at work collecting signatures for an appeal for mercy on behalf of Henderson and Sugden.

THE TRIAL
1899

I

"Members of the jury," Gilmore said, "in this case I appear for the Crown with my learned friend Mr McGlew, while my learned friend Mr Jessop represents the accused man Blair and my learned friend Mr Neil the accused men Mathieson and Moffat. The charge, as you have heard, is Criminal Conspiracy."

Here Gilmore settled himself comfortably against the wall of the dock and said in a matter-of-fact voice: "You may think, when all is over, that it is one of the most extraordinary stories you have ever heard. Gentlemen, the Prosecution say that because of what happened one winter's night in a remote rectory on the fells, and because of what these accused police officers thought of that event and continued to pretend when they very well knew better, two innocent men were tried and sent to penal servitude for life and served eight years before the truth came out. The Prosecution say that the evidence on which they were condemned was false and had been manufactured by these accused in the dock today. 'To make the punishment fit the crime' was the benevolent aim of the Mikado in the opera. It has been left to these police officers to show that in a less humane democracy the *evidence* can be made to fit the crime as well. This we shall show.

"Gentlemen, my case is in a sense an epilogue. There was a first act which was played out in this same court when two humble people whom I shall call before you were tried and condemned on the false evidence I have spoken of. The second was brought to its climax by the efforts of two just and selfless men—for it is by twos we go throughout—who uncovered the truth and the real perpetrators of that old crime and saw them brought to justice. You will hear for yourselves from those criminals who on that winter night broke into the home of an old man to steal and fired a gun at him. You may wonder whether it has ever happened before that convicted men, the innocent and the guilty, have united to testify to the immeasurably more shocking guilt of the police officers who arrested them. Strange are the workings of providence—and, you may think, of human justice. Milligan and Kelly, who were innocent, were charged with burglary and attempted murder and might have lived out their lives in prison. Henderson and Sugden, guilty, were charged with burglary alone and sentenced to five years. Let us admit that some restitution has been made. Milligan and Kelly have been released. But they should never have been imprisoned. They have been pardoned. For something they never did. They have each been given eight hundred pounds as an act of grace—and one applauds that, though perhaps not the Treasury rates for an injustice that has lasted for eight years.

"Members of the jury, it is necessary that you should learn about these things in greater detail, since my case today is only to be understood in the light of what went before. So we will start in Massingham Rectory about two o'clock on a cold starlit night. . . ."

In the well of the court, a few places away from where he had sat with Rees, Justin listened to this opening. The wooden paling of the dock alone divided him from Blair and the two other accused; Gilmore was slightly to his left in the front row; and on the bench a thin, pale man in crimson robes seemed only to half fill the chair under the royal arms where Garrowby had brooded. Through the windows above the public gallery a shaft of light fell on the canopy above the judge's head and on the fashionable folk in the Grand Jury box along one wall. The trial jurors sat herded together in three rows of seats on the judge's left, facing towards Gilmore like well-conducted children in school, and opposite them was the witness-box. Apart from the judge, it was all so like the setting of eight years earlier that he half expected to hear some whispered comment from old Rees and to see the bearded Milligan and Kelly with his unformed peasant's face lean forward in the dock with the trapped expression that he could see now in the young constable, Moffat, at the far end of the line. It was of course Gilmore who gave the greatest force to the illusion: the elegant figure, the voice of reason itself—

"Members of the jury, the Prosecution's case can be summarised easily. We say that the accused, acting in concert, arrested on suspicion of burglary two innocent men who happened to have been from home that night and charged them *on that evidence alone*. Then, finding that they had against their suspects nothing but two most indifferent identifications made by an old man and his daughter in almost total darkness, what did they do? Release them? Not at all. They were the best suspects they had. Did they unearth other evidence against them? How could they. There was *no* other evidence. So they had to create it. These police officers—officers of justice, members of the jury—set about making up a case to fit what they felt ought to have happened. There was no evidence that Milligan and Kelly had ever owned a housebreaking implement. One might think that a disadvantage from the Police point of view. But no—not to men of initiative. A chisel had been found at the scene of the crime, so the accused Blair sent his confederate Mathieson and P.C. Pugh down to the house of an old half-blind man called Piggott, where Kelly had lodged, and by working upon the fears and credulity of that old man they got him to say that this chisel (which he had never seen before and which they had planted on him) was his and that Kelly had had access to it.

"You may think that was a remarkable proceeding—a 'ruse', Blair called it, though perhaps you will find a better word. But we are only at the beginning. There are far more imaginative things to come."

Gilmore had given the jury a searching glance as he said this, to make sure that they were not adrift on his flights of irony, and satisfied with what he saw, went on:

"We come now to what we might term the 'Paper Chase'. A piece of newspaper had been found in the rectory after the crime and this had been handed to the Police. A coat which Kelly was alleged to have been wearing that night was also handed to the Police by a person now dead. A fortnight after the crime—a full fortnight, gentlemen—the Police Surgeon Dr Higson (whose integrity I in no way impugn) was asked by Superintendent Blair to search that coat, and in it he found a fragment of paper that fitted exactly into the larger piece found in the rectory hall. What a fortunate chance! What incontestable proof of Kelly's guilt! Admittedly it was a little strange that only after a fortnight and several Police searches did the evidence come to light. And it savours almost of a miracle when we learn that according to the testimony of the witness Piggott the coat handed to the Police *was never Kelly's;* it was his.

"So much for the younger victim: they would have his skin. But the case against Milligan still required a little window dressing, a little decorous rearrangement here and there. So the accused man

Moffat was sent to Massingham to hunt around under the window through which the burglars had come and gone. A month—a whole month this time—had passed since the crime. But knowing the resourcefulness of these officers and the beneficent providence that guided them, can you doubt for a moment that that constable managed to unearth something of shattering importance to justify his journey? Of course he did. The diligent man had not been there an hour before he had dug up a button with a bit of cloth attached. And remembering the scrap of paper in the coat, can you doubt that that bit of cloth was found to fit as neatly as a sausage into its skin into a rent in Milligan's trousers, also in the possession of the Police? You may think, perhaps, that this third of the Superintendent's gambits shows a repetitious quality unworthy of him, indicating that he was running out of ideas, but at least it shows his nose for a conviction was as keen as ever. Alas for him, that piece of evidence was rejected by the judge for reasons I need not trouble you about, and so the tailor, who was called in to perform what I might term the autopsy on the cloth and button, was not called."

Gilmore paused and added grimly: "But *I* am calling him. He is an honest man. And he will tell you what he would have told the jury if he had been allowed—that though a leap through a window *could* have caused the tear, it seemed more likely that some *sharper edge* had done it, such as a pair of scissors or a knife. It looked deliberate *and he told Blair so*. Of course no one listened."

But in court they were listening now. Justin sensed around him an unwavering concentration. The restless stirring and coughing that had gone on during the swearing of the jury had ceased, and in the pause that followed, while Gilmore glanced at his brief, there was not a sound to be heard except for a faint rustling of paper in the press box. Even that had stopped as counsel straightened up again.

"Members of the jury, these three 'ruses', to adopt the Superintendent's amusing word, are serious enough. But you may think that what I have now to tell you is more outrageous still. It has about it an impudent air that sets it apart—at once daring and deceitful, simple and ingenious, sly and immensely effective. More than anything else it convicted Milligan and Kelly. Even today the Prosecution cannot put the whole truth of it before you, because it happened that for this one last and final coup the conspirators employed no one else, trusted no one but themselves. But little by little we will piece the story together. P.C. Pugh, whom I shall call, will tell part of it; so will Henderson, and a young farmer called Merrick. And I think the defendant Blair may tell us what remains—if he is called; if he goes into that box. We shall see. Meanwhile . . ."

After luncheon the long procession of witnesses began. Justin knew that it was Gilmore's plan to prove first the burglary and the events up to the time of the arrest of Milligan and Kelly, both of whom would be called to deny their guilt. Henderson and Sugden would follow to admit theirs, supported by the evidence of Miss Binns, the roadman Green, and Longford to speak to the recovery of the watch. The foundations of the burglary and its true solution having been laid, the last part of the Prosecution's case would consist of proof of the Police conspiracy through the mouths of Pugh (who had turned Queen's Evidence), Piggott, Merrick, Higson and the tailor.

First, then, Mr Verney.

As he slowly mounted the steps and grasped the edge of the box with his scaly old hands the illusion that had haunted Justin all that day became complete. Time had stood quite still for him. The Reverend Thomas James McMichael Verney, aged 76, Rector of Massingham since 1859. Remembered the night of the burglary. Awakened by his daughter . . .

Suddenly Justin saw that she was in court, which must mean that Gilmore would not be calling her. He felt glad that she would not be called and browbeaten into admissions of the terrible mistake she must know she had made, and that it would be left to the old man to deal with the stolen property and the identifications of the burglars who had broken into his home.

Poor Mr Verney. He was not one actually to eat his words. But he was definite no longer. The intruders, he now said, had seemed to him like Milligan and Kelly. Of course the light had been bad and everyone had been in a state of great excitement. He withdrew in no way the testimony he had given that the men were Milligan and Kelly, but the possibility of error had existed. The light had been so bad. There had been a large man and a smaller man, both standing like drilled men. The big one had shot at him. At any rate a gun had gone off. He had seen an interesting and beautiful meteor-like effect which he had attempted to describe in a letter to the press. As to the watch (shown him), it was undoubtedly his daughter's. The seal (shown him) had been attached to the watch and had stood on a tripod on the drawing-room mantelpiece.

Cross-examined: He had certainly said at the trial that the burglars were Milligan and Kelly. He still thought that was probable. But the light had been so bad.

They were smiling in court. The old man's words no longer had significance. What he remembered or failed to remember would hurt no one now: it was light relief to listen to the old buffoon with his nightgown and candle, his meteorite and his identification of burglars by the drill book. Perhaps only Justin, who had suffered under the Verney memory for so long, felt pity for the old gentleman whose beard was wagging at them from the box and who seemed so astonishingly unaware of the harm he had done. To see him baited in the presence of his daughter was not pleasant, though there could be worse things. Suppose Gilmore were to call her after all!

When Mr Verney at last stepped down Justin was in panic that she would have to follow her father into the box. But it was only the Rectory cook, whose timorous appearance on the stairs above the tumult in mob cap and curlers had convulsed even Mr Justice Garrowby's court; followed by Bell, the odd-job man, who had found the newspaper in the hall.

Then Milligan. People were craning forward everywhere, and even the judge had glanced up from his notes towards the witness-box where the stolid bearded figure was standing with the Bible in his hand.

"You are Patrick Milligan?"

"Aye."

"Wheelwright, of 10 Orchard Close, Smedwick?"

"Aye."

"On the 7th of February 1891 were you and a man called Michael Kelly arrested on charges of burglary and attempted murder?"

"Aye."

"On the 15th March were you both indicted in this court for those offences, convicted and sentenced to penal servitude for life?"

"We were."

"Were you guilty?"

"Innocent."

It had taken eight years and three trials, Justin reflected, before the truth had been allowed to be told.

Next morning the Defence in the person of Mr Jessop advanced buoyantly upon it. Mr Jessop had slept well. His smooth well-nourished figure came bounding up the steps of the Moot Hall with the air of one who has some pleasant duty in store that will astonish the natives very much. "Mr Milligan," he greeted the reappearance of the witness, "Mr Milligan, you come before us as an honest man?"

"That I hope, sir."

"Whose word can be trusted," Jessop said. "What is your profession?"

"Wheelwright."

"And poacher, may we add?"

"I've poached, admitted."

"Do you admit convictions?"

"Aye."

"How many?"

"Six maybe."

"Milligan" (no Mister this time), "do you still say you are an honest-living man?"

That had been the keystone. And on it had been built an attack of considerable power and virulence, extending in time to Kelly and the whole field of the Massingham burglary. In form it was a restatement of what Paget for the Crown had said in that place eight years earlier, but made in the course of questions to men whom Paget had not been able to touch because they had been in the dock and protected by the law as it then stood. Now they were protected no longer but were witnesses, "men whose testimony you are asked to trust *and to convict others on*", in Jessop's words as he fixed the jury with bulbous and glittering eye. He was an excellent advocate, with a way of burrowing into a problem by the back door and of phrasing his questions in such a manner that his victims were made to look reluctant and sly, as though the truth were being dragged out of them. "Milligan," he asked on one occasion, "I think you tell us that you had an alibi for the small hours?"

The witness replied that he and Kelly had been on Bridewell Moor.

"Out walking? Taking the air?"

"We was poachin'."

"Were you now? Poaching. So in fact your alibi for one crime was to plead another. Did you have witnesses?"

"Some lads as saw us comin' off the fell."

"Saw you, did they? Most fortunate. Did you call them at your trial?"

"They've come today, sir."

"Did you call them *at your trial,* that's what I'm asking you?"

Under this treatment it was no wonder that both men, particularly Kelly, began to wilt a little. They had not expected such rough handling so late in the day. But though at times they were made to look foolish and stubborn, and their old fondness for other people's game was brought out in glaring colours, the core of their evidence remained untouched by anything Jessop could do. And the effect of it was very striking. At those moments when Defence counsel were on the attack and getting admissions a groundswell of sound could be heard in court—not the sudden intake of breath with which a damaging answer is greeted, but something restless and protesting, something very unfavourable to Blair and all he stood for. Only the jury seemed fairly immune. They had their property qualifications to think of and Mr Jessop to contend with at a range of a few yards. Yet even on their faces there was an expression which Justin thought he could read and which satisfied him as he saw the younger and more vulnerable of his two protégés released at last. "Call George Sugden," he heard Gilmore say, and voices were crying in the corridor, "George Sugden. Call George Sugden."

And suddenly he saw that Jessop was on his feet.

"Yes?" enquired the judge, glancing up from his notes which he had been scratching with a quill pen.

"My lord, if I might interpolate a point? We have heard from the two men originally convicted of the crime at Massingham, and I understand that the witness Sugden is one of their two 'successors', if I may use the term."

"He is one of the two men who now admit to the commission of that crime," Gilmore agreed in a suffering voice.

"Am I right—is my friend about to call them to repeat those confessions on oath?"

"Of course."

"Then might we hear how those confessions came to be made? They were first made to a Mr Derry, I believe?"

"That is so."

"Will my friend not be calling that gentleman as a preliminary? His name is on the back of the indictment."

Alarm. Horror. And then a definite exhilaration. In the clinical mood that the trial had induced, Justin recognised all these symptoms; also a sense of wonder as to what Gilmore would do.

"I will call him, certainly," the answer came without a trace of hesitation. "I must not disguise the fact, however, that Mr Derry has been in court throughout."

"Was that proper?"

"Well, I had not proposed to call him," Gilmore said. "Since I am producing the men themselves to confess all over again to their crimes, his evidence seemed to me to lack cogency. But if my friend wishes . . . certainly I shall oblige. Mr Derry." He was glancing behind him in his blandest way, as though he would call the Archangel Gabriel if it would assist the court. "Will Mr Derry please come forward?"

"Most improper: he should have been kept out of court: it is a scandal," he heard Jessop grumbling as he went through the well and up the steps into the witness-box, with the judge on his left and the jury straight ahead of him. The gallery was a sea of faces stretching back into the gloom, and over his shoulder, as he took the oath, he was aware of the rows of gentry in the Grand Jury box.

"Now then, you are Justin Derry, solicitor of Smedwick?" Gilmore said.

"I am."

"I have no questions to ask you. But it appears that my learned friends have. If you will be so good as to hold yourself at their disposal?"

"Yes, sir."

He could see Jessop rising on the balls of his feet: a very small man, seen from that angle, whose head hardly came up to the level of the dock behind which the monumental figure of Blair stared into nothingness. A formidable little man; it was not going to be pleasant.

"Mr Derry, I want to refer to my friend's opening if I may. He described someone—or rather two people—as 'just and selfless'—I think I have it right. Yes, here it is: 'just and selfless'. That did refer to you?" A titter of laughter had accompanied this sighting shot, and Jessop, hunting assiduously through his brief and gazing in enquiry at the witness, raised it to quite a sizeable laugh before he went on: "Those are impressive claims. Do you endorse them? Are you just? And selfless? I mean particularly so?"

"I don't remember making any claims for myself."

"So my learned friend did it for you. For some reason, presumably. Or was it just rodomontade?"

"What are you suggesting?" Gilmore was beginning angrily from his seat when the judge pounced on the pair of them. "How can the witness say what was in Mr Gilmore's mind when he opened? It was a piece of irrelevance anyway."

"I would respectfully agree," said Jessop, seizing happily on the last words. "The suggestion that witnesses for the Prosecution enjoy some special and divinely inspired status is not one to which I would subscribe with much enthusiasm. Not in this case certainly. Now then." He gave his gown a hitch like a man getting down to business and swung round on Justin. "Did all this start when a Miss Binns called on you to make a statement?"

"Yes."

"As a result, did you come to certain conclusions and embark on certain actions?"

"No."

"You mean you didn't believe what you'd been told?"

"I mean one doesn't act on a single statement out of the blue."

"Particularly when your informant is a young lady with a criminal record. I quite understand. You naturally desired to obtain other statements, other data, before you acted. Did you get them?"

"Yes."

"Were they—to adopt your own picturesque phrase—'out of the blue' also?"

"I didn't think so."

"If you add nought to nought, sir, what do you get?"

"My results were substantial."

"So they were *your* results, were they, is that how you thought of them? Is that how you thought of this case at Massingham, as *your* case, your property?"

"Not in the least."

"But it was *you*, wasn't it, who was carrying out this inspired programme of detective work to show that the Police and Mr Justice Garrowby, not to mention the jury that convicted Milligan and Kelly, were one and all mistaken?"

"There were others who thought as I did."

"Mr Lumley, Vicar of St Bede's for instance: the second of the 'just and selfless'?"

"Yes."

"Was this Mr Lumley's 'case' too?"

"How should he answer that?" snapped Gilmore contemptuously from his seat.

"Very well," Jessop said with a resigned gesture towards the jury, drawing their attention to what he had to put up with. "You may tell me this, though. Wasn't the suspect you fixed upon one of Mr Lumley's parishioners?"

"If you mean Sugden, yes it was."

"Did you and Mr Lumley together obtain a confession from this man?"

"Yes."

"Was Sugden at that time in bed and suffering from a dangerous fever and were two of his children ill also?"

"One of them, yes: quite seriously."

"Was the getting of that so-called confession from that desperately sick and troubled man one illustration of the justness and selflessness we've heard so much about?"

The court had gone very still. Justin felt the burden of eyes watching him, the tension building up like something physical that he could almost touch. He said simply: "I believed that Sugden was guilty. I was sorry for him. But I was more sorry for Milligan and Kelly. It didn't seem wrong or unjust to try to get at the truth."

"If it *was* the truth, of course?" queried Jessop, unmoved by this. "And not the result of social and moral pressures upon a sick and ignorant man?"

"I don't think so."

"Let us turn to Henderson. He was the second of your suspects?"

"Yes."

"You discovered him. Let us examine the circumstances. A man called Longford came to you and left an envelope in your possession?"

"Yes."

"You knew Longford was a poacher with a Police record?"

"Yes."

"And was engaged to the sister of the convict Michael Kelly?"

"The released, pardoned and innocent victim of a proved injustice," corrected Gilmore, rising. "Will my friend not find some less prejudiced way of describing people? It is a fault in my submission."

"That innocence could be in issue, very much in issue," insisted Jessop, standing his ground.

"So we are trying Milligan and Kelly again? My lord, it is an interesting legal curiosity. Perhaps we should alter the indictment and the accused: and my learned friend and I could change places. One must admit he makes an admirable prosecutor."

"My lord!"

"Really, it is very simple," the judge said. "Mr Jessop's case, as I understand it, is that these confessions by Sugden and Henderson were improperly obtained and false, while the Police process which ended in the conviction of Milligan and Kelly was accurate and proper. That is his case. I say nothing of its merits. But he is at perfect liberty to advance it and question witnesses about it. To say that we are re-trying Kelly and Milligan may be good advocacy but it is not good sense. May we now proceed?"

Mr Jessop's face cleared as he turned from the jury to the witness with the air of a good man maligned but free at last to do his duty. "I hope that no one is more aware than I am," he remarked, "of whom we are trying and for what. Police officers of unblemished reputation are charged that they criminally conspired together."

"Is that a question?" Gilmore enquired.

"It is the preface to one. Be patient. I am asking the witness about the circumstances in which Henderson's alleged confession came to be made. As I understand it, it was got with the active assistance of a criminal by the name of Longford—will my friend accept that as a proper and polite enough description of the man?"

"Question the witness, not me; don't bother me with your irrelevancies," said Gilmore in an aside audible to everyone.

"Certainly, I am trying to. That is so, Mr Derry? Longford helped obtain the confession, didn't he?"

"He was there when it was made."

"What was inside the envelope Longford had deposited with you?"

"I didn't examine the envelope. But it must have contained a lady's gold watch—Miss Verney's. Henderson actually had it in his hand when I burst in."

"Isn't it a fact that Longford had taken that watch by stealth from Henderson's house and lodged it with you?"

"How can the witness know that?" Gilmore said. "It is a question that should be put to Longford if at all."

"Then perhaps I may be permitted to ask *this*," said Mr Jessop, beginning to bounce a little under his frustrations. "Mr Derry, would you agree with me that this affair of Longford and the watch in the envelope bears all the marks of a 'ruse', as I think the word was when applied to Piggott's chisel?"

"I suppose you could look at it like that."

"It was a conspiracy in fact?"

"No. I knew nothing of what was in the envelope when it was handed me."

"But you were glad enough to take advantage of it?"

"You mean by taking Henderson's confession?"

"I mean by *extracting* that so-called confession from a man who was in your power."

"It's true he was at a disadvantage."

"Disadvantage!" Counsel raised his eyes towards the ceiling, which he might have perceived was much in need of a coat of paint. "Isn't it a fact that you had just surprised this man in the act of committing a felony?"

"Yes."

"And banged his head into the bargain?" There was a burst of laughter in court and Jessop added: "Also you were two to one?"

"Yes."

"How could any confession made in such circumstances conceivably be voluntary?"

It was a question Justin had often asked himself and even now the answer was not clear. He felt sure that the confession was true. And it had come freely, without any threats or promises from him. He had asked Henderson if the watch was Miss Verney's and whether he had been at Massingham, and after slight hesitation the words had come tumbling out. Surely that was enough? But a faint nagging doubt, a sense of something unexplained, had lingered and made him pause now in the tense silence of the court. He saw Gilmore watching him and the stony countenances in the dock. "Not in the strict legal sense," he said.

The astonishment on Jessop's face and the rushing movement with which the man rose to this undreamed-of opportunity almost made him laugh. "You mean you agree that the confession was not voluntary?"

"I think it was. I asked two simple questions about the Massingham crime and then I listened. I tried to be fair. I put no pressure on the man and he seemed willing to talk. But it is also true that there were two of us and the circumstances in which he found himself were strange, so that perhaps there was something there that made him act as he might not otherwise have done."

"That is a very fair answer," Jessop said, acknowledging with some difficulty that there could be virtue in a Prosecution witness. "If you had been a juryman trying Henderson on a charge of burglary at Massingham, would you have accepted that confession as conclusive evidence against him?"

"No—because of the element of doubt, as I have said."

"We shall be hearing Henderson and he will repeat every word of it," put in Gilmore, rising hastily to his feet.

Mr Jessop had begun to bounce uncontrollably and burst out: "That is not even re-examination: it is a speech out of context, out of place, out of time and out of order. My lord, may I be protected from such grossly improper interruptions?"

"Quite improper," agreed the judge. "I hope I shall not have to refer to it again."

Justin had remained motionless through this, looking straight ahead and trying not to see the aggravation he had caused Gilmore and the dawning smirk on Blair's face. Praise of his honesty from Jessop was hard to bear, but he could see that he was about to receive a whole cornucopia of it. "A most honest answer," it began. "As a juryman you would have suspected the confession. But as an interrogator you seem to have acted on it. Why?"

"It confirmed what I had already heard from Sugden."

"But surely to be fair—and you are being fair—that also had been obtained by improper pressure?"

"I don't agree."

"You seem to have a double standard of values for such things. Isn't it a fact that what you say you would not have done as a juryman you actually *did* in the course of an obsessive hunt for scapegoats?"

"I don't understand that."

"Neither do I," remarked the judge.

"Then may I put it this way? I am suggesting that you had a preconceived idea of what had taken place at Massingham and were determined to make the facts fit the theory?"

"I didn't have any preconceived ideas."

"Weren't you pursuing a vendetta against the Police?"

"Certainly not."

"Didn't you seek out a constable by the name of Pugh?"

It was not the first time that Justin had been subjected to this particular innuendo and he reacted indignantly: "No, I did not. He saw *me*. It was entirely his initiative."

"Would it distress you if I called that quibbling? You met Pugh and heard some rigmarole or other. You had your knife into the Police?"

"Not at all."

"Hasn't your attitude towards the Police been hostile and prejudiced throughout?"

"No. I respect the Force in general very much."

"Hasn't your attitude been obstructive too? Well, Mr Derry, you may shake your head and make gestures, but that is the question I am putting to you, though perhaps I should remind you at this stage of your legal right to refuse to answer certain questions. I say you were obstructive."

"No."

"Caution here. Didn't you fail to report an incident that happened in Bewley Street when a gun was fired at you by night?"

"Certainly a gun went off. But I was sure it was by accident."

"So you didn't report it?"

"No."

"Did you report the fact that you had caught Henderson in the act of breaking into your safe?"

"Not at once, not for some days."

There was a general gasp of astonishment in court, but Jessop for his part had already plumbed the depths of human obloquy and did not even look mildly surprised. "Of course you knew," he remarked, "that by failing to do so you were committing a crime?"

"I suppose I was."

"You suppose! Come, sir, you *know*. You are a solicitor."

"I did what I thought was right."

"By doing wrong! Now here is a mystery which perhaps my learned friend will elucidate in one of his celebrated asides, since you seem unable to. You misprised a felony. Wasn't your motive a blind prejudice against the Police?"

"No."

"I had better repeat my caution. Didn't that prejudice lead you to consort with criminals?"

"No."

Jessop drew himself up on tip-toe, and leaning forward like the banderillero who plants the darts into the flanks of the bull delivered himself of his final thrust: "Didn't that prejudice cause you to conspire with certain persons to mislead this court, to practise a fraud upon it? Didn't you even try to enlist the Treasury and the resources of the Crown . . . ?"

Gilmore was on his feet, his junior behind him; there was a flurry of furious activity strange to that slumberous place. And above the uproar the voice of Mr Jessop could be heard declaiming: "I have asked a question. Let him answer if he can."

When the judge rose at one o'clock there was a general scramble out of court in search of food, and Justin, following more leisurely, found the hall empty except for a group of magnates dawdling down the staircase, among whom he recognised Sir Miles Curvis, deputy chairman of the Smedwick court, arm in arm with Mr Freeze-Urquhart and Mr Ponsonby, who were clients of his as well as Justices before whom he had appeared many times.

At sight of him all conversation stopped and a kind of tremor seemed to pass across their faces. Their eyes became cold and solemn and then by some miracle of breeding ceased to register any awareness of his presence, but travelled through and past him like the lenses of cameras trained on some distant object.

His first sensation was one of outrage at this treatment. That he had been expecting something of the sort for weeks made no difference to what he actually felt when the thing happened. He knew a burning desire to impress on his tormentors in some signal way his absolute indifference to what they thought of him—preferably by assaulting them violently from behind.

"Mr Derry," a voice said from close behind him.

He swung round to see Miss Verney standing in the hall, her gloved hands clasped together, her eyes oddly luminous under the shadows of her veil.

"Mr Derry, I am most terribly distressed."

And so no doubt she was, he thought unkindly. It could not have been pleasant to sit in court and hear her father's bumblings and the evidence of the innocent men she had accused; but though at most times he would have felt sorry for her, the humiliation he had suffered was too recent and somehow she herself seemed part of it.

"No one need reproach themselves," he said.

She came a hesitant step towards him. "But I do. I feel ashamed for all of us. That awful man."

"Milligan?"

"Jessop of course. Those dreadful questions!"

Justin was suddenly aware that the conversation had taken an odd turn. "You can't surely be meaning the questions he asked *me?*" he said, trying to make a joke of the very notion.

"Of course I do."

"But Miss Verney . . ."

"He had no *right* to ask them. Oh, I know you have been misguided and *very* wilful, but to say more than that . . . Oh, it was infamous. To suggest you were a criminal!"

"Misprision is a crime, you know," he said mildly, astonished by the passion in her voice.

"I don't want to hear of it. Whatever you may have done, and whatever they may say, *I* know you acted as you thought was right. I was very wrong to treat you as I did . . . and those others. . . ."

"My dear Miss Verney, please."

"No, I was wrong. I can't forgive myself. So grossly wrong."

Somehow her hand was in his. He had no idea at all how it came there. It was only for an instant. Looking back at it, he even doubted whether it had happened. But in that brief flash of time he felt the absolute assurance that the whole world had changed.

II

By afternoon the well had become packed almost to suffocation, and when Justin returned to his seat in counsel's wake he had to push his way through a phalanx that showed the greatest reluctance to move. "Make way, please, make way; it is a scandal," he heard Jessop's voice booming, though the man himself was submerged up to the top of his wig which bobbed along in the tide. The judge, arriving untimely on the scene, looked grave. "I shall ask the bystanders at the back to leave at once," he declared into the hush that had fallen. "Officials at the doors will see to it that there is no overcrowding. If there is the least disturbance I shall clear the court."

Into this setting came George Sugden in a suit that looked too large for his emaciated body, his face the colour of wax and skull-like under a convict's crop. Only the pale blue eyes darting here and there seemed to have life—the same mischievous, restless glance that Justin remembered. Gilmore had risen. "You are George Sugden? Now serving a sentence of five years penal servitude for your part in the burglary at Massingham?"

"Aye."

"Was that sentence fairly earned?"

"Oh aye, sir, it were."

A small fugitive burst of laughter escaping from somewhere caused Jessop to shake his head and an official near the doors to bellow for silence. But the judge had paid no attention and Gilmore went on: "You admit the crime. Tell us what happened. Tell us in your own way."

So Justin heard again the words he had written down on that winter evening. All was much the same, except that Henderson was now definitely named as accomplice. There was some uncertainty about who had gone through the window first or who had suggested the enterprise, but these were not matters of much moment, nor was it likely that Jessop would be able to make them seem so. What Jessop would or *could* find to say when his turn came to cross-examine was a matter of general wonder.

"Who stole the ruby and eagle seal?" was the first and unexpected question—unexpected because first questions are often searching ones and Miss Verney's seal had never been a live issue. Sugden himself seemed as surprised as anyone, but answered: "It were Henderson."

"Henderson, was it? Are you sure? What did he do with it?"

"Dinna ken, sir."

"Well now," Jessop said, signalling with a wave of the hand that got entangled with the stuff of his gown, "will you take a look at this exhibit?"

It was handed up by an attendant and Sugden examined it.

"Is that the seal Henderson took?"

"Aye, sir."

"Let me put it to you formally that you have never seen that seal before because you never were at Massingham?"

The witness shrugged his shoulders, obviously thinking the question beneath his notice. 'Then why am I here?' he seemed to be saying. 'Why am I doing time?' But when the question was repeated and he saw the small bouncing man in the wig still slightly askew was in earnest about it he answered gravely: "I were there, sir. Stands to reason."

"Oh, it stands to reason, does it?" Jessop said, seizing on the words. "Because you have confessed, you mean?"

"That's right, sir."

"I am putting it to you that your confession is untrue."

Nothing had so clearly shown Justin the nakedness of the land on the other side of the hill than Jessop's insistence on this point. The question, being part of the Defence case, had to be put, but it was plain bad tactics to go on hammering at it when everyone in court could ask himself why in the name of reason Sugden should have confessed and gone to penal servitude for something he had not done. To suggest, as Jessop proceeded to do, that the motive for the confession had been fear that otherwise the Police might lay a graver charge (not named, but Hannington probably in mind) seemed sheer fantasy the more one looked at it. What kind of advantage or protection did one get by being put in gaol? In any event the Police *had not wanted Sugden put in gaol*. Far from having a reason to urge him to confess, a confession was the last thing they had wanted and would have made them sour, not sweet; more ready and not less ready to bring on their 'graver charge', supposing it existed. Indeed, after a time even Jessop seemed to have become aware of the self-defeating nature of his own argument and began to concentrate instead on what he called 'undue influence', the 'moral pressure' brought to bear by Gilmore's 'just and selfless men'.

And at once he had better luck.

First the man's sickness: he established that with broad and sombre strokes—a soul at death's door; a sick child; an unheated garret. Enter the tempters bearing gifts—one in the guise of a minister of the Faith. Exhortations. Promises. Appeals to the instinct of self-sacrifice. Finally the skeleton in the cupboard of this affecting scene —"Did Mr Derry warn you that you might be tried? Were you warned you might be sent to penal servitude?"

The witness had begun to hesitate and the blue eyes to sparkle with something that might have been resentment or mischief or a combination of both.

"Not that, sir."

"Did Mr Lumley warn you?"

"'Im, sir? The Riverent?"

It was understood from this reply that the Vicar's ministrations had been on the celestial plane and Jessop pressed home the point at once. "He was concerned about your soul?"

"Seems 'e was, sir," replied the witness, so lugubriously as certainly to have drawn laughter from the court if the judge's eye had not been on it.

"What were *you* concerned about?" Jessop enquired.

"Nowt much, sir."

"Quite. You were a sick man. Did you believe that you were dying?"

"That I did, sir."

"So if it had been suggested to you that an act of self-sacrifice such as a confession would add merit to your immortal soul . . . ?"

But he got no further. "Mr Jessop," said the judge in a tone almost of incredulity, "do I understand you to be suggesting that a priest in Holy Orders urged a false confession on a parishioner whom he believed to be dying?"

Everyone looked horrified, Mr Jessop most of all. "The very last thing I intended," he assured the court with a glance full of respect for the Anglican communion. "It is no part of my case that the Vicar of St Bede's acted with other than propriety. He believed Sugden to be guilty—of that I am assured. His aim was to prepare a supposedly guilty man for death. The fact that the man *was not guilty* does not in any way affect the sincerity of his action. But let us look at the results. Believing Sugden guilty, he used pressures that this witness was in no condition to resist." Here Jessop swung back to Sugden and demanded: "Was it put to you that confession would benefit your soul?"

"Aye, sir, in a way."

"And was it put to you that by confessing you would free two men who were your friends?"

"Aye, sir."

"Isn't the truth of all this that you just agreed to what was put to you because you were tired, and it seemed the easy way out, and because you didn't think you would be punished? In other words, it was no true confession but one made under duress?"

"They said as it would be best for me."

"I have no questions," said counsel for Mathieson and Moffat as Jessop resumed his seat.

"But are you under duress *now?*" enquired Gilmore, rising to re-examine with the fatigued air of someone who is called on to point the obvious. "Apart from the fact that you are in gaol, I mean."

The witness shook his head.

"Nor are you dying now, I take it? Is anyone threatening you to-day or urging you to say anything that isn't true?—I except my friend's ingenious verbal traps."

"Not a soul, sir."

"You come here convicted by a jury and sentenced by a judge. You have been punished, and I think you feel that it was a harsh sentence and resent it?"

"Aye, sir, I do."

"Do you still say, in spite of that, *today*, that your confession is true and that it was you and Henderson who broke in and stole at Massingham Rectory that night?"

"It were me and Henderson."

Four questions in less than a minute. And Jessop's painstaking cross-examination lay in ruins.

For some time Justin had been feeling distinctly uneasy about the case. The mauling he had received from Jessop had bruised his confidence and the way the Defence had been able to throw doubt on the voluntary nature of the confession had appalled him and made him see disturbing visions. Then Gilmore had re-examined, and instantly the skies had cleared and he had been filled with admiration for the man's masterly timing of questions, which had not been wasted in examination-in-chief but had been held back till the moment came to explode a nonsensical theory. The danger had passed, and if Henderson proved to be anything like Sugden, or showed even half his honesty, the case was as good as over.

In fact, Henderson in the box made a figure of considerable *empressement*. They had given him back his best suit for the occasion, his collar was as high as in the days of prosperity, his face as ruddy, as though he had just come in from a Sunday afternoon stroll, and a watch-chain gleaming across his fine expanse of stomach defied the world to think that he had stolen it. Not that he was in any sense cocky or disrespectful to the court. As an ex-gamekeeper and professional witness his attitude towards it was more fraternal than anything else. He was one of the family, who understood its queer goings-on, even down to the to-ery and fro-ery of counsel that had so baffled poor Sugden, and one gathered that on the whole he thought well of it. A model witness.

Under this treatment the court itself relaxed. After the tensions of Sugden's evidence, with its undertones of tragedy, Henderson brought such a comfortable humour to bear on everything, even his own afflictions. That they had been richly deserved he left little doubt in anyone's mind. But being without self-pity, he absolved others from the need of feeling pity and enlisted their sympathy instead. Without playing for comedy, he achieved it. Perhaps his best moment was his handling of his old gun, the one he admitted firing at the Verneys, but one forgot the crime in the affecting nature of the scene. Not even fear of the judge's displeasure could prevent the laughter that rippled over the court as these companions of old poaching days were reunited, but it was kindly laughter, and significantly the judge made no attempt to check it in spite of the shocked expression on Jessop's face. It came as an astonishing thing to Justin to see how his 'Other Man', the dark shadow that had brooded over his thoughts for so long, could bring light and humour with him.

As for Henderson's evidence in general, it followed the confession with only minor variations, describing how he and Sugden had been poaching in the woods near Massingham when the suggestion had been made to 'try the priest's'.

"Well, Geordie and me ganned roond bi the plantation and ower the medders tae the back o' Mr Verney's hoose. We'd a muckle bag made of owd poke . . . of sackin' as ye might say . . . and we tore it up and put it roond us boots."

"So your boots were covered. Are you sure of that?" enquired Gilmore, holding up his hand.

"Aye, sir: gay sure."

"It is important. Please go on."

"In a byre we finds a bit chisel. 'The verra thing,' says Geordie. He'd a rare eye for things had Geordie."

"Keep to your story," warned Gilmore, detecting a restless movement on the bench.

And keep to it he did, with a relevance surprising in so untutored a man. Perhaps an interpreter would have been an advantage at times, but there could be no other complaint against the witness, at least from the Crown's point of view. Breaking-in, theft, arrival at

Verney's, scuffle, escape, dawn search by the Police—everything was in order and accounted for with a rare candour.

It was this that chiefly seemed to exasperate Jessop when he rose to cross-examine. "What you have been giving is a catalogue of crimes," he remarked bleakly. "You have been telling us how you plotted to break into an old man's house by night to steal, how you took his goods, nearly killing him in the process, how you escaped and allowed other men to suffer for what you say you did. Does that describe it?"

"Aye," admitted the witness cheerfully.

"It seems to amuse you very much."

"Wouldn't say that, sir."

"But *I* am saying it and the jury can see you for themselves. It amuses you. You have been basking in the limelight. Isn't this an act you have been putting on?"

"It's truth, sir."

"Haven't you just been repeating a part you've learnt by rote?" Henderson shook his head with a smile of incomprehension on his face, and Jessop burst out furiously: "Don't smirk at me, man. Respect the court."

"I hope my friend will respect the *witness*," put in Gilmore with a dutiful glance at the judge.

"Certainly, when he merits it," replied Jessop, standing his ground. "I don't feel obliged to tolerate his insolence and prevarications though. I was suggesting to him that he had learnt a part. And he had some props, I think. Take a look at this exhibit, please. Is that the eagle and ruby seal you stole?"

"That's 'er, sir."

"What did you do with it?"

Justin was suddenly aware from Jessop's voice and manner that the little man was becoming violently excited.

"I give it away to someone," the witness said.

"To someone. You have not said to whom, you have never said to whom. May I suggest to you that you have been so constantly evasive about it because you never gave it to anyone, because you never had it to give?"

"I give it like I telt ye."

"No, wasn't it *Kelly* who gave it?" said Jessop, suddenly very still. "Didn't he give it *to his fiancée, Amy Dodds,* who took it to Mr

Coates the jeweller. I will be calling him. Mr Coates remembers now."

There was a stir of movement and voices rising and dying away like the wash and hiss of a wave against the shore, and into the trough that followed, Jessop said: "Were you at Massingham that night?"

"Aye, sir, I were, and Geordie too."

"Then there were *four* of you. You and Sugden as you confess. And Milligan and Kelly, as the jury found."

Justin heard the voices and the sound of people craning forward in their seats. Part of his mind was very clear and analytical. If Amy Dodds had had the seal, then in all probability she had got it from her fiancé, Kelly, which meant that Kelly had been at Massingham, and Milligan too, and therefore Blair was innocent and he had been on a fool's errand. It was too hard a thought to bear. There was a buzzing in his ears. The court had begun to go dark, though he could see shapes moving in the gloom, and words came to him from a long way off, mixed up with other voices, Amy Dodds's among them, trying to tell him something . . . perhaps about the seal. Someone was saying loudly, defiantly: "All right: I give it 'er: not Kelly: yon's the truth." And suddenly his senses cleared and he knew who had spoken and what a hostage to fortune it was.

"My dear fellow, are you all right?" he heard a voice whisper urgently in his ear.

"Of course I am," he answered testily. He had not known that Mr Lumley was in court that morning.

"Are you sure?"

"Quite sure."

"You went so pale. If you'd only come outside for a while and take a rest. This constant strain . . . so bad for you."

People were rebuking them from behind. Jessop himself had glanced round at them, and it was interesting to see how his petulant glare was transformed, as he swung back towards the witness, into an incredulity that spoke louder than words. "Come Henderson," they heard him say, "you are not seriously telling us now, after all this time, that it was you who gave Miss Verney's seal to Amy Dodds! Why should you give it her?"

"She were my lass," the witness said.

"Not Kelly's?"

"Aye, she had binn."

"I suggest to you that you had never even spoken to the girl?"
"That I had, sir."
"Can you prove you knew her?"
"Just me word, sir."
"And nothing else! Your word! Why didn't you mention her before?"
"An' tell on the lass!" cried Henderson. "To ye an' a'!"

Far up in the public gallery there sounded a burst of delighted laughter, instantly stilled as the judge glanced up. No one had laughed below. Justin saw the intent jury and Jessop's face registering his long-suffering endurance of the witness.

"Of course to 'tell', that is to tell the truth, even to me, is what you have sworn on your oath to do," the insinuating voice reminded them. "I hope you understand that."
"Aye, I do."
"Why couldn't you 'tell' on Amy Dodds?"
"It would ha' made her a receiver."
"But she was dead."
"Aye, the puir lassie."
"You were protecting her memory? One respects that. So you said nothing about her in your statement to Mr Derry. Or in your proof of evidence. Or when my learned friend examined you just now. Is that right?"
"Aye."
"Then why are you saying she was a receiver *now?* I mean, what has changed?" enquired Jessop with the air of a man who deeply desires to be instructed. "What can have made you betray those refined emotions of chivalry and honour in the protection of a lady's name? Will you enlighten us?"
"Ye axed me a question," the witness said.
"No: I told you something that surprised you—that the seller of the seal to Mr Coates was known to us. So you panicked and you lied. Why did you lie? Why did you deny that Kelly was at Massingham that night?"
"He nivver were."
"And Milligan?"
"He nivver."
"Why did you claim as mistress a girl you never knew except by sight? What are the *reasons*, Henderson? Indeed I might ask you— I *will* ask you: *"Why did you confess at all?"*

III

Justin returned that night to Smedwick hugging a grain of comfort to his heart. Jessop had miscalculated with a question. When he had asked why Henderson had confessed, he had probably had in mind the affecting study he might draw of the witness in the role of Sidney Carton sacrificing himself for others, and indeed it would have made a beguiling and ludicrous picture if only he had been able to get Henderson to sit for it. However, the man had answered, as Justin could have answered for him, that he had confessed because he had been caught red-handed in the act of recovering stolen goods and because he had feared that Sugden might turn Queen's Evidence, leaving him alone to face the music and perhaps a charge that he had tried to murder Verney. Self-interest, not self-sacrifice, had moved him. The witness had been quite frank about it. He had been 'catched' and 'took short a bit'. He had thought that 'they'— meaning Justin and Longford—'kenned arl aboot it'; more than they did, in fact; and this he had acknowledged with the rueful aside that after all he had 'ainly gotten five year'. Indeed Jessop's question had miscarried altogether, as it had deserved to do.

But there the comfort ended. For to know that Henderson had been at Massingham was no longer an answer to the insidious thought that Milligan and Kelly might have been there also. It was true that Jessop's 'four man' theory supposed that the Police had found the need to frame (and Sugden to save) not innocent men but guilty ones, two of the most unlikely things imaginable, but other unlikely things had been advanced that morning, not least Henderson's evidence which had filled Justin with a profound distrust. He felt sure that if the man had been protecting anyone by his silence over Amy, he had been protecting himself, and had some personal motive for keeping the connection dark—assuming it existed. For the most likely explanation of his behaviour was simply that he had lied to Jessop in the box, never having known Amy except by sight; which threw the possession of the seal squarely back on Kelly and suggested that the 'four man' theory might be true.

As the train rattled northwards in the moonlight he faced the possibility of an appalling error. His pride rebelled at the thought. He remembered Pugh and the other witnesses to the Police conspiracy, and it seemed almost inconceivable that they could have been lying or that Sugden and Henderson could have misled him at such fearful cost to themselves. Yet there were times when he imagined that perhaps all this had happened and he had been caught in a web of deceit and double dealing. At such crises Mr Lumley was a great standby. He saw things so much more clearly, perhaps because he had ceased to feel any emotional involvement once his 'innocents' had been released and a comparatively lenient sentence had been given to his 'penitents', as he was apt to call them. "What are you worrying about?" he demanded from his corner seat in the tone he used at sickbeds to those who were unreasonable enough to dislike translation to another world. "You know what Pugh and Piggott are going to say. Even a legal ignoramus like myself can see that the conspiracy is being made out against the Police."

"But suppose Henderson was lying just now?"

"Then he was lying about a very small and unimportant matter, my dear chap. Why are you so hypnotised by this business of Coates and the seal?"

"Simply because it points to the fact that Kelly might have been at Massingham."

"Stuff and nonsense!" cried the Vicar quite heatedly. "The poor girl took the seal to Coates long after Kelly went to prison, so how can you deduce anything from that? She got it from Henderson, of course, just as he says."

"If he could only prove it."

"How do you know he can't prove it? People may come forward. And even if they don't, no sane person would argue that there were four men at Massingham when everything else suggests there were only two. I don't know why I have to tell you these things. Surely you are not so set on having poor Blair convicted that you jump at shadows?"

Justin understood that, left to himself, the Vicar would have released all parties, in gaol or custody, with a blessing on everyone, coupled with a pressing invitation to subscribe to some worthy charity. But he felt heartened all the same. His problem seemed smaller and more manageable by the time he had got out of the train at Smedwick and set off homewards through streets that were ankle-deep in slush. Yet that night, in spite of his joy at Miss Verney's surprising kindness and the hopes that sprang from it, his dreams were dark and troubled. They were vivid dreams between periods of waking when he imagined he could see a pattern connecting them with Massingham and his adventures on the quest, though the settings were different and even the actors had changed identities in the most baffling way. There was a voice—he thought a woman's—explaining something in a room, and in the background the suggestion of some brooding but unseen presence. Then he saw the sky, in which a bird was wheeling against a screen of woods, and there was the sound of running water and he saw someone struggling in the current while another watched from the bank. As he woke to see the sun shining through his window the idea occurred to him that the watcher by the river had been Henderson and that he too had been the unseen presence in the house where Amy Dodds had lived. The waking was rather worse than the dream.

That was the Saturday morning, with the week-end stretching interminably ahead and no Miss Verney to cheer him. He spent it quietly, hardly aware of mealtimes or of Flo's anxious face watching him from behind the teacups and the chinoiserie. All his thoughts were concentrated on the moment on the Monday morning when at five past eight the whistle would blow, a green flag would be waved and the Belcastle train would pull out of Smedwick with its cargo of witnesses and spectators bound for the 'last act of the drama', as the *Mercury* had confidently named it.

It came at last, and with Mr Hicks for company he travelled down through a countryside almost awash in the thaw. In Belcastle the rain was teeming down, drumming on the glass roof of the station and on the fine classical portico where the hansoms waited, huddled together out of the wet; streaming in torrents in the forecourt of the Moot Hall on glistening umbrellas and the coats of cab-horses as drenched as seals.

Inside, in the stone-flagged hall and on the stairs rising towards the Grand Jury Room, chaos had arrived out of the rain, smelling strongly of damp worsteds and mackintoshes. Justin found himself between a squad of Police keeping the doors of the court and a mob of folk clamouring for their rights as witnesses and relations of witnesses, while clerks dodged about like rabbits and a voice from the stairs besought everyone to be calm.

"You've heard the tale the odd-job fellow of Verney's—Bell—brought me about the boots?" he heard someone ask out of the scrum, and another answer:

"Yes, I have."

"I can't call him. Too unreliable. Can't pin him down."

"Too bad."

"They've brought our prize one back, I hope?" the first voice said.

"He's down below."

"You're sure? Must have him back. Essential."

Turning, he saw Gilmore and his Junior in earnest consultation some yards away. He wanted to ask how Bell came into it and who their 'prize one' might be, but the pressure of the crowd was too great, and he found himself driven through the Police cordon into court, and across it, along the passageway that ran behind the dock to the comparative peace of the benches under the gallery on the jury side. Hardly had he got into his seat, however, than he was aware of Hicks bearing down on him with the insufferably primed and knowing look of a Greek chorus—

"Mr Derry, have you heard? Have you heard the news, sir?"

"I can just hear *you* as it happens—just."

Indeed the noise was deafening. Mr Hicks came closer and hissed through the uproar of voices and shuffling feet: "They're recalling Henderson. Seems that it's true he knew Miss Dodds. They've found a photograph."

"What photograph?"

"Of him and Amy—on Scarboro' prom, I think."

Justin sat back and closed his eyes. He was rid of a nightmare. Mr Jessop's 'four man' theory had dissolved into air. And in its place arose another, not so clear, not clear at all: made up of a dream, the memory of a woman's voice with sounds in the house around her, a figure glimpsed at the corner of a street. He said to himself: 'She meant to tell me something. Suppose Henderson was in her house that night and guessed? Suppose he murdered her?'

IV

THAT morning Gilmore called evidence of the actual conspiracy charged.

First Piggott. There had been some fear that the old man might be too alarmed or stupid to understand what he had to do, but in fact he made an admirable witness, far better than Mr Verney. Emphatically he denied ever having owned the chisel 'found' by Pugh and Mathieson in his house. He had never even seen it before, but had admitted to its ownership out of fear of 'getting into trouble'. The coat handed to the Police by Amy Dodds had been his, however. He had never lent it to Kelly; had indeed been wearing it when Kelly set out on his poaching expedition. There had been no scrap of paper in its lining, so far as he knew, and he himself had certainly never been inside the Rectory at any time.

Bulwer the tailor followed to swear that the rent in the trousers the Police had shown him must have been caused by some sharp instrument such as a knife or pair of scissors, not by 'a window-ledge or suchlike'. He had told Blair so at the time and Blair had answered: "Think again, man." But he had not thought again. (Much laughter.)

Three witnesses testified to seeing Milligan and Kelly with their dog by the Duke's Wall under Bridewell Moor at dawn. A lady (Miss Kelly) had asked them to give this evidence at the Assize court, but there had been no money for their fares. One had approached the Police with his story and Blair had said to him: "Ye leein' bogger! I'll mind yer name."

Next came P.C. Pugh in uniform, standing very erect and never once looking at his old colleagues in the dock. He spoke of the 'ruse' of the chisel carried out on Blair's instructions. He (Pugh) had had a bad conscience about it at the time, and worse since. Because worse things had happened. The coat for instance. He himself had searched that coat and found nothing. He had heard Blair say it would be 'helpful' if something happened to be found in its lining, and then something *was* found. "Providential", the Superintendent had remarked.

"Were there other 'providential' things?" Gilmore asked the witness at this point.

"Aye, sir, the trews, yon trews o' Milligan's." The witness had seen 'ni slit in 'em'. And then P.C. Moffat had gone to Massingham, a month after the burglary, and had produced a button and a bit of cloth, and these and the trews, 'aa cut aboot', and been shown to the tailor.

"What else?" Gilmore asked. "Were you at Massingham on the morning of the crime?"

"Aye, sir, I worr."

"Did you inspect the lane past Merrick's bothy?"

"I seen it, sir."
"Were there footprints on it?"
"Aye: gay little 'uns."
"A lady's prints, perhaps? Miss Verney's?"
"Aye, a leddy's sawtenly. And Mr Merrick's too."
"No other prints?"
"None that I seen, sir."

There remained young Merrick. And when he had been called and cross-examined about the shot he had heard and the ensuing silence till Miss Verney had come running to his door, Gilmore rose and said laconically: "That is the Crown's case, my lord."

V

"My case, unlike my learned friend's," said Mr Jessop, giving the jury the benefit of his most encouraging smile, "is very simple. I shall not take up days in calling before you what you may think was the most remarkable batch of rascals of one breed and another ever assembled to swear by Almighty God to anything. Members of the jury, you have seen them, and what a privilege!—an old man in his dotage with a police record; assorted poachers; two men convicted in this very place of attempted murder and two others now undergoing penal servitude. These are not Defendants, gentlemen; they are *Crown witnesses* on whose evidence you are asked to say beyond reasonable doubt that police officers of unblemished character conspired. Now you shall hear these officers. Less than two years ago, before the passing of the Criminal Evidence Act, they could not have gone into the witness-box to tell you of their entire innocence, but now they can, and you will be able to judge for yourselves who is likely to have conspired and for what. I will call Superintendent Blair."

It was almost four o'clock and the rain was still rattling on the high windows above the gallery when Justin saw his old enemy come out of the gate at the back of the dock and cross the court into the witness-box. Very calm and paternal he looked, with his drooping jowls and comfortable spread of stomach under the ill-fitting tunic. "Superintendent," Jessop greeted him in a tone that invited the jury's respectful attention, "is your full name Josiah Blair?"

"It is, sir."

"I think you have been in charge of the Smedwick division these twelve years past and your total service is nearly forty years?"

"That's so, sir."

"What do you say to these charges that you conspired to pervert the course of justice?"

"It's all lies, sir."

In effect, what followed was a root and branch denial of the Crown case, except that some slight irregularity over the matter of the chisel was admitted, though excused in the same breath as the kind of thing the Police were sometimes forced to do in their unending struggle against criminals. "You have to be as sharp as them, sir," was how Blair expressed this. For nearly an hour in the deeply attentive court the Superintendent told his story of what had happened. The gruff unhurried voice, the frequent pauses for thought, were strangely impressive and suggestive of truth. It seemed a denial of the natural order of things that this upright, official man could have come from the dock with charges hanging over his head or that the jury listening so raptly could have been called there to pronounce on him.

"Must get at this fellow," Gilmore whispered over his shoulder as Defence counsel sat down. "Must knock him off his perch." The afternoon was drawing in, and at the back of the court an attendant had appeared with a lighted taper. There came the hiss of gas, the gentle plop of explosions as the mantles came alive, and soon the court was ringed with points of light shining on the dock and on the chair under the royal arms where the crimson of the judge's robes caught the eye, like some figure in an exotic tapestry. "We had no lights last time: it was early afternoon if I remember," Gilmore remarked aloud as the man with the taper came down past the witness-box on his way out of court. "Do you recall it, Superintendent?"

"Recall what, sir?"

"I'm speaking of the last time we met. It was here, wasn't it, some eight years back?"

"That's right, sir."

"You told me all about the scrap of paper Dr Higson found in a coat you handed him?"

"That's right, sir."

"Did you tell me about the 'ruse' of the chisel down at Mr Piggott's?"

A blank look had come into the Superintendent's eye but he answered stoutly: "I was never asked, sir."

"So if you're not specially asked to tell the truth you don't tell it, is that right?"

Blair could find no reply to this.

"Suppose I ask you *now*? Wasn't the trick you played on that old man a disgraceful and dishonest one?"

"No."

"You have to be 'as sharp as them', the criminals—is that your philosophy of life?"

"Plain common sense, sir."

A murmur of approval came from certain quarters of the court, but Gilmore took no account of it. "What you are saying," he insisted, "is that it is right for police officers to practise criminal behaviour."

"No, sir."

"Let us examine your actions, then. I will ask you about the footprints you found at Massingham. The first you came upon—soon after dawn—were marks in the flower-beds under the drawing-room windows of the Rectory, but those you rejected for some reason?"

"I did, sir."

"But on the lane and highway you discovered marks made by two pairs of boots you thought were Milligan's and Kelly's?"

"That's right, sir—so they were."

"When did you discover those footprints on the lane and road?"

"I'd traced the last of them by afternoon, soon after three."

"Some hours after you'd arrested Milligan and Kelly?"

"Yes."

"Were you alone when you discovered them?"

"I had young Moffat with me."

"Where did the footprints in the lane lead to?"

For some time the witness's answers had been getting slower, and this time there was quite a lengthy pause before he answered: "They led down the hill, sir, to the Smedwick road."

"Past Mr Merrick's cottage?"

"Right past it, sir."

"Yet you heard Mr Merrick say in evidence that though he heard the shot from the Rectory and then the sounds of Miss Verney's footsteps, he heard no other footsteps on the road?"

"He should ha' done, sir."

"You see I am suggesting to you, Superintendent," said Gilmore very slowly, "that apart from Miss Verney's prints and Merrick's, which P.C. Pugh saw, there were no others on the lane or road *until you put them there.*"

There was a gasp almost of horror, then a silence so profound that Justin could distinctly hear the hiss of the gas and the scratching of the judge's pen. Only the witness seemed unmoved and replied contemptuously: "Quite absurd, sir—with respect, sir."

"Absurd? But wasn't it *necessary*, because you had so little evidence to support your charge? Weren't the marks in the soil under the window useless from your point of view?"

"Unhelpful," Blair corrected him.

"Weren't they the marks made by Sugden and Henderson when they jumped through the window *with sacking on their feet?*"

"I don't agree, sir."

"But by that afternoon, when you 'found' the marks in the lane, you'd arrested Milligan and Kelly?"

"So I had, sir."

"And at that time, didn't you have with you at Massingham a bag *containing the boots of both accused?*"

"No, sir," the Superintendent said.

Gilmore looked at his brief, turned over a page, then slowly straightened up and faced the witness, saying: "I want you to think very carefully. You are on oath. You know the truth and perhaps it is known to others. Let me ask you again. Did you have in your possession at Massingham the *means* of putting those footprints on the road?"

Before Blair could reply, Mr Jessop had bounded to his feet, trembling, with vexation and alarm. "My lord, I must protest, I really must. My friend has no right to repeat his question in that form or otherwise. He had an answer and he must abide by it."

"Even if it were a lie and there happened to be evidence to prove it?" enquired Gilmore with the utmost cheerfulness.

"But my friend has no *right* to call evidence in rebuttal in such a case," cried Jessop, bouncing like a dervish under the sting of that confident smile. "He has no right even to refer to evidence he hints he knows of but has not called. It is the duty of the Crown to open all the facts it intends to prove; not to save things up and lie in ambush for witnesses."

"Aren't those strong words," remarked the judge mildly, "for exhortations to the witness to think about his answer?"

"They should never have been made, my lord, never. It was a threat: a ruse, if you like; an attempt to confuse my client."

The judge leaned forward in his chair, looking down at the small indignant figure below him. "Mr Jessop," he said, "I think you exaggerate the heinous nature of what Mr Gilmore has done. It seems to me that no harm would have come if the witness had been allowed to answer. However, it is vitally important that nothing should be said or done that is in any way unfair to the accused, and if it is your wish"—the judge was speaking very slowly, emphasising every word—"if it is really your wish that your client should not answer Mr Gilmore's question, then I shall certainly direct he need not do so."

Jessop bowed his head and his murmur of "As your lordship pleases" had a dutiful and complacent ring. Only the quick glances he shot first at the jury and then at the witness betrayed the fact that below the gratitude he was thinking hard. Gilmore knew it, and so did Justin. Calculations were racing through that agile mind: a profit and loss account of what had been won for the witness—time —and what might be lost if the jury were to suspect he had something to hide. It was a matter of instants only: the bow; the quick assessment of risks; and Mr Jessop had decided.

"My lord."

"Yes?" said the judge, an interested spectator of what had happened.

"My lord, if I have appeared to rely on technicalities the blame must lie on me, not on my client, and I am sure that is appreciated by the jury as much as by your lordship. I felt I had to intervene, since the question was improperly conceived. But if your lordship feels, as your lordship has indicated, that it should be answered, then of course it shall be answered. My client was always ready to do so. No reluctance should be attributed to him."

"None will be," replied the judge. "Superintendent, do you recall the question?"

There was no answer. The witness, staring across the court like a ship's figurehead, had apparently not heard.

"Superintendent?"

"My lord?"

"*Did you have the boots, man?*" Gilmore demanded with a sudden pounce.

"Aye, I had 'em," the witness said.

And next moment, before Jessop's horrified gaze, he had slumped forward in a dead faint over the ledge of the witness-box.

For over ten minutes the hearing was suspended, the witness-box empty, no judge on the bench, while the corridor outside the court hummed with excited talk. There was a school of thought that held that Blair was dead—and indeed there had seemed very little life in him as they carried him into the robing room of the Civil Court, to which a doctor was hastily summoned. Others looked to new sensations of an elevating nature when the repair work had been done. But what everyone seemed to be agreed about was that the Superintendent had damned himself in the jury's eyes by his admission, which was fairly generally put down to an Act of God or softening of the brain. "My dear Derry, to borrow a word from that unfortunate man, it was a providential answer," was Gilmore's opinion as they paced the corridor together. Apparently there had been no definite evidence to go on. "Except this, Derry. I got wind of the fact that the Rectory odd-job man, Bell, had some tale about a bag of boots, but the judge would almost certainly not have let me call him and who would have believed him anyway, coming so late on the scene? Our friend had only to stay dishonest a few minutes longer."

"Why didn't he?"

"You may well ask. Perhaps he thought I had something nasty up my sleeve and decided he'd best admit things while he had time. Or perhaps it was just the old Adam of honesty at work in him. I've often seen it happen. At heart most people prefer to tell the truth, and in the witness-box after a while, if you persist long enough, they *need* to tell it or bits of it. Don't ask me why." He broke off. "Hello, there's Perkins wanting us. Our friend must have recovered."

Near the doors of the court Gilmore's clerk, a small grey-haired man dressed like an undertaker, was making signs. People were scurrying for their seats, craning their necks to catch a glimpse of the Superintendent as he came back into court, his face as yellow as an idol's in the gaslight and his eyes curiously wide and expressionless.

Justin felt saddened by it all. He had not forgiven Blair. It was not in his nature, as it had been in the Vicar's, to feel charitable towards a man who had acted with such disregard for justice and human suffering, no matter how strong the temptation and even the need might have been to punish *someone* for the burglary, to check the wave of violence that had cost Luke's life at Hannington. But the spectacle of retribution, the packed court charged with emotions of excitement and pleasure, repelled him. Though Gilmore asked no more questions, he found it just as painful to watch Jessop trying to reassemble something irretrievably broken and to hear the halting voice proclaim an innocence he was sure no one believed in any longer.

But there he was wrong. The next witness, to his consternation, was Miss Verney.

As she went into the box, holding herself very erect like a pale and diminutive grenadier, he felt all the emotions of a lover. He feared terribly for her. He prayed without much hope that she would avoid disaster. It even crossed his mind to wish that she had chosen something more appealing than the dark dress that had made so dismal an impression on him at Massingham, and at the same time he wanted to defend that dress and the matching bonnet against the ignorant prejudices of the world. What they would make of her evidence he hardly dared to think—and he was right.

For what she had come to do was to repeat her testimony of '91: how, awakened by the sounds below, she had followed her father down on to the landing and seen the burglars standing in the dining-room in line; how the candles had gone out, the shot had been fired, and one of the men had come rushing out into the hall where she had grabbed him by the hair.

"Who was that man, Miss Verney?" Jessop asked.

She replied that she believed it was Milligan.

"Not Henderson? Could it have been?"

"Certainly not. He's a much bigger man."

"Could it have been Sugden?"

"No."

"I suppose that *he's* too small?" suggested Gilmore as he rose to cross-examine her. "Miss Verney, you made this identification eight years ago?"

"Yes."

"And then you identified only one of the two men?"

"Yes."

"Not even by candle-light apparently. By the light of the moon shining through a broken shutter in the room next door?"

"I saw him," she said. "I had hold of him."

"And it was Milligan?"

"Yes."

"When he was brought to you to be identified weren't you uncertain at first?"

"Perhaps a little."

"Come now, Miss Verney, I am sure you are anxious to be fair. Isn't it true that you were very uncertain indeed? The size of the man bothered you, also the length of his hair?"

"Yes it did."

"But now you're sure it was Milligan?"

"Quite sure."

Justin closed his eyes. He knew what was coming: had indeed remarked on it himself in the early days when the 'Verney Memory' had been a joke and not something that concerned him heart and soul.

"You see, what is so remarkable," Gilmore went on, "is that you should be so certain now and yet have doubted then. Forgive my putting it discourteously like this, but can your memory really have improved with time?"

"One needs time to think things over."

"Let me suggest to you that it is the very thing one does *not* need. Time, to be metaphysical, is the worst enemy of truth. Or put it like this. Isn't it like a curtain that gradually obscures truth?"

"I saw the man."

"You saw *a* man, Miss Verney, and wasn't the rest all memory, which is a very different beast? Will you explain how it happened that you could doubt it was Milligan one night and be sure it was him eight years later?"

'Oh God, make him let her go! please let her go!' prayed Justin at the sight of that pale, desperately resolute face. He felt he hated Gilmore and the sheepish jury almost as much as the amused glances he saw around him. What made it worse was that he recognised in himself all the old feelings of exasperation at her obstinacy and refusal to admit a mistake which must be obvious to everyone. It was perverse of her: the sin of pride. And yet at the same time it was magnificent and his heart went out to her. Through the shifting patterns of the case, so full of lies and evasions, there had come just this one voice that had never altered or compromised, and it struck him as the worst irony that it should have proved to be the one that was the most mistaken, the very furthest from the truth, of all the voices that had led him and misled him through the long game of blind man's buff.

VI

In its next issue the *Mercury* delivered judgment on a somewhat apocalyptic note:

> On Monday at the Moot Hall there terminated the Massingham Burglary Case that has perplexed and scandalised the public to a greater degree perhaps than any other event in local memory. At last Justice has been done. MILLIGAN and KELLY have been pardoned and have received gratuities. SUGDEN and HENDERSON are expiating their crimes in prison. Now the POLICE OFFICERS whose misguided sense of duty led them to conspire against the liberties of innocent men have paid the penalty of their misdeeds.
>
> It is a matter for general satisfaction—not least in that mercy has been shown. The sentences on BLAIR and his subordinates are mild by comparison with the suffering they caused, but they are sufficient to the purpose. It is enough that a great principle has been re-stated and the equality of all before the law made plain.
>
> The *Mercury* avers that the jury who by their verdict of GUILTY against all three accused gave expression to this truth have performed a public service. But they would have been unable to perform it if a love of Justice had not existed in the hearts of a host of ordinary men and women. We are not referring only to the two Gentlemen of Smedwick who bore the brunt of the battle and first brought a grave wrong to the attention of the public. Their efforts deserve outstanding praise. But there were many others who played their part and contributed to the satisfactory ending of the affair. The friends and relations of the innocent accused who never ceased to strive for them; the witnesses who came forward with their evidence, often against their own interest; the barrister and Member of Parliament who espoused the Cause; the public whose weight was always on the side of right; even the *Mercury* itself which became the voice of the general disquiet—all played their part. As long as such people and such institutions are to be found, injustice will never flourish. Such is the true lesson to be learnt from the harsh and lamentable case now ended.

But was it ended? Not many months later the *Mercury* felt called upon to supply an epilogue:—

> Those of our readers not insensible to the charms of Cupid's darts (it wrote) will have rejoiced at the news of the nuptials celebrated last week at Massingham. There were joined together in connubial bliss Mr Justin Derry and Miss Charlotte Matilda Verney. Divided by the claims of a long and bitterly contested case, they have been united by the unconquerable power of love.
>
> The *Mercury* salutes them. In this union, performed as it was by the bride's venerable father, assisted by his fellow Churchman from St Bede's, in the presence of a congregation that numbered many of the witnesses and chief parties to the Massingham Affair, the *Mercury* sees its happy and final outcome and an end to all the hatreds and sorrows of the past.

> O brother Montague, give me thy hand.
> This is my daughter's jointure, for no more
> Can I demand.
>
> See pictures on page 6

THE VERDICT OF YOU ALL

1936

I

THIRTY years went by, during which the Massingham affair became a memory preserved in the amber of folklore and in the yellowing files of the *Mercury's* reading room. Its actors passed away: Blair, Milligan, Henderson, Piggott, Hicks, old Mr Verney, Longford and many more. But the same Vicar of St Bede's had remained behind to scourge their successors into repentance and good works. And in the market-place the gold lettering on the windows of Justin Derry, Solicitor and Commissioner for Oaths (Managing Clerk: J. W. Harris), shone resplendent on a new generation of litigants.

One summer's day Justin ('young Mr Derry' no longer) was working at his desk when the phone rang and he found himself talking to Dr Hastie, a fishing crony of his. Since his marriage to Miss Verney and the arrival of two daughters he had felt increasingly drawn to quiet pursuits, and his first thought at hearing Hastie on the line was to imagine that he was being asked to go out that evening to take advantage of the splendid conditions in the river, where the level was falling after the floods. It was a business call however. Dr Hastie was apologetic about it. "Fact is," he explained, "I've got a patient keeps asking for you. Old woman in the geriatric ward of the Cottage Hospital, name of Heslett, Mrs Heslett."

Justin could recall no Mrs Heslett.

"Well, I'm sorry I can't help you with your murky past," Dr Hastie said when pressed for further details. "I'm new around here, remember. As far as I'm concerned she's just an old body I took over from Dr Copeland—a bit starkers, poor soul, and driving Matron right up the wall."

Justin consulted his desk diary and found rather to his surprise that until four o'clock his afternoon was free. 'Heslett: hospital,' he noted down. He had reached an age when even the smallest break from routine is welcome and he was pleasantly intrigued by the message and the faint air of mystery surrounding it. He must have become a rare old fogey, he thought, to be excited by a visit to a hospital, when once upon a time to be shot at in the street and threatened with direful prosecutions had seemed all in the day's work. The truth was that he had kept from his youth a quality which his wife and daughters called 'nosiness', though it was really a sense of wonder at people's doings and a love of sharing in the workings of a world so rich and unpredictable. Who, he wondered, was this Mrs Heslett who 'kept asking' and had prevailed over such powerfully inert forces as Matron and Dr Hastie? The obvious thing was to ask Harris, whose memory was as exhaustive as its by-products were mimicked and abused by the younger members of the staff. In reserve was an immense steel filing-cabinet with drawers that slid in and out at the touch of a finger and looked capable of answering any query raised by man. But no Heslett of either sex appeared in it.

That afternoon, as soon as he had had his sandwich lunch, he set off for the cottage hospital in the Warbury Road, not far from where Georgina had lived before she had disappeared from view into a triumphant marriage with a baronet. That brought thoughts in its train too—of relief mostly. At the entrance to Block B he found himself in the presence of the Matron, as he had rather expected. Matron would naturally wish to explain things for herself and correct any misunderstandings that might have arisen. He was shown into the Ward Sister's room (from which Sister had tactfully retired) and there the matter was put to him, rather as though he were a Consultant who had been called out in the middle of the night.

"Such a shame, Mr Derry, bringing you all this way. It's so good of you to come."

"Not in the least," he answered, fascinated by the perfect starch of her linen so reminiscent of Gilmore in the palmy days.

"Did Dr Hastie tell you about it?"

"He said there was a patient of his by the name of Mrs Heslett in the geriatric ward who had some problem for me."

"Yes, that is so," Matron replied, with a clear intimation in her voice that the Doctor in his blundering way had contrived to say both too little and too much.

"Is she very ill?"

"Not well, Mr Derry, not well at all. Of course she is an old lady and one mustn't expect too much. It is her mind, chiefly. Not that I'm implying she is certifiable, you understand."

He nodded and made sympathetic noises.

"But the dividing line is blurred sometimes. Old ladies suffering from her complaint get queer notions; they imagine things and have to be humoured. Old people are secretive; they are very cunning," Matron said, leading the way into the ward.

At first sight it looked almost full. About twenty women were in bed or wandering about in dressing-gowns, their scanty white hair scrimped into nets or set in curling pins. At the far end a screen had been drawn around a bed, and passing behind it in Matron's wake he found himself in the presence of a very frail woman with a mop of snow-white hair who lay back against the pillows, her hands folded on her breast. He had no idea who she was.

"Now, Granny," began Matron brightly, "this is Mr Derry the solicitor whom you asked for and who has most kindly come to see you. Isn't it nice of him?"

Granny Heslett, however, continued to stare straight ahead at the screen as though unaware of their existence.

"Stubborn, that's what they are," Matron remarked. "They fuss for days on end and then they're stubborn, that's all the thanks we get. Put another pillow behind her, Nurse."

The patient shut her eyes while she was lifted and a stray lock of hair was discovered and clipped firmly into place. "She's in one of her moods," Matron announced, "but perhaps if we went she might come round. Here's her bell if you should require anything. I don't think she'll give trouble. She may even talk. And I hope you *will*, Granny, now that the gentleman's come all this way just to be with you. You'll not get another chance, you know."

As soon as they had gone he pulled up the bedside chair and sat down in it cosily, like a man in his own home. There was something pitiable about that still figure, so neatly brushed and clean, in the white bed with the spotless sheets and the vase of flowers on the table beside her, but if he was to help her he must give her no inkling of his thoughts. "Such heaps of nurses," he remarked encouragingly. "Weren't we just the centre of attention! And now they're all off elsewhere." He heard a movement beside him and rejoiced: she had turned towards him on the pillows, and when he next looked her way he saw her dark eyes regarding him—quite youthful eyes at the centre of a network of fine lines running to the hollows below the temple and the sharp promontory of her nose. "All gone away," he said. "Not a Sister in sight. Let me see now: why did you send for me?"

He got no answer.

"Of course I could make it a social call and have tea, if they give us tea. Can't stay too long though." He took out his watch and solemnly consulted it. "Now I have a secretary," he said: "someone rather like Matron really, and *she* says I must be back by four. Not that I'm tied to minutes. I like it here. It's cosy. Have we met before?"

Still no answer.

"If we have I expect I've changed. Put on weight—that's bad for a man of my age. And my sight's not what it was. Don't recognise people. Pass them in the street. People I know quite well."

"Like you knew me, sir?"

An enormous and quite disproportionate sense of triumph flooded over him. Yet the voice had eluded him completely: old and broken, more a whisper than a voice, and charged with echoes he could not catch.

"So we knew one another?" he said. "I had the feeling we'd met."

"Yes, sir."

"Was it connected with Massingham in some way?"

"In every way."

And suddenly he saw that she was smiling and memory came flooding back. "Why, you're Miss Kelly," he accused her.

"Now you've got it, sir. I knew you would."

"You're Mrs Longford."

"He's dead is Jim, poor lad. And Heslett too. There's just me left, sir. Just me left to tell you something 'fore I die."

II

WHAT she told me (wrote Justin on the last foolscap pages of his Summary of Facts in *In Re Milligan*) was that Lumley and I had been made fools of and 'used', as Jessop said of us. We thought that we were imposing our own harmony on events, and really we were like conductors beating time at an orchestra that is playing some completely different tune.

I have been wondering whether this could possibly be true. She was such a queer old stick and it seemed such a rigmarole as she told it. Matron and Dr Hastie would have had no two doubts about it. They put her down as a borderline case, subject to delusions, and certainly that was how it struck you as you listened. Or again I've thought that perhaps she was more rational than she seemed and invented the story to make herself feel important and annoy Matron, which was about the only pleasure left to her. Old people *can* be cunning. Second childhood, like childhood itself, can be a very inventive time.

As against that, she would surely have made a better job of a put-up story. There were such gaps in it. She didn't bring it out in one consecutive narrative, but there were all sorts of inconsistencies and downright lies sometimes. I had to probe and ask reams of questions. She was far more difficult than poor George Sugden ever was. Yet in the end, in some odd way, it all seemed to add up to the truth or to something nearer the truth than all the rest of us arrived at. Let me try and set it down in an orderly way.

She told me first of all that Milligan and Kelly were the men who burgled the Rectory that night, as my wife and her father maintained all along. I find that hard to write. She said there were two, not four men involved. I find that easier, since Jessop was at least wildly astray on that. And Blair and the Police had planted the false evidence, just as was alleged at their trial: they faked the footprints on the road and Milligan's trouser button, just as they faked the piece of paper in the coat, which was old Piggott's coat. They did all these things exactly as Pugh said, and they did them because otherwise they would have had no hope of getting a conviction. To my mind that lessens somewhat the heinousness of what they did.

So Milligan and Kelly, according to her story, burgled the Rectory, shot at Verney and escaped—not by the road but across the moor, wearing sacking on their feet. They had with them the watch and the seal. Instead of going straight home they decided to make an alibi for themselves, so they went poaching on Bridewell Moor, buried their rabbits and waited near the Duke's Wall for their friends. The booty, well hidden, escaped the cursory Police search of the chapel. The watch they gave into the safe keeping of Miss Kelly, the one enterprising person in their circle, and Mick Kelly gave the ruby and eagle seal to his fiancée Amy Dodds. These stolen goods were hidden in a cistern in the attic, where they survived a second search, to appear again another day. It was found that Kelly's coat was soaked in blood—rabbit's blood or from the Verneys: no one seemed sure—so Amy burned it, and when the Police came she gave them one of Piggott's. She never mentioned this at the trial, however, partly because she was too bewildered and afraid, and partly because she felt that the destruction of the coat would tell heavily against her lover. In the event, of course, the faked piece of paper put by the Police into the lining proved even more damaging, and the conviction of both men followed inevitably.

So far it seems clear that the old lady's story fits the facts of the trial of '91 and explains the things that puzzled me at the time, in particular the distrust I felt for the Police witnesses in court and for the accused men when I saw them in the cells. There was lying on both sides. But now the controversial things begin.

Between 1891 when Milligan and Kelly went to penal servitude and the January of 1899 when Miss Binns came to me with her story two very important things happened. Amy Dodds tired of waiting for her lost fiancé and secretly took a lover: Henderson. They went to the seaside together where they were photographed. Perhaps Amy paid the hotel bill, and it would be ironic if she paid it with the proceeds of my wife's ruby and eagle seal which she had sold to Coates the jeweller for £25. More significantly, Miss Kelly became engaged to one of the Pelegate poachers: Longford.

Now Miss Kelly had loved her brother, whom she had mothered since he was a child. I had been struck at the Moot Hall by the force and passion of her nature. His condemnation was the key event of her life; and what made it all the more unbearable was the fact that the cowardice of Piggott, the old man with whom she had been living, had been one of the main causes of the disaster.

Her first act was to break with Piggott, who went to the workhouse, where Wilcox found him some years later. Then, as I have said, she took up with Longford, a man some years younger than herself and one of her brother's closest friends. How much she knew about him is doubtful. She was evasive about this. Perhaps she knew all about him and set her cap at him deliberately, or perhaps she just stumbled on the truth. But what is certain is that in the autumn of '98 he told her—or at all events she got to know—that he had been one of the gang which had killed P.C. Luke at Hannington.

How that name came to haunt me! Anyway, what Longford told Miss Kelly was that he had seen Luke die and that Henderson had killed him at Sugden's urging. The Police, as we know, arrested the pair of them (but not Longford) and then had to release them for want of evidence, which enraged Blair against the Pelegate folk and was the cause of much that followed.

These arrests and releases had taken place a few months before the burglary at Massingham. And eight years later Miss Kelly had the evidence to send the killers to the scaffold. She could not, for Longford's sake, take it to the Police. In any case P.C. Luke meant nothing to her. But it would mean something to the murderers of Luke that she had in her pocket—or to be more accurate in her bed—the young man who could turn Queen's Evidence and hang them.

From that moment the plan formed in her mind of using the threat of Longford's knowledge of the crime at Hannington to force Henderson and Sugden to confess to the lesser crime of burglary at Massingham, of which they were quite innocent, and so free her brother. It was a bold plan, and dangerous, as the future was to show.

First she went to Sugden's niece, Miss Binns, who had been a friend of P.C. Luke's, and by telling her part of the truth and holding out the prospects of revenge, got her to agree to back up her story with picturesque details of George's guilt—how he had returned in the small hours babbling that he might have killed a man and so on. I don't suppose that many women could have conceived of such a scheme, much less have executed it. But Miss Kelly was exceptional in every way. She saw at once that it was no use going to the magistrates or trying to get confessions from two trapped and dangerous men with only Longford to help her. She needed a middleman, someone who would act as a respectable front for her activities—and it so happened she chose me.

From that stage on, a Punch and Judy show developed. In the foreground Lumley and I worked away to get confessions, while Miss Kelly sat back and pulled the strings. In defence of myself I may say that I didn't swallow the story whole. I had doubts about Miss Binns for instance, but those vanished when I discovered that the Police, who were also alive to what was happening, had put pressure on her to recant. By an evil chance all my attempts to test the story were directed towards those aspects of it *that were true*. Thus I discovered that Merrick had heard no one on the road past his bothy, which made me properly suspicious of the footmarks Blair had claimed to find. Similarly, my visit to Amy Dodds convinced me that the Police had been given Piggott's jacket (as they had) and therefore must have faked the piece of paper in the lining. When George Sugden confessed I naturally took it as the most perfect confirmation of the story. I saw no significance in his sly smiles and the pointedly ironic way in which he treated me. I ignored the glimpse I had had of Longford and Miss Kelly outside his house on the night he confessed. How could I have guessed that it was not our urgings *but their threats* that had worked the miracle. Besides, P.C. Pugh's phantom attempts to see me only added to the pattern that seemed to be building up, so that when at last we met and he told me of Blair's ruse of the chisel I became quite *certain* I was on the right track and no longer intellectually capable of doubt.

All this time Miss Kelly had been working quietly in the wings. She had coached Sugden for his confession and she must have felt properly disgusted when she discovered that this high-class piece of fraud was not enough to release her brother. So she turned on Henderson and tried to coach him too. This was over-stepping things a little. Henderson was not a timid man like George to be stampeded at the first scent of danger, and his reaction, which she ought really to have foreseen, was to try to short-circuit things by shooting Longford in the street, nearly killing me in the process, which was one of the ironies of the story I didn't appreciate at the time. Another was the fact that Amy Dodds had changed sides and had begun to sleep with Henderson. No doubt she had heard from him what Miss Kelly was up to; and in her alarm the poor girl first blurted out to me the truth about the coat and then, to correct things, all but warned me of what was really happening. Of course, in the end she never did tell me, because within a week they had taken her body from the river. It could have been accident or suicide, but I think someone had overheard her talking to me and guessed what she might say, and I think it must have been Longford in the passage in Clay Yard, not Henderson as I once thought, and Longford's voice that Snell and his dogs heard in the woods near the Red Mill pool. In any case I feel sure that Miss Kelly had no part in *that*.

The rest of the story bears all the marks of her ingenious mind, showing her understanding of the people she was dealing with and how she had learnt from her mistakes that it was *in combination* they worked best. Since Sugden alone couldn't do the trick, she had to set Henderson in motion. So she went to him with Longford and told him that a full description of Luke's murder had been deposited in a sealed packet in my safe. He was invited to 'confess' to the crime at Massingham. She had already sent Longford to me with an envelope which contained no statement but some sheets of foolscap and my future wife's gold watch, which had been in her possession all along.

This was the last of her manipulations and it brought by far the best performance. For Henderson had no intention of confessing. His aim was to get the supposed statement in his hands that night and then settle with Longford for good and all before he could write another. He probably had no thought that Longford was shadowing him across the market-square and along the ginnel, or, if he did, it may have crossed his mind that my office was as good and quiet a place as any to get his man. He certainly had no thought of me or any notion that there had been a 'tip-off' about the burglary in the offing. Caught red-handed in possession of the watch, in the presence of Longford, with the threat of a murder accusation hanging over him, his nerve gave way at last and he decided to 'confess', and stuck to it through the trials that followed. It was better than being hanged. He even defended Miss Kelly's story with ingenious touches of his own; as when he checkmated Jessop over the seal, which of course he had never given to Amy or even seen, though he may have enjoyed a holiday on the proceeds.

It had become a cast-iron story by that time. Why, as Gilmore said, should innocent men confess to something they had never done? Why should they go to penal servitude for it? Jessop's theory that there was some other charge outstanding against them which made it imperative that they should confess to the lesser crime of burglary at Massingham was right (if we believe Miss Kelly), but it was made to look ridiculous once one appreciated that the Police had no motive for wanting a confession, which in fact proved fatal to them. No one thought of Miss Kelly and Longford who *had* the motive. Why should anyone have thought of them? Even Jessop wasn't as perceptive as all that.

And why, finally, should *I* accept the story now? I don't know altogether that I do, though it certainly seems to answer many of the points that bothered me. If only I could talk it over with someone it would help, but my old friend at St Bede's would be too deeply grieved by it and perhaps in all the circumstances it would be better not to trouble those at home.

For, after all, everything is over now, and the guilty were punished, if not precisely in the tidy way the law would have approved of. How Hicks would have laughed about it. I could have told *him*. But what a story he would have made!

Such was the summary that young Mr Jobling found in the lumber room. He had not met Mrs Derry. But even without that privilege he understood—if nothing else—why Justin had not done the apparently obvious thing and taken his problem to his wife. Like any other woman she would have been bound to say: "I told you so."